A STATEMENT IN LITERATURE

W·CLARK
PUBLISHING

A Life For A Life 2

The Ultimate Reality

A Novel By

Mike Jefferies

D1447339

Wahida Clark Presents Publishing
60 Evergreen Place
Suite 904
East Orange, New Jersey 07018
973-678-9982
www.wclarkpublishing.com

Library of Congress Cataloging-In-Publication Data:
A Life For A Life II/ by Mike Jefferies
ISBN 13-digit 978-09828414-6-4 (paper)
ISBN 10-digit 0-9828414-6-9 (paper)
LCCN 2012913334
1. Urban- 2. Atlanta- 3. Hip-Hop- 4. African American-
    Fiction- 5. Street Lit- 6. Music Industry- 7. Urban
    Fiction

Cover design and layout by Nuance Art.*.
Book interior design by Nuance Art.*.
Edited by Linda Williams
Proofreaders Rosalind Hamilton

Printed in USA

This one is dedicated to faith!
This gift, this work of art, is surely the evidence of things not seen.
Keep believing in your dreams.

Acknowledgements

This wouldn't be a completed vision if I didn't take the time to acknowledge a few people. First and foremost, I want to say thanks so much and send my undying love to my grandparents, Willie and Dorothy Jefferies. It took some time but it's because of the way you raised me that I'm such a morally grounded man today. It's because of y'all that none of the things I've seen and lived have turned me into a cruddy person. I know there's something better. Y'all taught me faith.

To every one of my readers who Facebooked, wrote, or just supported me on the come up. I truly thank you. A lot of times it has been your appreciation and encouragement that motivated me to keep pushing that pen.

To my sister, PJ, my cousin Meatloaf, my dog Mike Sanders, and my lil brothers Mike Anthony and Charles (Baby-T) Tyler and John (BK) Davis, y'all helped a player through tough times. I love you too Momma, Phyllis Jefferies, you know I can't forget my Chocolate Queen. And of course, Paris, Lil' Mike, and Komica, the best kids ever! I love the rest of my family too, but this situation has taught me that every relative ain't family and if ya feel like I'm jabbing at you, then I guess ya realize what you ain't did. It's been damn near 16 years. You found everything else you loved on the Internet, how come ya never thought to find me? Family, ha?

I want to give a special Thanks to my promo team, headed by my amazingly beautiful daughter, Komica. Thanks for handling my Facebook and everything else. Anthony Sowell, you stepped up to the plate for a true player. Thanks for handling them flyers and pushin' ya boy's brand through the streets of Q.C. first and foremost. Sandy, over at Gutta Magazine, you shout me out every chance you get! Bulletproof respect to you and your street team for your support. Sky is the limit for you. I want to give thanks to the W.C.P. (Wahida Clark Presents) Team for the new cover designing and all of your great efforts, and of course I can't forget Towanna. I keep you in a post office (smile) you still make it all come together, girl.

Now to all my real Niggaz I was in the struggle with. Man, y'all know how I get down. I know you happy for a player. Help spread the word. I ma get at every soldier left behind in just a minute. If ya was ever beside me then you know I make shit happen. WE got money, didn't we? Wish I could shout you all out, but y'all know my road has been waaayy too long!

Tonight I got to give my celley, William (Pretty Squeak) Johnston a shout. Good look, homie. Real talk: I 'preciate the space you give me, the encouragement and the constructive criticism, even when I buck (smile). It's been real player! Keep wakin' up a soldier. We bout ta put feet on the ground, fuck what ya heard. Queen City, here we come!

Nuff said, let's get on with the story, and don't forget to read the afterthought.

Enjoy . . .
Mike Jefferies

Introduction

"Reality Records?" Wiz mean mugged the man standing in the foyer of a building an anonymous tip had led him to.

"Yeah, Reality Records," the man repeated himself and tightened up the scowl on his face, realizing Wiz wasn't appeased with the politeness he'd offered at first.

Wiz sucked at his platinum teeth, never taking his eyes off the man who'd introduced himself as Drip.

Without turning his head, he reached out and patted Swirl, who shot the man an even colder glare. "Let's get up outta' here." Wiz turned and stalked back out the door. "Reality Records, ha?" Swirl capped hotly. "We'll meet again." He brushed his hand over his waistline and nodded on his way out the door. Drip made a step closer to the door and stood there stunned as he asked himself what in the hell had just happened? In the next flash, he watched two of the hottest celebs in the industry jump into a black Lincoln Town Car and nearly burn rubber getting back onto Forsyth Street.

*****

Before Wiz could make it out the parking lot his whole body had turned warm. The moment he flopped behind the driver's wheel he happened to glance to his right, and when he did his gut instinct was confirmed. The sound of Reality Records still reverberated through his mental. But staring over at Diamond"s red Lexus Coupe, he knew that Drako was somehow behind this label.

"Fuck!" Wiz slammed his fist into the dashboard and pressed the accelerator even harder. "This some underhanded bitch-ass shit! I knew something was up with Drako! I can't believe he sided with some other niggaz on me!" He smacked an open palm to his forehead. "Man, I shoulda' seen it comin'! He all of a sudden tryin" to squeeze me for money!" Wiz nodded his head in disgust. "After all I done for him! Man, I tossed that nigga hundreds of grands when he hit the bricks! Put him in a house, copped the 760, and you know I ain't stop there!" Wiz fumed more heat with every word. "I gave this nigga *toys*! He pushin" a Bentley Coupe and all! ... Man, it was first class everything! You know that shit!" Swirl nodded in agreement. "Enough just ain't never enough for some, huh? And now this man wanna step outside and be my competition! I „on get this shit, homie. I just don't get it!" His thoughts were scattered into a million pieces.

Swirl sucked at his platinum teeth with a knowing smirk. "Yeah . . . I been saw the malice in that man's eyes. But them yo' people, like way before my time, so I saw best to mind my own, ya dig?"

"Yeah, yeah, I feel ya," Wiz said easily, trying to calm his rage. "That *was* my friend. Man, this shit ain't all about no money when it's between us." Wiz's voice cracked. "I guess he got his reasons." Wiz seemed to curb his attitude a bit as he merged back onto the beltway.

"You think . . ." Swirl said hesitantly, "he had somethin" to do wit' dem folks stomping through our doors?"

Wiz glanced at Swirl sideways and then gazed off in the distance. He thought a moment and said, "Hell naw, man. That shit ain't nowhere in "im. This 'bout somethin" else. I can't figure him out. It's like to me he developed some type of control issues in the pen after all them years. I don't think he can accept me being the boss. So maybe he wanna be his own. But that other shit ain't him. I know it ain't. That's in my heart, homie." Wiz went silent again as they cruised on.

"Well, how you gone handle up?" Swirl asked the inevitable.

"It's business, that's all, player. If he want to get in the waters with me I'ma just crush that shit! We gone keep makin' good music and keep this shit on lock! Just business."

Swirl sat for a moment before he gave his final thought. "A'ight, I hear you and I respect you bein' in charge of this business. I respect you leadin' this camp. On the business level I'm wit' it; we'll crush everythang. But when or if it gets personal, Drako's *your* friend. I ain't finna' be the nigga to keep handin' out passes and bags of respect. I done had enough from „erybody, and like I said, I want to be clear wit' you. My nigga, I „on give a fuck who it is . . . It's soou-woou if he brang it!"

Swirl's face told it all. He meant every word he said before he laid the pistol on the floorboard, reclined his seat and closed his eyes. Neither one spoke a word until they reached their final destination.

*****

"Now isn't this better?" Diamond asked as soon as she positioned the tall indoor plant in the corner of Drako's office.

"It's cool, ma. Whatever you think," he said, not even glancing up from the papers strewn about his desk.

"Well, if you gonna be spending time here this place needs life. It needs to breathe." She stepped over and flopped her behind on the ledge of his wide desk. Just as she was about to lean over and steal his attention something else stole hers.

"Look, baby!" She startled, pointing to the six monitors behind him.

Her eyes bulged wide enough to make Drako think she was staring down the barrel of a loaded gun. He immediately spun his chair around to check his security screens.

"What the fuck?" He was taken by surprise as he leaned closer to the monitor. "Damn. . . . How?" he stammered in confusion, but got to his feet even quicker at the sight of Wiz and Swirl standing in the lobby of Reality Records.

"Dang, how the—"

"I ,on know and I ,on give a fuck!" he said.

Diamond slid off the desk and rushed to Drako's side. She saw that smoldering look in Drako's eyes. "And I ain't 'bout to tiptoe around these niggaz, either!" He pushed past Diamond and headed for the door.

"What are you gonna do? Where—"

"Whatever I have to!" he said with his tight jawbones jutting from beneath his dark skin. "Just stay here!" he bellowed, not allowing Diamond another word as he vanished out the door.

By the time Drako trotted down the steps and rounded the corner, Drip was standing near the door gazing at the parking lot.

"Where did they go?" Drako shouted, making quick steps toward him.

"Man, I-I-I ,on know?" Drip turned to meet Drako's loud voice with a baffled expression.

"Shit!" Drako huffed with anguish, looking out the door himself. He rubbed his hand over his baldhead as Drip noticed his chest heaving up and down.

"Fuck did they want?" Drako didn't attempt to hide the anger on his face.

"He just asked what was this place?" Drip said, still lost. "Sheeit, I told him this Reality Records, shawty! Hell, I thought he knew," Drip said honestly. Drako nodded and gave thought as Drip turned to lock the front door. Drako saw the butt of his .45 still tucked safely in the back of his pants.

"I shoulda' moved faster. I saw that shit Swirl was giving you."

"Yeah, I peeped that shit, too," Drip admitted. "Is everything okay? That nigga Swirl was packing some heavy heat!"

"How you know?" Drako's brows furled.

"Man, you know a nigga's conscience gone always make him check to see if he holdin" up tight. . . . The first time he grazed his waist I ain't trip, but he did it again, so I knew he had somethin" heavy. Feel me?"

"Oh yeah?" Drako shook his head as his mouth twisted up into a grit. "You mean to tell me that nigga came up in my shit packin"?"

"Sheeit!" Drip slurred his trademark curse. "I whadn't even trippin" over that, „cause if that wide-eyed fool would'a reached for that pipe it would'a been the last thing he remembered!"

Drako shook his head. He knew Drip was street savvy and short-fused, but a thinker just like him.

"We beefin" already or what?" Drip asked as he stepped over to the counter, pulled the pistol from his back and laid it on the countertop.

"I „on do no beefin" and I ain't wit' none of that paper gangsta shit! If I speak the shit I"ma live it—simple."

"I know that, but I"m sayin" from the look of thangs I thought you'd be telling me somethin" I don't know. Swirl poppin" slick and—"

"Look, whatever fall between me and Wiz, just make sure you stay out of it!"

Drip gave a cool nod to Drako's unbroken glare. "Well, what about—"

"That nigga Swirl has gotten beside himself lately. I used to respect him as a man, but he just received his pass. If he step outta line again I"ma see 'bout "im," Drako assured Drip.

Drip nodded again, further letting Drako know he was with it. "I ain't mean to catch up with my old camp this way or so fast, but fuck it, we here now. Reality Records 'bout ta blow and ain't nothin" gone take our focus," Drako said, knowing it was gonna come down to this eventually.

"I"ma play the back on this like we been talkin" „bout, but I want you to keep these booths busy? And from this day forward I want you to tighten up on this door! Reality Records ain't no revolving door or no hang out spot for nobody. No exceptions! Let everybody know we puttin" in work around here. They come here to utilize studio time. We gone run a business first and foremost. See, at Red Rum they eat and shit from the same pot, that's why the whole world stay in his business." Drako turned his head to see Diamond approaching. He turned back to Drip, lowering his tone. "I „on see how they found us so fast."

"Man, are you serious?" Drip leaned his back against the bar and shrugged his thin shoulders. "You done signed two of the hardest rappers in Atlanta. Them young cats is proud! They tellin" 'erybody! Sheeit, and if we gone be out here tryin" to eat off the same plates as Gucci, them Brick Squad niggaz and Jeezy, we besta get behind 'em!" His revelation sank like water through dirt. Drako knew Drip was about getting paper!

"The door's open," Drako said confidently as he stepped away and led Diamond up the stairs.

*****

Drako sat back down in his chair shortly after he sent Diamond home. He picked up his remote control and replayed the tape once more. He watched the black Lincoln whip up to his building, and then he watched Wiz and Swirl enter his establishment.

Drako was seething inside. Not necessarily at Wiz. He knew Wiz was often silly, but never stupid! He was mad at himself for not keeping the lid tighter for just a few more months, at least until he could pull off the lick he'd been priming for months in Connecticut. He told himself that with the cat now out of the bag it didn't matter. He needed to disassociate himself from Red Rum for now. Also, a few days ago his single focus was on finally avenging his first and only true mentor, Toney

Domacio. Wiz and Red Rum"s negative attention wasn't about to stand in the way of any of his plans. He still felt sour as to Wiz only tossing him pennies, but now was no time to fiddle over his motives. In time, he and Wiz would cross paths again, but for the moment, Drako couldn't shake the thought of the four hefty, army duffel bags that contained three million unexpected dollars in cash, thanks to Vinny Pazzo. Pazzo's blood was the only blood he'd gotten on his hands since he'd been released from prison. It felt good. Just like the money, the freedom, and the thought of soon surpassing the ten million dollar goal he'd set his sights on.

Yep, Drako was feeling himself. He felt stability, not remorse and he planned to keep it just that way. He turned off the three-minute event after watching the Lincoln bolt from the screen. He set the remote on the desk and stood to his feet. He'd made up his mind: Anybody that crossed his path or tried to stop him would be the next blood spilled on his hands. He cut off his office lights on his way out, hoping that for Swirl"s own sake, he'd choose to stay in his place.

Toney Domacio
Chapter- 1

It was just past 7:30 a.m. when Toney Domacio dismissed his two henchmen from their routine morning duties. Today, he stood alone in his cell, his heart racing with anticipation. He glared at the blurry sheet of steel on the wall that served as his mirror for a long while. His incarceration had now stretched over a decade, but Toney still remained poised. A very well-groomed man of distinction, who still held the respect of many, is what he was proud to still see staring back at him.

He squared his shoulders just before slipping on his gold trademark Armani frames at the sound of his name being called to visitation over the prison's intercom system.

Approximately twenty minutes later, the legendary Toney Domacio was escorted to Lewisburg Penitentiary's visitation room. His eyes quickly traipsed over the crowded room full of women and loud kids until they once again settled on the fuzzy haired, middle-aged man with thick glasses. Toney's smile broadened as he made his way through a maze of tables that led to the far table where Damien always sat.

"So, we meet again." Toney greeted him with a firm shake and a nod of approval to the disguise Damien always wore to visit him.

"Not bad," he added with a whisper. "But I see you still haven't gotten a haircut." He chuckled at the worn-out toupee as they both sat down.

"Well . . ." Toney exhaled a sigh of relief. "Our date has surely come and passed us by once more," he said with a raised eyebrow, studying Damien's face.

Damien couldn't hold back like he originally planned to, and Toney could see right through him anyway.

"Like a Hiroshima bomb it hit them!" He delivered the good news with a smile. "Everybody paid the piper!" Damien seemed to poke his chest out.

"Everybody?" Toney asked with excitement, reaching for the bag of popcorn on   the table in front of him.

"Everybody!" Damien replied, reaching for his bag as well. And like always, they used the popcorn to conceal their lips from being read as he filled Toney in on what was going on.

"Spare me none!" Toney ordered with a handful of kernels covering his mouth.

"They never seen it coming!" Damien gave a sinister chuckle. "He told them it was an anniversary gift from an old friend."

This time they both shared a proud laugh before Damien began to relive all the things he saw that night. He included all the gory details as he watched Toney's leg twitch with the feelings of excitement and revenge. He described the sight of Mrs. Pazzo's grotesque corpse, all the way down to the sound of the pig's last squeal when Drako slit Vinny's (the informant who'd gotten Toney a life sentence) throat. Just like Toney had asked him to. Damien watched and waited for the victorious look on Toney's face, so that he could honestly report back to Drako just what he'd seen in Toney's response.

The two men sat in silence for a few moments after Damien delivered the news. He gave Toney time to absorb the relief of what he'd waited so long to hear.

Finally, Toney responded, "Words . . ." He cleared his throat. "I can't find words to tell him how much this means to me. Tell him if I never get anything else; that I still got even!" His voice trailed away and he went silent.

Damien turned to Toney. "I figured it out," he said. "I witnessed his essence that night." Damien swallowed the lump in his throat. "Remorseless," he stated, sure of himself while looking straight ahead. "Those wings could only belong to an angel . . . an angel of death!" He didn't even look Toney's way again. Toney's silence let him know his assessment was right on point. Damien now held the soda can to his lips. "You got me hooked up with an angel of death." He exhaled and set the can back down.

"He'd never turn on you," Toney stated with assurance. "His hands are for you. Just stay loyal to him as you have to me. Those that cross the lines you set will be the only ones with worry."

"I like him a lot." Damien nodded, wiping his hand with a paper towel. "I have no problem even though this date has passed. I'll be there for him just as I am for you whenever you need me."

Toney smiled inwardly just before he took another sip from his can. They enjoyed the rest of the visit filled with the joys of their accomplishments.

Again, the CO announced that visitation had concluded. The two stood and hugged goodbye. Damien aligned along the left wall as usual, and Toney was led into the strip room by a tall, stone-faced CO. Today, the strip search and cavity check was nothing. Toney put back on his khakis and steel-toed boots and was led through another door that returned him back to his life of imprisonment. Unconsciously, Toney ignored all the loud noise and inmate activity as he made his way across the prison yard and back to his cell. Though he wore a smile on his face the whole while, he never spoke to any of his prison associates along the way.

Toney soon closed his cell door behind him, feeling relieved. He flipped his light off and sat on his bunk. There was no

mistake. Today he received the best news he'd heard since the day he realized Vinny Pazzo had walked him head first into this very cell.

He draped a towel over his head and dropped his head to the floor as he replayed over and over all the things Damien recalled to him. He laughed, he cried, and his heart raced with a victory he wasn't sure he'd ever claim.

'Final Redemption' is how he referred to it, and now after all these years he was finally soaking in the feeling. Though he knew he was locked up, he still felt a fleeting sense of freedom for just a few moments.

Toney knew he'd been a father figure to Drako, and at this moment he was as proud as any father had ever been of a son. Drako had kept his word! Damien"s assessment had been just right, and for the first time Toney drifted asleep fully dressed in that very spot, wishing all the world to fall in Drako"s hands, just as he"d planned from the very start.

Drako
Chapter- 2

On August 7th, Drako was the first to awake. He looked over and saw Diamond still sleeping peacefully on the fluffy pillow next to him after a long night of intense lovemaking. He reached out and gently raked his fingers through her soft strands of curly hair. He was loving the new style she wore even more with each passing day. Her jet-black strands were now cut short around the left side and the back, while the other side was cut shorter than normal, but was still long enough to spill over her forehead and on to her sweet smelling mulatto skin.

Leaning forward, Drako strummed the longer strands from her forehead and planted a soft kiss. Just then Diamond"s eyes fluttered open, and on instinct she scooted her nakedness even closer. "Mm . . ." she crooned, switching her head over to his pillow and feeling safe in his arms again.

"Happy birthday," he said, followed by another kiss to her cheek.

"Hmm . . . you gave me that last night." She rubbed an appreciative hand across his chest.

"Every day, ma. I want every day to feel like your birthday." He slid his hands down her back and over her shapely, firm behind. He held her there and caressed her back to sleep for a short while as he still basked in the two days leading up to her birthday he'd spent spoiling her.

Eventually, it was she who nudged him awake this time. "January 3rd," she said, leaning up on an elbow.

"Huh?" Drako said, still sort of groggy and confused.

"January 1st is your birthday. It's on a Friday this year. January 3rd—that Sunday is when I want to take that step with

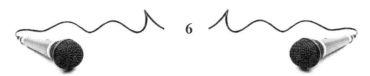

6

you." She ran a hand over Drako"s freshly shaved baldhead, then cradled his face as she leaned up to plant a kiss of her own on his Hershey black skin. "Mwah!" She ended the kiss. "So it's a date, huh?" Her expression said she was eagerly awaiting his response.

"Baby, it's whatever you want. The sooner, the better. Put it together, let's make us official."

Diamond beamed like the first rays of morning sun. She peeled the covers back and slid out of bed. "I'm cookin" you breakfast." She stood, stretched her arms, and then ran her fingers through her hair. "I know you got things you need to get done today, but I want to spend a little more time before you get lost, baby."

She stood there as Drako"s eyes danced over her brown nipples and down her flat stomach to her diamond belly ring.

"Don't trip, ma. I'ma always make time for you, baby."

Drako winked assuredly, and then watched her turn and saunter her flawless naked body to the bathroom. He had no doubt that Diamond was still the cream of the crop. A definite sex symbol. He also knew lavish plans were underway and Diamond would plan a wedding they'd never forget. He lay back cozily on his pillow as he heard the shower come on. He still had Diamond and things were looking up. All he had to do was keep Reality Records headed in the direction it was and stay on course with his next scheme. He quickly made the next few chess moves ahead in his mind, and then he slid out of bed.

It won't be long, he told himself as he slid the door open and joined Diamond in the shower.

*****

It was late afternoon by the time Drako finally walked through the doors of Reality Records and into the studio room to see Drip busy at work behind the keyboards. He bobbed his head along to the track as he kept a steady eye on the emcee that was just on the other side of the glass booth.

Drako sat down on the stool next to him, finally breaking Drip's only focus for the moment. Drip smiled, still nodding to the beat as he extended one of his long slender hands to give Drako dap.

"Man, you got to hear this shit!" He pointed to a pair of headsets for Drako to put on. "Man, when I tell you it's a mothafuckin" lion in the booth! It's a mothafuckin"—" Drip tripped over his words with excitement and whipped about two buttons on the mixing board. "Shawdy been at it for over four hours now!" he yelled as Drako slid the headphones on and heard 'Save' freestyle for the first time.

I 'on talk it I live it/ I 'on fake it to make it/ But I'll risk it to get it/ This ain't a right it's a privilege / If you stop talkin' and listen / You might realize what you missin'/

Drako sat straight up as Save flailed his arms and stepped closer to the mic without missing a beat.

It ain't a dream it's a vision/ It ain't a plan it's a mission/ Long as I play my position/ It ain't a goal it's a given/

In no time, Drako was bobbing to the same gangster track as Drip. There was no doubt about what Drip had claimed this artist to be. The metaphors, the diction, and delivery were just the beginning. His lyrics had the substance of Nas and the attitude of 50 Cent. They were looking at a success story in the making. Save, short for 'Save the Game' was another underground mixtape monster. His distinct style was surfacing everywhere! He'd made a mixtape and passed it off for free on his Facebook page, which had quickly soared to over 200,000 friends and an inevitable call from Drip. He was on course to become YouTube Platinum, and now was the moment to cash in and get some real paper, just like Drip had all the plans of doing.

"Sheeid!" Drip slurred proudly as the track faded out. "I'm tellin" you now, ain't nothin" fuckin" wit' this! What we need to do is record as many of his verses in front of the green screen as possible! You want a surplus of this on hand at any and all times! I'm tellin" you this kid gone have an archive as deep as Pac!"

Drip winked at Drako, feeling sure of himself. Drako nodded and then looked over at Save still in the booth. He tossed his dreads back over his shoulder and turned up a bottle of Vitamin Water.

He picked up a towel off the stool and dabbed sweat from his smooth brown skin. A moment later his six-foot frame was back in front of the mic and his shoulders slightly rocked back and forth as his head caught up with the cadence of the next beat that blared through his headset. Drako was further proud of Drip as he sat in the cockpit and steered Reality Records in the direction he'd always hoped for. Drako knew Drip was smart and had tons of business sense. Drako had first met Drip many years ago in Lewisburg Penitentiary. Drip had caught eighteen years after blowing trial for money laundering and racketeering charges, but after six years, his case was overturned on appeal.

In the pen, Drip was a law library hamster. While other inmates lifted weights, played sports, or partook in the many vices of prison life, Drip kept his head in the Federal Guideline books. He became fascinated with the law and obsessed with beating the government. He'd gotten several other cases overturned before finally achieving relief for himself. Other than just beating his case, Drip also studied to make sure it never happened again. The chosen few in prison such as Toney Domacio and Drako knew of Drip's reputation for washing money. He'd become an expert at finding tax loopholes and a wizard at hiding and diverting corporate funds. He understood the workings of offshore accounts, secret stocks, and securities and tax-exempt entities abroad. He had hands-on experience with washing money through untraceable Swiss Bonds and had once stashed holdings in Bermuda and Latin America.

And the one thing he and Drako shared a common interest in was the music industry. Drip had been to school for accounting before becoming a launderer. But his first passion was making beats. He'd practiced this hobby on the side ever since he was a twelve-year-old kid with his first drum machine and a microphone. It was Drip who helped Drako on the side. He broke down tax law, incorporation, and the power of branding. Drako started to look forward to catching up with him in the law library, and when Drip got his case overturned, Drako had promised him a position if he ever got on.

Well, when Drako first got out he thought about trying to bring Drip to Wiz"'s attention, but because of the way Wiz handled things, Drako decided to hold this vital piece until he felt it was the right timing. Drako now knew he'd made the best decision ever! For the most part, Reality Records would remain squeaky clean, but wherever it didn't wouldn't make much difference. Drip was sure to leave the IRS scratching their heads in wonderance at all stops. Drako knew Drip's heart and where his loyalties lay, and he couldn't have made a smarter or safer move than to have Drip on his team.

"Man, you got eyes and ears for this shit," Drako commented as he witnessed Save blaze over the next beat with an entirely different flow.

"Drako, this thing ain't even got started yet." Drip laughed, removing the headset and twisting his neck from side to side. "I'm doin' my best to spread him out evenly. It's hard to hold him back. The kid has got so much he won"'t stop!" He signaled for Save to come out the booth after the track ended.

"He says if Weezy can do seventy-seven songs in a year he can do one hundred seventy-seven." He eased back a little and

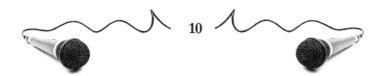

slid his fingers together before resting them on his chest. Drako smirked with a nod as he thought of how Drip had a very striking resemblance to TI; the only difference was Drip was taller. He was at least five-eleven, but he had all the same chiseled features and that hard look to his brown skin. To top it off, he kept that 'one against the grain' cut, tight at all times.

"What up, son?" Save waltzed into the room with a foot-wide smile. He gave Drip dap as he tossed the towel over his shoulder. He turned to Drako.

"What up, So—"

"Drako . . . just call me Drako."

"Oh . . ." Save had a baffled look, but gave Drako a weak pound.

"So, uh . . ." Drip cut in, seizing the awkward moment. "I was about to tell Drako how I asked you not to put another free mixtape on your page."

Save waved the thought away, sitting down on the next stool. "Yo, don't worry about that shit. The God is infinite. I got a plan and it's gonna work. I'm tellin" you, son, I just need to get this shit out my head."

"And you will. You got two videos; your album is doing great! Just let me guide you into stardom. You can't be denied, believe me," Drip advised.

"Well, meanwhile, anybody that want me on, set the price and tell them to email it to me. I ,,on give a fuck! I'm hungry! Hungry enough to eat everything on the plate!" Save sucked his teeth and turned the Vitamin Water up again.

"Just be cool." Drip smiled proudly. "I gotcha. You gone get way more than yo' feet wet. You and that email in-box gone be drenched in the months to come." Drip stood up, patted Save's shoulder and strolled on past him as he and Drako departed to Drako"s office.

"What's good?" Drako asked as his eyes gazed over his security screens. He saw the interior monitor over the sleeping quarters where two more artists and a female were lounging. Drako blacked that screen off with the remote and then turned to Drip. "Looks like everybody good 'round here."

"Yeah, yeah . . . you said keep them booths busy, so I'm always lookin" for the next best thing, feel me?"

Drako just looked, but gave no response.

"I told 'em if they gone smoke, just do it in the sleeping quarters. I got everything respectable. I know everybody don't blaze. Hell, you'd think Save was a weed head. Man, he's as sober as a Catholic priest. And I'm sure we'll eventually be sharing the booth with Diamond and other females alike. So we'll keep respect due."

"Good . . . Good." Drip always seemed to think in the same way as Drako.

"Well, I see you got this under control. No need to waste time on that." Drako swiveled his chair around and leaned forward placing his elbows on his desk. "So like I was saying, I got a lil" help we could use for promo or whatever. It's just a lil backing ,til things really hit, feel me?"

Drip crossed one leg over a knee and got comfortable in the thick padded leather chair just in front of Drako's desk. "How much help are we talking?" Drip's eyebrows rose.

"Two . . . two and a half big." Drako was referring to two and a half million dollars he'd gotten from Pazzo.

Drip chuckled. "Not a problem. We could really use it to help spark a flame around here." He leaned forward, causing the leather to crack. "But I ,on think we're gonna need it for long. I don't think it'll be long before we can demand a distribution deal that'll far benefit everybody in this camp." He reared back and intertwined his slender fingers just like he"d done every time he

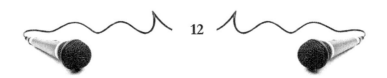

thought he'd figured out a loophole in a case back when he was in the pen.

"Well, we'll cross that bridge when we get to it. Right now I need to know how you want this money delivered?"

Drako"s concern for moving that much paper around safely was etched on his face. He knew the consequences of getting caught slipping was nothing a man with his criminal history could swallow.

Drip smiled even harder. He was ready to do what he did best. He raised a thumb to his chin while his index finger rested on his nose. "Check this out," Drip said. He carefully explained how, where and when he thought best to deliver the money. Then they talked about everything that had gone on around Reality"s Headquarters for the few days Drako spent away with Diamond. They both laughed like two lost and found buddies. They knew that together, they had everything to make this the Ultimate Reality and soon, nothing would stand in their way!

Wiz
Chapter- 3

Down in Miami things were moving much faster for Wiz today. He stood on his huge balcony in his master suite and glanced down over his infinity pool and the beautiful waterfall below it. His eyes scanned across the endless miles of ocean front property just before they traveled heavenward. He closed his eyes and ran his fingers through Thai's stringy brown hair as she brought him to another climax.

"Oh shit!" He couldn't hold his nut any longer as his fingers now sprawled over the top of her head and held firmly. She gagged a little and let drool run down his dick as he slammed it to the back of her throat. His knees trembled and his dick jerked as it spurted the last drop of semen down her throat.

"Damn, you drainin" me!" Wiz groaned, trying to catch his breath. He eased his waning penis from her mouth and ran a smooth thumb across her face as he admired her rare mix of Cuban and Chinese skin.

"Mmm . . . whatever you like," she cooed, looking up at him from a kneeling position. She still pulled on his big dick and licked the head free of all semen traces. They'd both forgotten about all the people who were running around the pool area below making last minute preparations for the busy shoot scheduled to take place in just over an hour. Wiz hadn't spoken to any publications since the Feds had raided Red Rum"s headquarters a few months back. Since his best gossip-spreading columnist buddy, Joshua had gotten his position back at XXL, Wiz figured this was the best time and the best tool to reintroduce Red Rum back into the tabloids.

"Chh . . . Why the fuck y"all gotta be comin" all out here?" Wiz craned his neck to see Cinnamon standing naked at the doorway with her arms folded over her breasts and her lips poked out.

"Stop whining all the fuckin" time!" he snapped, causing Thai to stand her five-foot three-inch frame up.

"Why she be actin" like that?" Thai whispered with a frown that caused her oriental eyes to appear even more slanted.

"I 'on know. She knows both of y"all my girls." Wiz winked and popped her bare ass cheek.

"I know, right?" She smiled and followed Wiz back into his bedroom.

"Cinnamon!" he yelled, "I suggest you get yo' face together and get yo" ass in your best gear. I've chosen y"all to be the models for my layout, so you need to get downstairs in Diane's makeup chair." He turned to Thai. "Come help me wash my dick off." He waltzed his naked butt into his huge steam shower.

*****

Thirty-five minutes later, Wiz was prancing down his spiral mahogany staircase wearing a pair of Red Monkey jeans, Gucci sneakers, a fresh white tank top and a red bandanna hanging from his right back pocket. Wiz knew damn well he was far from anything Blood, but he chalked it up to the idea of suggestive images bringing good controversy. He strolled his short five-foot six-inch frame across the marble floor, making his way to the pool area as he slipped a pair of Millionaire shades across his handsome posterboy face to top off all the ice he wore. As soon as he stepped out the door and on to the cobblestone, he saw Swirl reclined back comfortably on a padded table getting inked up. Diablo was regarded as one of the best Latino tattoo artists in the country and he was the only one to sink ink into Wiz or Swirl after they tried his work the very first time.

"How that red look in my star?" Swirl asked as Wiz stood over him. "You tight, my nigga. Real tight!" Wiz said, giving open approval as Swirl's upper body was a full shirt of the finest red and black ink.

"You know I ain't had my things touched up in a while. I just have to feel this needle some time." Swirl raised a hand smoothly, which told Diablo to stop the needle for a moment. Swirl reached over the .40 Glock on the table beside him and took a sip from his Styrofoam cup.

"Shoot a lil red through this Red Rum on my stomach," he instructed, putting the cup back down. "You using five needles, ain't you?" Diablo nodded and the buzz came back to life. Swirl didn't flinch as the needle poked him all over again.

"Looks like everything everythang ,round here. The whips been wiped down and I told these bitches I want 'em on their best behavior."

"Who you shootin" with? That Chinese looking bitch and Cinnamon, right?"

"Yeah, yeah, that's a good look. Pretty new faces, ya dig?"

"Yeah, that Chinese girl is." Swirl smiled, dropping his hand to his crotch. "Bad as a mothafucka! Cinnamon is too, but don't she look just like Myria to you?"

"Hell, naw." Wiz denied seeing any resemblance between her and his ex-girl. "She way too dark!"

"Tss . . ." Swirl sucked diamonds. "Cinnamon"s a little darker, but that's it! Same body. Same whining. If I was you I'd look to throwin" that bitch back soon!"

"Yeah, it ain't shit to it." Wiz let Swirl's comment roll right past him."Well, you got less than an hour. I just got the email. Joshua's flight just landed."

*****

16

An hour later, Wiz squatted in front of his red Phantom with his suicide doors kicked open, showing off his custom white interior. He had a crisp, Gucci sneaker slightly extended in front of him to match the Gucci bag filled with cash right beside him. He stood and posed in several positions after Cinnamon and Thai joined his side, just like the photographer asked.

Swirl reclined on a lounge chair without a shirt on, showing off all his fresh tats. He had two long-haired, thick redbones he'd of course, hand-picked. One was sprawled across his lap in a signature blood burgundy bikini, while the other stood behind him with a hand rested on his shoulder and a soft pedicured foot on the other girl"s behind. The photographer captured Swirl and his models in several tasteful positions, and they surely had enough frames to guarantee another hot layout.

As soon as the flashes ceased and the ladies were dismissed, Joshua was finally at the table next to the pool with his tape recorder and notepad out. He had Wiz and Swirl in front of him and was ready to give the streets the interview every columnist clamored for.

"So, Wiz," Joshua said and started the recorder, "it's been over two months since your troubles began with the Feds, and now many people are wondering where Red Rum is headed. But even more, they want to know why haven't you spoken out?"

Wiz sat up and cleared his throat. "Well, in actuality my 'badgering' is how I describe what the Feds are doing to me, started long before two months ago. They deny it by all means, but they're wasting millions of taxpayers" dollars to follow me and many other artists around at every turn." He laughed. "I wouldn't call that a problem for me. Red Rum is a respectable, clean entity. It has and always will remain that way."

"Well, why haven't you just come forward and said so?"

Wiz took in a deep sigh as if he were contemplating, but he knew all the while and wished he could tell Joshua that if he made them wait it would be even more profitable—jackass! But instead, Wiz let that same breath out and held a straight face. "To be truthful, Joshua, I just don't like to be the center of controversy or negative attention of any kind. I just chose to keep my focus on releasing Swirl's album as well as Choc-Money and Jay-Poon." He cleverly plugged his two new artists. "You know they're next to blow. I can honestly say since Swirl came into this game I haven't seen anything close. My only intent at Red Rum is to make great music and satisfy our loyal fans. It's them who got us here. It's them who know the truth, and it'll be their support that keeps us puttin' down hits to the end!" Wiz's voice dripped with firm confidence.

"I agree wholeheartedly," Joshua said sincerely. "But Bless at Take Money Records is saying else wise. He's pointing fingers and saying things like you are the reason for the lack in sales of hip-hop right now. He's saying—"

Wiz burst out in laughter. "Bless? Take Money? . . . Clowns! I don't want to hear anything about them. Only because of respect for the deceased I won't bomb on them." He was referring to Fatt Katt, a rapper he was once in cahoots with in a profitable fake beef and later became a prime suspect for his murder.

"Their record sales are the only ones down. If you have nothing to say, who in the fuck is gonna pay to listen?" He laughed again and stood up.

"Ask Swirl what you need to. I need to use the bathroom. Those silly remarks make me feel like I need to piss!" Wiz stepped off with a wave of his hand, leaving Joshua and Swirl to finish up.

"Well . . ." Joshua turned back to Swirl, seeming a little peeved at Wiz's arrogance. "So what's next for Swirl?" He began with a few basic questions in a rather dry tone. Swirl answered each one with quick, witty responses. Soon Joshua

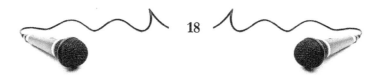

was looking over his shoulder anticipating Wiz's return, which obviously wasn't gonna happen.

"So what do you think? Is hip-hop dead as Bless claims?" Joshua seemed to hurl the line of questions that had been intended for Wiz straight in Swirl's direction.

"No, I don't agree. I simply think that's one man's opinion of what he feels."

"Well, what about this young phenom called Save? He claims he's come to single-handedly save the game of hip-hop?"

"I „on really know much about him. He's only dropped one album, so I can't really say," Swirl answered sincerely, but not liking the direction Joshua was steering things.

As fast as Swirl finished his thought, Joshua fired right back. "Save claims that hip-hop is far from dead. He says it simply moved to Atlanta." He smiled.

"Look man." Swirl bit down on his back teeth and gritted at the scrawny little white columnist. "You here to speak about Red Rum or Save? I told you I „on know shit about the newcomer. Now, if you have a set of questions that's relevant to Red Rum then get on with it. Other than that, get on 'bout ya" business." Swirl tried to be firm without raising his voice.

"Well, uh . . ." Joshua cleared his throat. "I'm just trying to gather the story that people want to hear. Sometimes it puts me in a position to ask the tough questions. And right now people want to hear about Save and what you think, because that's who you'll most likely be sharing your light with." Joshua's smirk was irritating.

"Say bruh, I „on wanna hear shit 'bout no fuckin" Save!" Swirl swiped all Joshua's paper off the table as all traces of composure left Swirl's face.

Joshua held on to the recorder tight and caught an attitude of his own.

"Hey! Who do you think—"

19

Pop!

Swirl had smacked him on the side of his head, tumbling both him and the lawn chair onto the cement before he even realized it.

Joshua, who was now in pure shock, tried to quickly recover. He was on his knees scrambling to pick up all the loose pages when Swirl stalked from around the table and kicked him square up his ass!

"Owww!" Joshua shrieked as the thud caused him to flop down on his stomach barely catching himself from hitting the cement face first.

"Write that up you gossiping little bitch!" Swirl stormed past him and headed back in the mansion.

*****

Wiz and Thai both swallowed two x-pills and Wiz now had her pressed against the wall in his eight-car garage. He'd held her hands above her head and had been tongue kissing her passionately for over ten minutes when he spotted Joshua hauling ass toward his SUV.

What the hell? Wiz thought as he dropped Thai's hands and yelled to get Joshua's attention.

"Tell Swirl he's lucky I don't call the cops!" Joshua yelled as he reached his truck.

Wiz trotted out into the driveway as Joshua jumped in and slammed the door behind him. His face was beet red.

"What the hell is goin' on?" Wiz trotted toward the truck "wait!"

"Fuck y'all!" Joshua snapped, putting the truck in reverse. He backed back then left skid marks on the driveway as he disappeared through the gate.

After Wiz found out what happened through Swirl, he then put a persuasive call in to Joshua in hopes of preventing any lawsuits.

Things began to settle down again. All the hired help, along with Swirl's two models had been dismissed. Wiz was now walking back into the garage kicking it with his man Swirl. "My bad, homie. Man, I'm tellin" you that lil chump got an attitude when you left. He tried to play me out and when I spoke up he just . . . Man, I just couldn't get with all that bass in his voice." Swirl half-apologized, taking a swig from his Styrofoam cup.

"Don't even trip. I doubt if he"ll report any of that." Wiz hoped he was right. He knew another case regarding Red-Rum and especially Swirl would be terrible press at a time like now.

"Look man, I"ma go ahead and stab out. I"ma take the Lambo and head over to South Beach. I wanna clear my mind a bit, ya dig?" Wiz took a step back as Swirl opened the door to his blacked out Lamborghini Gallardo.

"Yeah, that's cool. If you find a pair that's nice, bring 'em back. I'm gettin" tired of these two old mop heads." He winked with a smile.

"I gotcha," Swirl said, settling into the cockpit. "I gotcha," he said again as he closed the door and passed Wiz the Styrofoam cup through the window.

"Toss that for me," he said politely as he pressed a single button that awakened the Lamborghini.

Wiz took another step back as he heard the dual exhaust growl with life. In the next moment, he watched the shiny black paint drift from its parking space and seconds later, the Lambo's tail lights disappeared past his wrought iron gates as it zipped away from his estate and into the night.

"Man . . ." He dropped his head after taking a whiff of the codeine syrup left in the Styrofoam cup he held. He wanted to say something to Swirl about it, but what could he say? The place he'd reached in his career consisted of three things: sex, pills, and parties. Wiz was again enjoying the x and the life himself, he reasoned. "I hope this shit don't get no uglier," he spoke aloud. Wiz knew the game, and somehow, someway, he was going to continue to make his paper. He tossed the cup and headed back inside.

Drako

Chapter- 4

"How does that feel?" Diamond asked, massaging her oily fingers back and forth over the long scar on Drako's chiseled back.

"It don't itch so bad no more." He casually twisted his back from right to left. "It's like sometimes those tissues feel like they tighten up or something." He tried to make logic of why his scar would itch so bad from time to time. He turned his back to the mirror and craned his neck to take one final glance. The wound was a diagonal strip of scar tissue that stretched from his right shoulder blade to almost his left hipbone. The scar tissue was not as wide as they thought it would become, but it had formed a keloid and raised itself nearly a half-inch thick. Back in prison when he was much younger, he had the word 'Reality' tattooed along it as a reminder of what bad choices in life could bring. Now out of prison, he often believed that it was simply a reminder from a higher being. A reminder to never forget that Toney had given him a second chance in life. Had Toney simply walked away, Drako knew he could've bled out right on the floor of the chapel after the two GDs attacked him. Drako nodded his head in a daze, still thankful that all he walked away with was an itch and a scar.

"So do you need me to help you with the other bags?" Diamond asked, breaking Drako's small reverie.

"Uh, nah . . . I got it," he stuttered, referring to the heavy bags of money he'd been lifting by himself, which he thought caused his scar to irritate.

"You sure?" she asked again, wiping the oil from her hands with a towel.

"I'm good." He frowned at her as if she knew better.

Drako stepped out of the bathroom and into their bedroom where he picked up the last two bags of money. He'd trippled the Hefty trash bags and transferred the money into them. He carried them to the garage and climbed into the back of the white commercial van Drip had provided. In the back of the van were several carpet cleaning machines. Drako unsnapped the latches and then twisted the seal off just like he did the other two machines earlier.

Once he saw the empty secret compartment, he dropped the last two bags in and sealed the smell proof canister back off. He hopped out the van, closing the double doors behind him and quickly made his way back inside.

"You got everything in my bag?" he yelled back at Diamond as he stood in front of the mirror buttoning up the collared shirt he wore over his slacks.

"Everything"s ready, baby." She stepped up behind him, dressed and ready to go. Drako buttoned his final button and then glanced at his stainless steel Submariner.

"Ten minutes, you leave," he instructed. "I need a few moments with Drip, but I want to be at the airport in plenty of time for our flight."

"Got it." Diamond stepped off.

*****

When Drako pulled into the carpet cleaning company Drip had owned ever since he got out of prison, he was pretty surprised. Drip"s company had at least twenty-five vans. And just off of Ponce Deleon the service appeared to be a flourishing one. Drip came straight out and met him as soon as the wheels hit the parking lot"s pavement.

"I'll take it from here." He smiled, watching Drako step down from the van and remove the sunglasses from his face.

Drako tossed him the keys. "It's all yours." They began walking back toward the building. "I'm not gonna waste a

moment talking about the money," Drako said easily. "I just wanted to let you know I may be out for a day or so. Me and Diamond need to check on some things."

"Not a problem," Drip said, holding the door open curtly for Drako. "I got things over at Reality. You know that!" They made a sharp right into the first office. Drip sat behind a desk. Drako took the couch where he could see out and into the parking lot behind Drip. "I'm keepin" busy. Things are moving faster than I anticipated and"—Drip leaned back, crossed a leg and raised his brows.—"I think I may be on to somethin" else." He smiled. "I been workin" with another artist. They call him Turk—Big Turk to be exact." He looked at Drako as if the name should have rung a bell. "Man, I know you've seen this guy before . . . He's been in the streets for a good minute. He was gonna compete in BETs ultimate fighter competition for team Grand Hustle. Then Grand Hustle decided to sign him instead, but now with TIP goin' through his legal woes I was able to get his attention."

"What's his sound like?" Drako sat up a little.

"It's diverse. I mean, he can be gangster but he more like a Jeezy. He talk that dope boy, trapp money music good." Drip nodded, reaffirming his assessment.

"Yep, I'd say a cross breed between Jeezy and Jadakiss, except he look like he on steroids. Man, the nigga six foot four, every bit of two sixty-five!"

"Damn!" Drako huffed with surprise.

"Still don't ring a bell?"

"Nuh- uh, not at all." Drako was sure. The two capped on until Drako saw Diamond pull into the lot.

"See ya in a few days. Just stay at this paper." Drako encouraged with a firm shake before he stepped off.

Drako"s mind was already on his next move.

*****

25

Once the plane landed at Bradley International, he and Diamond were relieved again to make it to their luxurious suite in downtown Stratford, Connecticut. Last night, Drako was sure to get a good night"s rest. He wanted to be up early and feeling vibrant when he smoothed the bank manager over for nearly the last time. Drako had run into Pazzo"s money, which made it that much more convenient to lay play money in the account for now, and pull off his grand scheme later.

All of that was under control. The problems that plagued Drako were that with Reality going the way it was and if he pulled this lick through, he knew he could finally sit down. He'd promised Diamond he would, and he'd easily gotten away with two major schemes already. A credit card scam had netted him a quick 1.7 million dollars, and then he coerced Diamond into playing a bank manager out of another 3 million dollars in a fraud scam for properties she'd never even owned or seen. All of this checked out good, which was exactly his problem. A man once told him, once you rob a bank it's an addiction. It was a natural high in itself. Drako had met many men who'd served long terms for bank robbery and turned right around and robbed the next bank just hours after being released. In his mind, his capers were much sweeter and much harder to turn away from. And much more profitable!

Drako stood in front of the full-length mirror. His six foot, hard body frame was now covered in a dark gray suit. A black kufi covered the top of his smooth, baldhead, and his fake beard and horned rimmed glasses topped off the guise of Scott Smith to a tee. Drako felt exhilarated before he even entered the bank. It was a feeling he hoped he could soon shake because surely he had another scam up his sleeve.

*****

"Yep, definitely one of the greatest." Drako ended the twenty minute conversation with Charles as he stood to his feet and

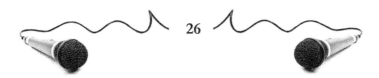

accepted the firm shake from the hand Charles extended his way. His eyes traveled proudly, taking in another glimpse of Eli Manning's picture that his personal banker kept on his desk. "I'll see you soon," Drako said confidently as he pulled his suit coat straight and headed back out the office.

Drako strolled through the lobby, ignoring the busy throngs of customers at UBS Warburg Bank. He subconsciously inhaled a deep breath. It was as if he could smell the possible 4 million dollar payday as his plan unfolded. Today, he'd simply deposited a few cashier's checks to further gain the manager's trust. Drako knew if he got this money easy, he could surely do it again. The only things he hadn't figured out were how to stay out of banks and what would he eventually tell Diamond?

Hopefully, time would tell.

Reality Records
Chapter- 5

Drip''s office was located right next door to his control room. He felt especially happy today when he stepped out because Reality''s walls were budding with life. Both booths were in use. Save and Big Turk were feeling each other out. His next project to blow, the rapper Navan, was in the next booth. Navan could also sing and preferred to sing most of his own hooks. His approach was definitely not gangster, but he had a very colorful, witty, mainstream flow. His dress code was skinny pants and Vans, and his boyish look was a marketable one.

Drip promptly made his way upstairs. He had a few vixens from Fresh Face Models to stop by. He really wanted the handpick of the litter for Save's next video shoot in just a few days. He opened the door and directed all six ladies to the sleeping quarters and told them to make themselves comfortable. There were always hors d'oeuvres on hand, chilled champagne, and a plasma screen showing the latest videos released. When Drip finally caught up with the ladies, he'd discarded the first four within the first two minutes. They all wore tight revealing clothes to showcase their figures, but for the first chick someone should have told her everything didn't need to be showcased. She had the huge, 40 plus, video chick ass of today, but she couldn't have done a crunch in at least five years. At least two rows of fat bunched up on her sides, just below her halter top. The next chick crossed her legs and gave her full, glossed lips a sexy lick. Drip laughed inwardly because she should've put some of that gloss on her ashy knees or the ankle that was exposed from the red stiletto.

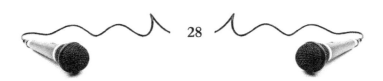

"Dang, this is that Diesel!" one of the dark skinned chicks said as she passed the blunt Big Turk had left them to the other. They looked like they might have been twins.

"Glad all you ladies could make it." Drip stayed professional as his eyes settled on the last two that he could possibly work with.

"What's your name?" he asked, narrowing it down to just one after he saw all the tattoos the girl had on her.

"That's nice." He politely faked the compliment. He didn't even hear what she had said.

"We've selected a principal and we were seeking out some beautiful extras. I'll be giving Ken a call in regard to your services. The principal lady was supposed to come in as well. I was hoping y'all could meet her," he lied.

"But if we use y'all, y'all will meet her on the set." He was clearly coaxing them out the door. Four of the ladies caught the hint and stood to their feet. "We waiting to kick it wit' Big Turk," the two blunt smokers announced.

Drip nodded his head and kindly led the others back out the door. He laughed to himself because he knew a lot of this kind of mess would arise.

He sat down in his chair in front of the mixing board and listened in on Save and Turk. Save had requested a certain video vixen to give his video the feel he wanted. And Diamond had laid down her first hook for Reality Records. Drip was so into his work he'd forgotten all about the vixen stopping by. He wasn't reminded until Save motioned him to turn around.

Drip's eyes traveled from her eyes, down to her pedicured feet, back up to her short, ice blonde hair. For some reason Drip felt like he'd momentarily lost his breath. The lady in front of him stood nearly six feet with curves that looked animated. She had flawless light, yellow skin and a cute Marilyn Monroe mole just on the right side of her chin. Drip stood tall and held his poise. He extended a hand, ignoring the next lady accidently. "Drip . . . and you are?"

She slid a soft hand into his. "Blondelle," she said, seeming to pout her full lips before she licked them discreetly and batted her long lashes.

"Well, I see now the look Save was going for." Drip smiled. "He picked the right one for sure." He nodded, never taking his eyes off hers.

Inside the booth, Save and Big Turk saw as the two divas arrived right behind each other. Save waved to Drip, sending Big Turk's attention that way as well.

"Shit!" Big Turk snapped, shooting his full attention to the ladies. "Look at the ass on this red mothafucka here!" His huge hand clutched his crotch as he drooled over the way the jeans fit her ass.

"Yeah, that's Blondelle. She gone be the lead girl on Friday," Save said.

"Man, I ain't studdin' no Blondelle!" He sucked his teeth, waving her off. "I'm talkin' ,bout shorty wit' the Kelis cut!" He watched her turn and shake Drip's hand with a pretty, white smile.

"Nah man, that's Diamond."

"Diamond?" Big Turk thought a moment. "You mean that lil broad who was doin' all them hooks at Red Rum?" He turned to Save, baffled.

"She cut her hair, man. That's her." Save hunched over to get another look.

"Damn, I gotta get that!" He stared at her like he'd already claim her as he pulled his T-shirt off revealing his tank top and huge biceps.

"Man, that ain't what you wanna do," Save told him fast. "She fuck wit' son. The kid, Drako."

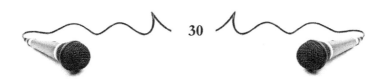

"Oh, you mean the security nigga runnin" „round here? Come on, man. I know—"

"Look, I on' know who he is, but whatever he is, Drip cuttin" him a check 'cause he like him."

"Man, I wouldn't give not a damn!" He pounded his thigh, and then snatched his blunt out the astray and relit it. "Man, if a nigga catch her slippin", she fucked! And that's all there is to it!" He stepped over to the glass and tapped on it a few times as if trying to get Drip"s attention that was clearly back on Blondelle.

When Diamond turned and looked, Big Turk tossed her a chin-up and a wink. Diamond blushed as she dropped her head and turned the other way.

"You peep that shit, shorty?" Big Turk felt cock sure. "She blushed. That bitch feel me breathing down her neck! Every time she can get away I'll have her just like these other bitches 'round here." He blew smoke, waiting for Diamond to look his way again.

"Man, that shit ain't worth it," Save said evenly.

"Ain't worth it . . . Man, I „on give two shits 'bout that nigga!"

"Nah, it ain't that, son. Drip like 'im. You „bout to kill ya own money before you get it! Think first, man." Save waved the smoke from his face. "And put that stank shit out in the booth! I done asked you like ten times already."

"Man, this dat' Sour Diesel. I need this shit! You 'bout to clog up my flow wit' all that cryin" shit!" He turned to Save with an intimidating smirk on his face. "Straight like that, player."

"Whateva." Save waved him off and walked out the booth.

"Soft mothafucka!" Big Turk yelled after him, and then hit the Diesel again. He blew smoke out and turned around. Diamond and Blondelle had vanished from in front of the booth. "That's okay." He laughed to himself. "I think I'ma like it around here."

*****

A few moments later, Big Turk stepped into the sleeping quarters. Everyone was gathered around the TV because BETs 106 and Park said it had a new number one video. Turk looked over the room; everybody was there except Diamond. He snapped his finger in disappointment as he stepped over to the two chicks that were waiting on him. "What the fuck y'all do wit' my blunt?" he barked, flopping down on the couch in between the two.

"I thought you wanted us to—"

"You what?" he yelled for no reason. "Y'all better know what time it is tonight then!" He snickered inwardly at the thought of roughing off a few chicken heads until he could get another opportunity to catch up with fine ass Diamond.

*****

Diamond leaned forward to turn her air conditioner up even higher. It seemed like the little car wouldn't cool off fast enough as she hurried out of the parking lot and headed straight back home.

Another strange, warm feeling washed over her at the thought of what had just happened. Diamond wasn't silly, she'd saw exactly the way Big Turk ate her up with his eyes. She knew he wasn't the first and he certainly wouldn't be the last. The problem was that she'd never entertained the thought of cheating on Drako, and she wouldn't start now. She however, was human and Big Turk was definitely what most ladies would categorize as phoine!

He was tall, dark brown with a baldhead just like she liked. Huge muscles rippled all over his upper body along with all those tattoos to go with his cockiness. His demeanor had Thug Lovin" written all over it.

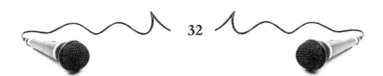

32

She had to get a hold of herself. Although she knew she didn't want any parts of this guy, it was now the second time she'd envisioned how it would feel for his big hands to lift her up and settle her down on his lap. She shook off the thought, feeling guilty inside as she merged on to the beltway.

Even though she hadn't done anything wrong, she still felt guilty and bad. Diamond was confused. She felt that maybe she should tell Drako, but then again maybe it wouldn't be a good thing. Soon he'd get the picture and go on about his business. Then again, this guy was cocky. He led with an air that said he just didn't give a fuck, and that scared her. She didn't want to be a drama queen or bring trouble to Reality or Drako's way. Even she was smart enough to see that this guy was so large he'd be a huge problem, even for Drako, physically.

"Lord have mercy," she said a small prayer as she neared Stone Mountain. She'd made up her mind. Diamond knew better than to play games like that, and couldn't imagine Drako getting a whiff of that. She decided to play it cool for now, hoping he'd get the picture. Either way, if it happened again she was certainly gonna let him know it was in his best interest to back off.

This would be the first and only time she took matters in her own hands. She wouldn't jump the gun and tell Drako just yet.

But somehow, someway, she knew that little flicker had to be doused because it could at any moment become a flaming inferno at the hands of Drako.

Red Rum
Chapter - 6

As far as producing great tracks and developing new artists, Red Rum was still at the top of the charts. Even after the raid, life went down as smooth as gravy. Of course, the tabloid fodder never ceased, but neither did Wiz"s relentless work ethic. Downstairs, the camp was alive and festive with all the regulars present.

The only problem in the whole building today was Swirl"s attitude toward the new security team Wiz had hired since he no longer had Drako by his side as head of security. Wiz sat back in his big armchair in his office as Swirl paced the floor in front of him.

"Man, if we ain't workin" I „on see why you'd ever have these clowns hangin" around! They ain't nothin" but another distraction!" Swirl didn't attempt to hide his displeasure. "And a goddamn waste of money!" he added.

Wiz nodded calmly, taking in Swirl"s assumption. "I feel you, but it ain't just about that. It's also about image, baby. What we want to do is get 'em on camera. Use 'em for somethin" big! Once niggaz see us surrounded like this, they'll think way more than twice before they try runnin" up."

Wiz smiled behind his logic.

"Try somethin"?" Swirl stopped pacing and pounded a fist on the cherrywood table. "Man, ain't nobody gone try shit!" he growled. "All this time they woulda' been done it by now!" He locked eyes with Wiz. "Man, it don't take nearly that long for the shit they accusing you of. It woulda' been front door a long time ago if it were me!" He popped his knuckles and sat down.

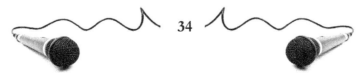

"Bless is a clown! He knows better. His time is just up. He ain't no-where lyrical as Fatt Katt was. Fatt Katt carried Take Money on his back, and Bless just gone have to find the next emcee on the East Coast to fill his shoes." Wiz listened with an open ear. Swirl made sense, and to some it may seem as though they were at odds, but in actuality this is how the two had come to build a mutual respect of the other's opinion.

"Yeah, you got a point. I thought of that," Wiz lied. "But still, I think it's a good look. Maybe I won't keep 'em around here. We'll just call on 'em when we need 'em." Wiz eased up a bit.

"How do you even know what they'll do? They look like a bunch of bouncers to me. You don't need to be surrounded by wrestlers. You need to be surrounded by gun slangers!" Swirl wouldn't let up.

"Well . . ." Wiz cleared his throat. "Damien screened each of them personally. Most of them have background in either law enforcement or corrections."

"What?" Swirl threw his hand in the air. "So you mean to tell me you done hired the goddamn police to protect us? When the hell have you known police to die behind a nigga?" Swirl laughed at the thought, and Wiz soon joined in.

"Yeah, maybe you right. I'm startin" to see your point." Wiz stood after reading the text that came through on his phone.

"One question though." Swirl seemed unable to resist asking. "Who in the hell decided to call them the Goon Squad?"

Wiz laughed and waved Swirl off. His expression told him he was the guilty party.

*****

A few moments later, they were downstairs mingling with everybody else. Wiz was speaking with Damien about lightening up a little on his so called 'Goon Squad' image. Everybody else was gathered in the lounge room and watching

106 and Park. They'd also received the industry chain text about a new number one video to be aired. Swirl had already come in at number eight with "The Rebirth" and he'd just made number three with "Stones!" He'd forgotten all about Wiz and a Goon Squad, and like everyone else he knew that after the number two spot showed, "Bleed" was certainly gonna be the number one video. Swirl's album had been number one for three weeks now on Billboard, and his days were busy from wake „til night. He now had personal assistants who were always within text message summons. Swirl was leaned over whispering in his latest female conquest's ear when 106 and Park returned with the number two selection of the day. Terrance J wasted no time as he hopped to his feet and introduced "Bleed" with a clap that brought applause from the whole set. Swirl's mouth gaped as he turned his head to see him pulling up to a private jet and hopping out of a red Bugatti with a model in tow.

Silence swarmed the room as Swirl stood stiff and his hand slipped from the girl"s ass. "Damn," he mumbled in a whisper and straightened up quickly. Wiz and Damien watched his video play out. Nobody said anything as they wondered who could've beat him out. "And the new number one video on the count down is . . ." Just moments later Terrance J stood up smiling Rocsi"s way and announced, ",My Turn" by the young phenom y"all know as „Save"!" The set erupted with applause and Rocsi clapped with cheer just before the screen switched to Save"s latest video. Swirl smiled lightly and nodded his head. "Can't stay there forever." He stepped off and took it in stride.

"You know you still number one," the short, thick chick said as she reached for his arm before he could get away.

"It's all in the game." He smiled down on her. "Come on, let's go spark up."

She smiled back and trailed behind Swirl to the smoke room.

Disappointment clouded the room for a moment, but like always, they knew Swirl would soon reclaim that number one spot.

*****

Wiz was back in his office just after Red Rum thinned out for the day. He watched his screen as Damien walked through his door with his briefcase in hand. "Did you get that for me?" Wiz asked, rearing back and folding his hands behind his head.

Damien sat his briefcase on the table, promptly using both thumbs to open it. "Yeah, I sure did look at it. And it's true what they say: numbers don't lie." He handed a single printout to Wiz. "This fuckin" kid's numbers are ridiculously consistent across the board," he admitted as Wiz scanned down the page. "He's got numbers everywhere. I'm talkin" from SoundScan to Twitter. And with the torrential rhyme flow that they're tweeting about, he"ll probably be getting six figures per guest appearance in no time." Damien shrugged. "The kid's basically undeniable. Of course he's not the best, but he's a new look." He closed his briefcase as Wiz folded the paper. "Well, I got things to do. You know how to reach me." Damien turned and left the mogul in his own thoughts.

Wiz reared back in his chair once again, his marketing mindset racing at warp speed. He thought about what Damien had just said, and his mind's eye still reflected Save's numbers across the board. After all the years of experience in this game, Wiz could see the potential Reality Records held, especially if it were at the helm of the right executives. He was thankful to still have friends that were dependable and trustworthy as Damien and Swirl, but even that didn't stop the small jolts of fear and jealousy of what Reality could do to a part of Red Rum"s star power.

He watched the screens as Damien exited the building, and then checked the others only to find Swirl, who was the only one left, receiving a blowjob from the girl he retired upstairs with. He blacked out the screen, turned off the lights in his office, then closed his eyes and relaxed in deep thought.

*****

Nearly an hour later, Swirl walked in the office to find Wiz sitting in a dark room. His armchair faced the window and the soft moonlight illuminated the chair's silhouette. "Whad up, my nigga . . . you a"ight?" Swirl asked as he crept up to the chair. Wiz inhaled a slow deep breath.

"I'm, I'm good . . . just thinking," he said without looking Swirl"s way.

Swirl just stood over him for a moment. He knew his mentor was in deep thought.

"You know, I been at this here for a long time," Wiz said in a calm tone. "And I'm a guru at what I do." He took a small glance in Swirl"s direction. "While some people track the stocks and the Dow on Wall Street I track SoundScan, Billboard, and nowadays I keep my eye on YouTube and Twitter. I wake up every day with one thing on my mind, and that's to sell albums! Lots of 'em, ya dig?" Swirl didn't respond, but Wiz knew he was listening.

"This shit is nothing new to you. You better than anybody, know how I get down."

Wiz stood and stepped closer to the window. "I see somethin". I feel somethin" brewing in my gut and I got a feel for this one." He turned to face Swirl.

"What's up, man? Just put it on the table," Swirl demanded.

"This *Save* character. It's undeniable. He's hot. Nowhere near better, but hot! New. And that's all this game is coming to when it comes to star power."

"So what are you saying?"

"I'm saying I know I told you we were gonna lay down on the beef shit, but this shit has far too much potential to ignore. I

also believe that what I got in mind will be a healthy choice for your career as well."

"My career?" Swirl relented with his voice totally against it. "This nigga drop one album and you gone stand here and fix yo' mouth to base my gangsta on—"

"No, no, no!" Wiz cut in. "Slow down, baby. It's not that at all! I ain't talkin" „bout us startin" nothin" serious. I'm sayin" we need to rattle his chain and make him come to us. It won't look like we doin" nothin" except handling what comes our way. Now, it's like I said, of course, he's not better. To engage in war with you is ridiculous! Your consistency would kill him. Your star power would far outshine him. But, what I see is the future. He's gonna stand possibly where you are today. The point is, he's new, he's hot, and that's all this industry clamors to see! We can't allow him to stand in that light alone. He has to share it with you until he fizzles out, feel me?"

Swirl didn't respond. He just began to pace the floor in contemplation.

"Swirl, this industry, this game, really doesn't have a conscience. I told you from the start it's all about numbers, and I haven't steered you wrong yet! They'll turn their back on you the second you're not relevant. You go from hot to lukewarm to JaRule!" Wiz flopped back down in his chair while Swirl processed the reality he'd just tossed his way.

"Well, what about your man Drako? What's he sayin"? You puttin" him down or what?" Swirl rattled, clearly unsure about all he was trying to ingest.

Wiz let out another sigh. "I've texted and emailed Drako. He's been totally unresponsive. He won"t even come forward and admit he's behind Reality Records." Wiz's shadowed face was full of disappointment. "I spoke with Diamond; she simply said that I need to talk to Drako about whatever Drako's into. She gave me absolutely nothing."

39

"Will she still be doin" hooks for us?"

"My door's always open for her. It's Drako with the problem. Anyway, she was never signed to anything. She's not that big a deal."

"So you tellin" me you cool wit' me poppin" off at Drako?"

"No, no, no." Wiz quickly clarified. "We ain't gone take aim at Reality. We just gone lure Save into the water." Wiz smiled. "If the Sharks eat 'im in the process, oh well. All I'm sayin" is when they mention his name just find a reason for them to mention yours a few lines down." Wiz stepped over and clicked on the light. "This is just business. I know it like the back of my hand. Either they come out on their own, or we bring them out. It's simple. Those around him won't be able to resist." Wiz laughed, picking up his keys from the table. "Let's have fun and sell records." Wiz persuaded Swirl.

"Yeah, I'm cool wit' dat. But like I was sayin" about this other shit, I ain't wit"! Lookin" like no studio ass—"

"And you won"t!" Wiz snapped. "Remember, they'll come to us!" Wiz looked at the smirk on Swirl"s face. "I saw you on tape." He smiled, nodding his head toward the monitors. "You ask her what's up?" Wiz had that conniving look on his face.

"She said she can do two," Swirl said evenly.

"Cheer up then. Let's get somewhere and get this shit poppin"!" He hit Swirl's shoulder playfully, and then the three left the building.

Wiz felt relieved. He felt like the walls had been closing in on him, but now that he'd convinced Swirl back into his scheme. He knew that nothing could outshine his camp. It was game on and he was ready to pitch!

Drip
Chapter - 7

"Come here . . ." She gushed, pulling Drip's face close to hers. She gently bit down on his bottom lip just before she sucked at his tongue nice and hard.

"Oh, shh . . . yeah! Ride it, girl!" Drip urged moments later, watching Blondelle's head fall back and her eyes flutter closed in pure pleasure as she bounced on his dick to a sexy rhythm like he'd never had before.

"Come on, baby. Take it all!" His hands slid further around her ass cheeks as he gripped her even tighter and forced her the rest of the way down his pole.

"Fuck! Oh, shit ... Dr-Drip!" She leaned forward this time and clung on to his shoulders for leverage. "I'm, shh . . . I'm cu-cummin' again!" she shouted as her body twitched into hard tremors, and her big yellow melons with large brown nipples bounced all over the place.

"Yeah, baby. That's it . . . Shiit!" Drip slurred, nearly drooling at the mouth seeing Blondelle cum and ooze cream all over his dick again. He stroked her hard a few more times and then simmered down to let Blondelle try and take hold of her erratic breathing. She collapsed on him and closed her eyes as they snuggled together.

Drip eased the silk sheet back up over Blondelle's ass, and then kissed her soft cheek. "You okay?" he asked, tracing a finger down her spine and through the crack of her ass.

"Mmm hmmm . . ." She nodded and smothered his lips with hers again.

She tasted traces of sweat on his lips that their bodies were glistened in and she loved it. She contracted her love muscles

41

around Drip's strong dick that was still lodged and pulsating inside of her. Blondelle knew Drip wasn't done with her just yet.

And she loved that too.

Wriggling her ass, she inhaled sharply as she felt Drip's long finger trace, then penetrate her ass.

"Ohh, fuck!" she cooed, working her ass to the rhythm of his finger. "God, baby, you fuck me so good. I can't get enough," she confessed. "Fuck me more, baby. Fuck me now." Her syrupy tone dripped with lust. Blondelle knew she was freaky, but after the two days of butt naked sex with Drip, she realized she may have just met her match.

"Turn over," Drip said smoothly, lifting her up off his dick and breaking their connection momentarily. "I can't get enough of you either," Drip also confessed, marveling at her body as she rolled over, rested her head on the fluffy pillow and raised her flawless yellow ass in the air for his enjoyment.

"It's all yours," she hissed over her shoulder. Then, with both sets of fresh manicured red nails she spread her cheeks lovingly.

"Umm, umm, umm . . ." Drip lusted with a nod and was right behind her clenching a dick that leaked pre-cum. He placed his hands on her cheeks and without another thought, guided himself back into her slippery, warm slit.

"Yes . . . Oh, y-y . . . yes!" she moaned, taking every inch all over again. Drip loved her light, nearly cocoa butter colored skin tone. He loved her soft, blonde hair and her Brazilian waxed mound. He loved the way she squealed his name and took his whole dick like no other.

Drip couldn't stop looking down to watch his dark meat plunge in and out of Blondelle repeatedly. He knew it was by far the tightest and wettest pussy he'd ever had. And now, all he could think of is all the fun he'd had over the two and a half

days he'd had her whisked away and stowed up in a ritzy five-star penthouse suite on South Beach.

Since they'd gotten there, they'd done nothing but fucked, sucked, and ordered the finest room service and Chablis the whole time. Blondelle had sucked him in long ways he'd never imagined. She deep throated, sucked his balls and painted her pretty face with his cum. Everything he dreamed of, she gave him. They had so much chemistry it was almost unreal, and there was no doubt they were both already sprung!

"Oh, God . . . right there, baby!" Blondelle shouted as Drip slapped her ass and poked at her g-spot again.

"Right here? That's how you like it!" Drip began to ram harder.

"Ye-yes, oh . . . yes . . . fu . . . Oh—" Blondelle was already gushing cream down Drip's dick, causing it to clump up in his pubes; she was so wet.

"Fuck . . . Shit . . . Yeah!" Drip snarled, clasped her waist tight and slammed nearly the foot of dick he was blessed with to the hilt as he spilled his cum inside of her.

This time they both collapsed, and the room just wouldn't stop spinning for Drip. His chest heaved and he was sweaty. The sweet smell of their sex wafted in the air and the euphoric feeling was a high all in itself.

He glanced over at Blondelle and saw the same glazed over glint in her eyes. He knew she was just as satisfied as he was.

They'd exchanged texts, emails and Skyped each other for several weeks, and there was no denying the chemistry and animal attraction they shared. The moment Drip found an open day or three to get away, they met up and it all just festered over.

Drip never believed in love at first sight, but after getting to know Blondelle, he knew that no man controlled the heart. The heart could only control itself.

He looked from Blondelle's ice blonde low-cut Caesar and down over an all natural body that was by far the most perfect he'd ever bedded. He knew in time that this would come a dime a dozen and that her beauty was not the only thing keeping his attention nor his erection. Blondelle just felt passionate, sincere, and her straight-forwardness turned him on. But nevertheless, he realized he'd been away from Reality long enough. This was fun, and Blondelle had certainly left him with something to think about, but he had to get back to his priority and that was definitely his camp.

Stretching his arms wide, he rolled over on his back with his head now rested on a pillow. Blondelle scooted closer and situated her head even more comfortably on Drip's hairy chest.

She, just like Drip, was lying there with a million thoughts racing through her mind. Long ago she'd quit asking herself how it came down to these intense feelings so fast. She'd imagined at first that maybe one day she and Drip could have a fling, but now after sharing a warm character like his, she didn't give a fuck! All she cared about and knew now was that it felt right, it felt good, and she was ready to leave her past in the past and be Drip's everything!

Yes, she saw the potential he held with Reality Records, and she knew there was much more to Drip than just the handsome slender man on television. She reached out and took hold of his amazing eleven inches and began to massage it slow and firm.

She gazed up at him with her pretty, innocent eyes. "So what now?" she asked with a crack to her voice. "I know this has to end somewhere and if this is that place where you leave me with some lame excuse about getting with me when you find time, just save it. You can miss me with that one." He heard her sniffle when she laid her head back upon his chest. She didn't even wait for his response.

Again, Drip respected her straight-forwardness. He took a moment to gather his thoughts and then said, "I know how the game is played, shawty, but I play different. Respect comes first and foremost to me. I respect you and I appreciate the time we spent." He kissed her on the forehead. "It is what it is. My roster is my first priority, but as long as you keep it real with me, I'll respect you." He rubbed his hand down her back and rubbed her ass soothingly. "And yeah, for now it does have to end. I have to be back in Atlanta first thing in the morn." He let her down easily then lay silent again.

"Do you have a woman?" she blurted in another sweet tone.

"No . . . And good time to ask." Drip smiled.

She nudged him with a smile of her own. "It's not the first time I've asked. Just thought I'd check again."

"You never have reason not to trust me. I just told ya, keep it real with me and I'll respect you."

"So does that mean we'll see each other soon?" She raised her head up to look at him and tugged circles with his dick a little harder.

"We'll see, shawty. You gimme a lot to think about." Drip laid his head back on the pillow and closed his eyes. He had tons of work to concentrate on, and now he had to figure Blondelle into his thoughts. He knew she was sincere.

She felt his fat dick expanding in her hand again. Blondelle really liked Drip, and not only did she believe there was a chance, but also that he was someone she could honestly consider committing herself to with all her heart. Blondelle knew the game of life and she understood the lifestyle of the industry as well. She'd been around, done several videos, and knew the attention that was headed his way from the media and the groupies. She also knew the cardinal sin was to spread herself too thin or appear too thirsty like many up and coming vixens.

No, she was seasoned. She'd take her time, and the best thing of all was that she hadn't been with anybody in Reality's camp. And she planned to keep it just that way.

Sliding down Drip's chest for the long haul, she'd made up her mind. She was gonna do the right thing. Starting at the top of the food chain, she was gonna do her best to work her magic on Drip. Hopefully, he'd be her knight in shining armor, her lover, and her everything on her way to stardom. She closed her eyes, parted her lips, and let Drip's long dick bang the roof of her mouth on the way to the back of her throat, again.

Reality Records
Chapter 8

With Save's video taking the number one spot on both BET and MTV, everybody on Reality's roster was working hard and eager to drop the next video as well. It was clear that Drip was shaking hands with all the right connects. He too could see much further than the couch on 106 and Park. He also took notice of SoundScan, Billboard, and Twitter gossip. Not to mention the flooded email inboxes with MP3s and a message for another collabo offer he woke up to daily. His days were now consumed with making phone calls and auditioning hundreds of bars of potential beats for his artists. He was happy about all Reality had quickly come to be and was all smiles when he stepped into Drako"s office. "We took our time, made all the right connects before hand and this thing is just gaining momentum fast." Drip sat in the chair in front of Drako"s desk and explained. "We have what the streets embrace: Reality. We got gangster, we got lyrical genius, and we just got art!" Drip began to round out the list of accolades. "Now we haven't even really put Navan in the water yet. He's the reincarnation of Drake! He's a multi-platformed pop phenomenon!" He looked at Drako, not slipping one centimeter of a smile into his expression.

"I see what's up." Drako sat up and laid his iPad on the desk. "But shit gone get real busy around here."

"Busy is what we want!" Drip said without hesitance. "Drako, I know business. This business, well, to be frank. I did paperwork for Inc., J-Prince, and you name it. Just let me take advantage of the exposure they're seeking. I"ma grant all interviews. I'm gonna explore reality shows, clothing lines, commercial tie-ins, endorsements. I"ma utilize any and all vehicles that gets Reality positive visibility." He crossed his legs and flopped back.

Drako knew it was done and Drip was gonna surely handle up. He could handle the stardom and the books and that was all that mattered.

"Well, keep them cameras away from me."

"Just like we agreed upon." Drip smiled. "I can handle the Red Carpet."

"It's all yours then." Drako stood to his feet.

*****

"Damn, she looks just like a young version of Mary J," Drako commented as the girl stepped away after Drip instructed her to put her things away and prepare herself to spend some time in the booth. "What is she gonna be? Our R&B chick?" Drako asked, staring at her nice, wide hips and pretty cinnamon colored thighs.

"Far from," Drip snapped. "She raps and has a very unique style."

"Unique, ha?" Drako said sarcastically.

"Yeah, you see that body, huh? She's quite marketable. She's gone look good as the female emcee of the camp. Somebody has to show skin. And she damn sure has it to show. She's from Queens, New York, and there's nothin" shy about this chick." Drip smiled and gestured for Drako to follow him.

*****

They'd been listening to Ebony for almost a half hour when Big Turk and Save entered the next booth. Drako didn't acknowledge the two with much more than a head nod because the look and the gestures Ebony threw his way, clearly let him know she was interested in laying down much more than a track for him. Drako kept it cool. He knew better than to acknowledge any type of interest until he knew her true M.O.

48

Diamond would be a part of Reality records and around the studio much too often for him to even consider that type of risk. Although his expression read: unfazed. He was slightly charmed by her admiration and soon found himself fighting to hold back that single wink of confirmation her lip, tits, and ass were all begging for. He stood up and told Drip he was about to retreat back to his office. Diamond was due in, in the next half hour or a little more. He glanced at his watch, and then looked over at Save and Turk. Turk appeared to be huge. He reminded Drako of his buddy in prison, Deuce, except he was an inch or two shorter. He had a few tats that caught Drako"s eye just before he thought he saw Big Turk throw a salty look his way.

"She's good," Drako said, shaking the thought away. "And even sexier than I thought," he admitted.

"Uh-huh." Drip laughed. "Just be careful. She's a street savvy uptown chick," Drip said, knowing he'd seen how she looked at Drako.

"Man, what's up with that dude?" Drako said, seeing Big Turk fire up a blunt right in the booth.

"He's working on some hot shit," Drip said.

"Nah, I ain't talkin" „bout that." Drako bit down on his back teeth. "Why he keep lookin" at me like that? And why's he smoking in the booth like he bought stock in it?"

"Man, just be cool." Drip tried to keep things kosher. "He's gone be one of our top artists soon, and niggaz gone smoke regardless, so I just said fuck it. I let him have his perks, feel me?"

"Hell no, I „on feel you!" Drako snapped. "If you do it for him you got to do it for everybody. I told ya, no exceptions! That man don't define Reality Records!"

Drip could sense Drako"s temper swelling as his eyes never left Big Turk again. "Look man." Drip's tone softened. "I just figured we need him and I ain't gone lie, that's a big ass nigga! I can't whip him. I can only deal with him one way." Drip gestured at the gun in his back. "So I just said fuck it!" Drip saw Drako"s jawbones flex. "Real talk, I'll holler at him tomorrow or when he ain't high, but right now let's get this paper, feel me?"

Drako ignored every stupid word that had just come out of Drip"s mouth. He watched Save come out the booth with an agitated look on his face. "What's up? Y"all done?" Drip turned to Save with a slight smile.

"Nah, son. I'm just givin" Turk a moment to clear the air."

Drako knew he was simply complaining about all the smoke in the booth. Without another thought Drako stepped over to the booth and opened the door. A pungent aroma spewed into his nostrils. "Excuse me, player, everybody don't smoke so you need to make sure you do that upstairs in the designated areas," Drako said flatly.

Big Turk arose from the stool he was perched on, toked on the blunt, and blew out another cloud of smoke. He tilted his head to look down at Drako as he shouldered past him with his smoldering blunt and walked into the control room until he was standing right over Drip. "Yo', straight the fuck up." He switched the towel to his other shoulder, and then hit the blunt. "This nigga is cloggin" up my goddamn flow wit' this petty ass shit!" He exhaled another cloud. Drip was shocked at Big Turk's choice of words as he smoothly rolled his chair back. "Why "on you straight up tell this nigga to run and get me some bottled water and some fresh towels so I can—"

"Whop!"

All he could hear was a loud sharp ringing in his ear as the slap Drako hit him with caused him to stumble at least five steps before he could catch himself. Shock gripped his body as he glanced up to see Drako stalking at him again.

"Whop!"

He slapped him even harder causing him to see double. This time Big Turk back peddled quickly, giving himself room as pain and fear wracked through the other side of his head.

"Yo', for real, you „on want this!" he yelled in the scariest voice he could find as he raised his fist in front of him. "I'm tellin" ya now, fuck boy!" he ranted, moving his big shoulders from side to side as he tried to pare down on one image of Drako instead of three.

Drako flinched at him and Big Turk winced, then threw a wild right causing Drako to weave left and counter with an overhand right to his chin. "Unn!" Big Turk"s neck snapped as he stumbled back but refused to fall. Drako moved in even quicker, leading with another overhand left to his nose and a solid right that sounded like a hammer to his jaw. Turk"s knees buckled then gave way as they crumpled to the cement floor like dead weight.

He was already out cold on his feet before Drako hit him again and laid him out flat on the side of his face. Blood gushed from his nose and the sound of a snore escaped his lips. The camp was thrust into a frenzy as Ebony ran out the booth screaming hysterically. Drip quickly pounced to his feet trying to bring back order and quickly diffuse the situation.

"Wait!" he yelled out, wedging his slim frame in the space between Drako and Big Turk. "Come on, Drako, he"s done. Don"t let this get any messier than it already is," he pleaded as he watched the cold glint in Drako"s eyes and his chest heave with anger. "For real, man. On the strength of what we started. Trust me on this one." Drip"s words seemed to halt Drako.

Big Turk shook his head as he began to come back to consciousness. He had begun to raise up on his elbows when out of nowhere, Save ran over and stomped him back to the ground viciously. "I told you, son, don't ever disrespect God

Body!" He stomped him four or five times sending Big Turk into a series of coughs and hyperventilation.

Drako reached down and yanked his shirt up over his head as he began to drag him toward the door. "Get this pussy out the building!" Drako snarled and huffed all the way to the door.

"Wait! . . . Hold up!" Big Turk pleaded from beneath the shirt pulled over his face.

"Yo, shut the fuck up, son!" Save stomped him again then ran ahead to open the door.

Drako hoisted Big Turk to his feet. "The next time you run up will be your last!" He looked him straight in his now pitiful face and shoved him out the door as hard as he could. Big Turk reeled back on his heels and tried to catch himself but to no avail. His two hundred fifty plus pounds hit the asphalt ass first. Drako locked the door, and then turned away without any further regard. Big Turk struggled to get back on his feet feeling more embarrassed and degraded than he ever had in his whole life.

"Ain't nothin" here to see. Y"all get back to what y"all do." He waved the altercation off and headed back to his office.

"You put hands of fire on, son!" Save yelled out, walking behind him. "I was waitin" on somethin" to chop his big ass down so I could put footprints all over his back! Yo, son deserved that shit. More than you even know!" Save was referring to Diamond, but decided to leave well-enough alone.

"You okay, sweetie?" Ebony licked her full lips and pushed her chest out so it looked like the single button that held her white Dolce halter top was gonna snap.

"I'm cool." Drako"s gaze stayed on her cleavage a second longer than he meant to. "It won"t be goin" down like that around here. Shit happens and sometimes you got to trim the weeds. Poison ivy can blend right in with the roses."

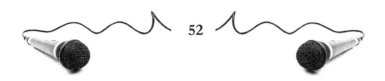

"Uh-huh." She winked and headed back to the booth with even more sway to her tight, matching white shorts.

*****

"He just crossed the line and it had to happen." Drako reasoned to Drip as he pulled his shirt over his head and flopped down in his office chair.

"I can dig it. I saw it comin". Sheeid, if it were me I"da had to smoke his big ass, so in actuality he came out good," Drip countered.

"Yeah, well I „on want to portray an image around here. I don't want the camp to see that side of me except when absolutely necessary. When we reach that point, you assign us some good security. I can point fingers and run it. They just need to be cats that know how to play their position."

"Cool. Good enough for me," Drip said, not really surprised at Drako"s earlier temperment. He'd seen Drako provoked years ago in prison. "So what do you think he's gonna do?"

Drako sat a moment. "I don't underestimate no man, but honestly I don't think he's gone do anything more than pray nobody finds out." Drako sniffled. "I looked in his eyes. A man"s eyes don't lie. I saw a bitch. I saw less fear in a woman"s eyes before. But whatever happens I always play da game raw! Fuck him." Drako stood to his feet.

"Keep everybody cool 'round here. Tell Save and Navan to keep that shit under the lid. That ain't to sell albums or Twitter. That shit was reality. You need to keep things movin"."

Drip just nodded his head, taking orders from the real CEO.

"And one more thing . . ." He looked right at Drip. "Tell Ebony I see her, but I „on play wit' Diamond 'round here, so I need her to keep that shit in her lane."

Drip nodded again.

"Good . . . Now let me hop in this shower before Diamond gets here. I really don't want her to know what happened."

Drako stepped around his desk and headed for the shower in his office bathroom.

Clenching his pistol, Drip headed back to the cockpit. He knew the code of the streets well, and if by chance Turk resurfaced Drip wouldn't hesitate to blast first. There was no backdown policy at Realith Records, and if his camp was threatened he was ready to lead by example.

Drako
Chapter - 9

Drako had decided to step outside and enjoy the feel and smell of the warm evening breeze. His shiny black Bentley Coupe was parked right near the entrance. He turned on his stereo and let Lyfe Jennings' soulful voice croon from the speakers as he leaned against the car. He was making a mental note of how much traffic passed by his establishment on a daily basis as he watched the last rays of sun fade into purple twilight. His eyes caught sight of a female who seemed to do a double take after glimpsing him in his shiny coupe. His gaze trailed the little Honda as it only drove down another block before making a U-turn and heading back toward the building.

Drako didn't move as the small car parked a few spaces down. He watched the girl cut the car off, remove her seatbelt and get out the car hesitantly. As she seemed to approach him with caution, Drako recognized her face. It was all too familiar, except she no longer had that shiny glow to her skin or smile. Her hair was no longer freshly done with the finest weaves, but it was certainly Myria in the rawest form he'd ever seen her in before. The Honda Accord was a further downgrade from the C-class Mercedes Benz she once drove. But still, Drako"s expression showed no sympathy toward her diminished aura.

"What are you doin' here?" Drako asked dryly.

"Please, Drako," she said, stepping nearly two feet in front of him with a desperate look on her face. She clasped her trembling hands together and held them close to her chest as if she were about to pray. "I just want to talk to you. I swear I had nothing to do with whatever happened with Wiz. You know damn well I love that man. I've seen you watch me and Wiz

55

together. And I've even watched you. That look you give your lady is all I wanted Wiz to give me. I've seen it in your eyes. And I gave it to Wiz at every chance. He just wouldn't return it."

Drako remained unresponsive. He had no interest in her and Wiz's business, but she ranted on so fast that her next words caught Drako's attention. "I would never cross Wiz. I had everything to lose and nothing to gain!" It made sense to Drako. "I'm not a fool completely; I was just a fool for him and I wanted him to keep me happy." Her eyes were now brimming with tears. "I'd do anything just to be with him. When we first met he was such a gentleman, and soon I realized he had a commitment phobia. Over time, somehow things worsened. The respect and quality time slipped away. He coaxed me into having sex with women and I just felt degraded. In the beginning I tried to leave, but he just told me a better reason why I should stay. It became a cycle and I just got caught up. If I were spreading rumors it would have happened long ago. I could've easily written a tell-all book for all the shit I know. And Wiz knows it!"

Tears began to fall as she vented further. Drako was now listening intently and he believed Myria. She told him personal things about her and White Chocolate's ménage a trois. She told him that Wiz had secretly purchased her a nice hide away home in the Buckhead area. Then she told him about the day she came home to find a realtor placing a for sale sign on the lawn and handing her a thirty day notice to leave, from the owner. By the time she told him about White Chocolate flipping on her, he knew that Wiz had pulled the black ball card on her.

"So what you gone do now?" Drako finally spoke.

"I don't know. I just want you to tell Wiz that it wasn't me. I'll forgive him if he just acknowledges his mistake."

56

Drako frowned with disgust. "How the fuck is you still worried about a mothafucka who „on give a damn if you eat?" Myria appeared aloof and despondent. "Where the hell you gettin" money now?" He pressed with even more attitude.

"I-I'm workin" at Strokers until I can find me some other work."

"You mean you strippin" yo shit off for money already?" Drako nodded his head and spit on the pavement.

"No, no, it ain't like that!" I went to bartending school in New York. I'm also gonna check out this local agency, Fresh Face Models. Maybe I can find some print work through them pretty easily, I hear."

As Myria continued talking, Drako realized she had a different motive. He was a good judge of character and by far, all her intentions were sincere! She seemed to have come from a good upbringing.

Myria was proof that every video girl shouldn't be stereotyped. She had been judged solely on the status of her sex symbol. Her only flaw was she was truly naive, and Wiz"s charm had truly blinded her.

"Myria, you better wake up before this industry sucks your naive ass dry! You got too many flaws to allow a man to love you. People think you're fake, and then you come across as conceited, but the minute a man stops telling you you're beautiful you lose all self-esteem. Just be yourself. Discover your own beauty and learn to love yourself first then you gotta stop thinkin" every man you fuck gotta love you back. This time find your morals and stand on top of them. Make mothafuckas respect you, then the right man will love you."

"What do I do till then?" Myria propped her hands on her hips and seemed to shift her weight to one leg.

"Stop being naive!" Drako emphasized. "Lil Momma until you find 'Mr. Right' you need to charge the hell outta 'Mr. Right

57

Now!' Play da game raw, baby girl. Just protect your feelings „cause at the end of the day you're the only one who's got to feel them . . . Now listen, stay away from that Fresh Face Modeling. A dude named Controversy runs it, right?"

"They told me his name was Kinney . . . maybe Kinney Slim." Her brows went up.

"It's the same guy. All I been hearin" is bad shit on his company and his models. Can't nothin" good come from that. Ain't nothin" over there for you, so keep lookin" elsewhere." Myria just nodded, gazing into Drako"s eyes. There was something different about his eyes. He seemed majestic and she felt they spoke to her on another level, a level that felt almost tantric.

Drako broke her trance. "Wait a minute . . ." He went into the coupe and pulled a brown paper bag from under the seat. He handed the bag to Myria. "I feel your pain, baby girl. Just remember to help yourself first. I probably won"t see you again, but I just gave you a piece of reality. Learn from your mistakes and play da game raw!"

Myria peeked in the bag and saw the stacks of banded money. She smiled, and then took her chances at hugging Drako. He barely reciprocated before gently pushing her back.

"It ain't necessary. That should help a little till you get straight. Keep ya mouth shut this time and don't come back."

"Thank you so much, Drako. I apologize for bringing this to you, but I just needed to vent somehow. I also want you to tell Diamond I'm sorry. I never meant to disrespect her either. It was the x—"

"What did I just tell you? You need to worry about yourself first."

She nodded and then folded the rim of the bag down as she turned and looked back at Drako. "You know, we really ain't that different. I „da done the same thing for you. Diamond really

is a lucky girl," she said, flopping down in the driver's seat and closing the door behind her.

"You think so?" Drako asked, watching her buckle up after she cranked up the Honda.

"Yup. Lucky I didn't meet you first." She winked and then backed out the space and drove away to her new life.

Drako just smiled.

As soon as Myria turned the corner, Drako spotted the red convertible Lexus Coupe pulling in. Diamond steered right up next to his Bentley.

"Wasn't that a female pulling away in that car?" she asked before she could even step out the car.

"Yeah."

"Well, who was she?"

"A black girl lost."

"Who?" Diamond looked even more baffled.

"A sista that was lost. She needed directions and I simply gave them to her, nothing more," Drako flatly stated, causing Diamond's expression to soften. "Raise your top and hop in with me. I'm ready for dinner and for you to fill me in on what you and these wedding planners been so busy talking about." He smiled warmly.

"Don't you wanna tell Drip we out at least?"

"Nah." Drako waved the entrance off. "I had enough for today. Ain't nothin' in there for us tonight." He pulled her to him and pecked her glossy, cherry flavored lips.

"Mmm." She smiled up at him. "Whatever you like."

"Good," he said, opening the door to his coupe and watching Diamond settle in. A few moments later, he'd hopped in the driver's seat and they were headed to Buckhead. Little did Diamond know that the flicker she'd been worried about had just, by fate, been doused. All Drako now wanted was a nice dinner and some drama free time with his lady.

He planned to stay away from Reality Records for the next few weeks. Drip would naturally embrace the responsibilities and Drako could spend more time not only working out his wedding plans, but also on another sweet scam that he couldn't get off his mind.

Reaching for Diamond"s outstretched hand, he grabbed it and placed it on his lap. "Is everything okay?" Diamond asked just then. "You feel kind of tense." She glared suspiciously.

Drako tried to smile. "Nah, ma. Everything"s just fine," he said, coming to a halt at the next red light. "Had to come to an understanding at the office, but we good now, and I was just reassuring those thoughts." He squeezed her hand and gave her a wink. Drako knew Diamond had a sixth sense, so he had to tell her something.

"Oh . . . well, I'm glad that's settled." Her face relaxed just as the light turned green and Drako pulled off again.

Drako sighed inwardly. He hoped he hadn"t put his camp in any imminent danger. But he knew if he stuck around and Big Turk resurfaced tonight things would"ve gotten super ugly. Now all he hoped is that Drip could keep things afloat without having to prove his gangster . . .

Damien
Chapter-10

For the last few weeks other than short visits to Wiz's mansion to deliver x-pills and a quick rendezvous, Damien had pretty much been MIA. At the moment, he was preoccupied with satisfying his appetite for good black pussy! He had purchased a home in Atlanta upon learning that it was home to the best strip clubs in the South, not to mention some of the most beautiful black sistas in the country.

Damien frequented all the spots, tipping well and soliciting private show after private show.

"Oh yes! Yesss!" the petite, tight-bodied black girl he'd been caught up over for the last few weeks, moaned loudly as he rabbit fucked her in missionary position.

"Whose pussy is this!"

"Yours baby! Oh God. Baby, it's all yours!" the girl replied as she bucked her hips wildly at Damien, while simultaneously reaching around and slapping him on his ass with every stroke as he'd instructed her to do.

"Buena panocha, negra puta!" Damien panted in his sexy Spanish bedroom dialect. He sped up his short strokes for the last time as he did his best to roughly fuck her so that she'd never forget about him. He felt her pussy muscles clench his dick almost with the firmness of a hand as she hugged him tight around the waist and pleaded, "Please don't hurt me, baby." Her sweet moans and a couple more strokes were enough to yank the warm semen from Damien's penis at the speed of a rocket!

"Oh fuck!" He trembled as the last bit of semen drained into his condom. Damien immediately collapsed on top of her as he labored to catch his breath. Sweat drenched his face and body;

his dick was still numb, and the Ecstasy had every nerve in his body standing at high alert! After a few short moments, Damien caught his breath. He raised his head from the nape of her neck and attempted to tongue kiss her.

Myria quickly turned her head, offering her cheek. "You know I ‚on like to kiss," she whined.

Damien didn't even argue because he was used to getting that excuse. He just went on pecking her soft cheeks in appreciation, and then proceeded to lick and lightly suck on her neck then earlobes, savoring the flavor of her sweet, flawless skin.

"I'm so happy to be your lover," Damien's husky voice whispered.

"Me too, baby," Myria replied, baring a half-smile to appease him.

Damien held her there for a little while before getting out of bed and reloading his system with x-pills and a glass of black cognac before he excused himself into his small study that served as his makeshift in-home office.

Myria watched Damien's naked ass leave the room. She pulled the covers up over her nude body as she sought comfort in the fetal position. Myria's mind was in a 'fuck it' mode as she thought she'd used Drako's advice to the best of her abilities. For the first time in her life, she was using what she had for the sole purpose of getting what she needed.

So far, she had only done two low-budget videos. She'd been the cover girl on the CD for an underground group that had a hella local buzz in Georgia. They were small jobs, but still, it was work. Damien had told her she'd start off small, but in time, he'd build her back up, and wherever ends didn't meet, he"d promptly trick the bill. The few grand he was giving up was nothing compared with the $10,000 tricking, prepaid plane tickets and limos Wiz had provided her so they could secretly meet at God knows where on any given day. But hey, as the saying goes: "You gotta crawl before you walk." And this time Myria would have patience.

*****

Once Damien had finally made it out of bed and into another expensive linen pants set, he was doing his best to make certain he'd covered everything and that all of his notes were in his briefcase. Wiz had requested Damien's presence for a meeting at Red Rum and Damien was cutting it close. He closed the briefcase and looked at Myria as she handed him his designer shades.

"I'm gonna miss you," he said, watching her tie the belt to her silk robe.

"Me too," she said, stepping closer to him.

Damien closed his eyes, whiffing her golden skin as he hugged her and kissed her neck one last time.

"Don't miss me. I'll be right here when you return," she cooed.

Damien smiled. He was sprung and proud of his accomplishment. Lately, she really was all he thought of. Between chasing after her goods and keeping their secret, he knew he hadn't given Red Rum much thought, so today he needed to make an impact. "And that'll be as soon as I can," he promised, gazing into her pretty brown eyes.

A few moments later, Damien hopped in his SUV and dashed to the airport to board his flight just in the nick of time. As the 747 Boeing leveled out, all Damien could ponder was how this new artist could be the vital piece to help further his plan for Red Rum.

*****

By the time Damien stepped into Red Rum the meeting was already underway. With briefcase in hand he gave Diane a sly wink, hoping to catch her next and headed into the first level conference room. He, of course, didn't interrupt as Wiz had Red

Rum"'s entire roster present. Damien grabbed a seat against the wall. He sat his briefcase beside him, crossed one leg over the other, and listened to Wiz lead his camp.

"In this quarter I want to see numbers!" Wiz stood up and began to take a slow stroll around the table. "We been the hottest label in the South for too long to accept this!" He raised the folder in his hand. "These numbers are unacceptable!" His eyes trailed over Choc-Money and Jay-Poon and settled on Swirl for a moment. "From this day forward, Red Rum is an army! I don't mean guns and bullets, I'm talkin" beats and lyrics! I provide y"all wit' the hardest tracks in the mothafuckin" game. There ain't no reason for only Swirl and Thump"'s numbers to soar!" He dropped the file on the table with a thud. "Everybody else in this room numbers are either stagnant or have dropped!" He looked at Thump and then to Swirl before his attention went back to his smaller artist.

"So anybody got any suggestions? Can someone please tell me why we ain't the only thing they talkin" 'bout?" He stopped and stood over a short, chubby artist from St. Louis that he'd signed. "So, Barz, you got the floor. Tell me what's your plan to fix these digits?" Wiz leered over at the folder.

"I"ma keep spittin" hot bars, that's what I do!" He sat straight up lookin" at Wiz.

Wiz nodded, clearly not satisfied with the weak response. "I'm lettin" y"all know now. Somebody in this room better make it happen! This industry is about new faces, a new approach and somethin" worth hearing. I'm about to reinforce this arsenal, so it's nothin" personal, it's just business! I don't see the point in dumpin" millions of dollars in videos for emcees without a buzz." Wiz had made it back around the table. He took another defeated look around the room and sat back down in his chair at the head of the table. "Y"all get in these booths and figure it out." He pointed to the door. "And just remember. It's just

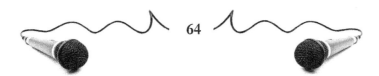

64

business." All of his underclassmen stood up and headed for the door.

"Please. Thump, Swirl. Stay put." He held a serious face as the last artist cleared the room. He knew he'd just given them initiative to get to work because positions in the camp were certainly on the line. "Sorry you had to see that," he said to Thump, "but it's just business. Feel me?" He studied Thump's expression, noticing his chipped tooth when he nodded.

"I like everything that's comin" from you. I like your energy. I need you to spark it within the rest of these guys. I want you to try to collabo with 'em. I think Barz and you would be fire!"

Thump just nodded again.

"Ain't no secret 'bout who's the face of this shit." Wiz's eyes trailed over to Swirl. "Wherever you need tips, it's all right there. Swirl got you . . . You'll soon learn how things go around here." He winked and laid back with a smile. He was trying to read Thump, but he could sense that it wasn't time to bring him into the fake beef scam.

"I'm good." Wiz looked at Swirl. "I just need these new cats to start actin" like soldiers on stage."

"Everybody ain't a soldier. Them cats is just artists," Swirl said, easily getting to his feet.

Wiz nodded at the thought. "Yeah, maybe . . . Well, let's try to get some good music out of „em," Wiz said, watching Thump trail Swirl out of the room.

*****

Damien had strolled up to Wiz's offices with him and was now sitting across from his desk as Wiz ranted on. " . . . Three weeks since Swirl dropped 'Reality Bites' and I haven't got a single rise!" He was referring to a mixtape Swirl had dropped, hoping to build hype. "Yeah, well I guess 'Reality' didn't bite." He tried to make humor at his failed attempt.

"And I'm not sure if they will," Damien spoke frankly. "Those were just subliminal remarks." Damien exhaled and sat up straight. "From what I'm gathering, you aren't getting much of a rise from your supporting cast either. Other than Swirl and this Thump kid, you got the same old cookie cutter emcees as everyone else. I heard what you said: It's just business. And I understand your objective more than most. Your aim is to sell albums, so practice what you preach. Get you some new faces if that's what it's about. Find some emcee with a relentless appetite and give the world something they have to pay attention to."

"Swirl knows our dilemma. I'm just gonna have to—"

"Wiz." Damien cut in with a slight nod. "As your friend I wholeheartedly agree, but as your advisor giving you my best business advice I must say that Swirl has both the heart and smarts. But that's not what's needed here. . . . You need an animal! You need a shift in momentum, and that's gonna be someone you don't have to persuade, somebody who don't give a fuck! An artist with the potential to grow so big the industry can't look around him."

Damien squinted as he gave another sure nod. "And I think I might have a few good candidates."

Wiz smiled sinisterly and rolled his chair closer to the desk as Damien popped open his briefcase. He couldn't wait to catch the small label in deep water. He laughed, looking over the list Damien passed him.

Reality Records, ha? Well, let"s see who"s really ready to play the game! He cackeled at the thought and gave Damien a pound.

Reality Records
Chapter - 11

Busy, busy, busy is how Drip described the life around Reality Records and its every day function. He was getting more magazine interviews and layouts as each day passed. Reality Records now owned a hermetically sealed tour bus with recording equipment that Save would now manage for his upcoming tour and the promotional tour they were on that never seemed to end.

Everybody was in attendance and looking their best. The entire roster was accompanying Save on 106 and Park. He still held the number one spot, and today he was there to speak out and introduce his latest video, which was the feature for today's show.

"Everybody straight?" Drip did a quick once over of all the artists. Navan wore his signature style, black skinny jeans, Van's, a white button down, and he carried his Ed Hardy backpack. Drip looked to his latest two acts who were dressed down in baggy Roca Wear Jeans, Air Forces and wife beaters. Then his focus skipped over to Ebony, who looked glamorous in her black, skintight corsette pants, knee length boots and a black leather bustier top that made her chest look amazing. "You lead the camp in on our cue," Drip instructed, unable to take his eyes off her ass as she slightly leaned over to rummage through her bag. "You gone make a mean First Lady and a mean impression!" he assured her, glancing over at Save who didn't seem so enthused as he stood a little ways off from the entourage, pacing a small circle. "Just take your time with your responses. Speak clearly and be mindful of all camera angles." He told the group as they huddled close together.

He stepped over to Save. "What up, man? Everything a'ight?"

"A'ight?" Save had a sour look on his face. "Yo, what kinda' respect is this? You hear what the fuck they playin'!" His jaw tightened a bit. "Son, you know that shit aimed at me; they know it too! That's why they playin' it!" He sucked his teeth, doing his best to keep his cool.

"Listen, let me talk to these producers. I don't know what's goin' on. Maybe you're right. I think they're trying to set a tone, but listen to me." He looked Save in the eyes. "We're not falling for it. Stay cool. Plug your album. This is your opportune time to make a first impression here. You don't get a second chance to make another one." He didn't break his glare a bit.

"Yo son. I'm sayin'—"

"I'll handle it," Drip said flatly, noticing the slight tremble in Save's bottom lip.

"I'm good. The God Body always is." He stepped back over to the group.

Drip turned and walked over to Blondelle. She stood up and planted a soft kiss on his cheek as she adjusted the collar to his Purple Label button down. "You look nice, baby," she said, assuring the super producer on the rise.

"But even better with you on my arm." He winked and gave her a bit of that charismatic smile that lured her in from the start. Blondelle blushed and sat back down and crossed her leg. She was cool with waiting backstage for this one. Drip knew Blondelle had one of the sexiest, unique prowesses on the screen. He had no problems red carpeting her everywhere he went, and he treated her with the utmost respect. She could sing a little, but in the studio he was sure he could pass her voice by with flying colors. He had big plans for his supermodel girlfriend as well.

"And, thirty seconds you're on," a set director instructed as he listened through his headsets carefully. "Five, four, three, two and go!" He pointed to the curtain. Ebony fired through with so much sass and sway to her hips. She stopped so professionally and turned at least three angles, showing off more than her outfit for the cameras. The set rose to its feet with applause as she pivoted and swayed right up to Terrance J for a hug. The crowd continued to roar for the rest of the entourage and seemingly most for Save.

"Glad to have y"all here. Show me some love." Terrance hit all the men with dap and man-hugs. Soon, everybody was seated and everybody had introduced themselves.

"So, Miss Ebony"—Terrance couldn't keep his eyes off her—"What's next for you? I saw on Twitter that you and Nicki might be doing somethin'?"

"Haven't had a chance to meet her yet." Ebony crossed her leg and checked her posture for the camera. "I really don't plan on rockin" with a lot of chicks. Never have, so I don't plan to start now. I sorta like being their problem." She flashed an even toothier smile behind her glossed lips.

"Is that right?" Terrance J asked with raised brows. "Navan, you know we can't wait to hear your unique style. I'm sure you're gonna be everywhere!"

"For sure, for sure," he said, adjusting the nerdy black Polo frames.

"Let us get a sample of that voice now." Terrance took him by surprise, seeing Navan swallow the lump and wave him off jokingly. "Come on, man, seriously. Just a few bars and a chorus maybe."

A few moments later, Navan had the set in a trance as he freestyled effortlessly off the dome. His voice nailed his hook with a tone that took the audience with complete surprise. He delivered over twenty bars with the confidence of an experienced emcee.

In no time the show had been a success. Another classic episode for the archives. Save had looked into the teleprompter and announced his video. Ebony took the show to a commercial break and the show returned with Drip plugging in Big Jud and Dee-Ruu for their upcoming projects. It was almost down to Save's number one spot and he'd answered all his questions with a calm poise. Reclining back on the couch, he wore Gucci sneakers, Red Monkey Jeans and a Gucci shirt. His dreads were pulled neatly behind his ears and held together in a bunch by a single black band. He wore a pair of dark Gucci frames across his face the whole show.

"You are definitely making your way." Terrance J said, complimenting Save while also seeming to ogle Save's diamond encrusted star shaped pendant with a huge number seven on top of it.

"So do you have any plans to address Swirl and make a reply to this 'Reality Bites' that's been circulating?" Save fiddled with his T-shirt and then cracked his knuckles, but kept his cool as Drip threw darts at him with his eyes.

"No reply," he said with a cool wave to Terrance J's surprise. "I mean he hasn't said my or anybody I'm associated with name. I take Swirl to very much be a man. Only women go around and whisper or say things behind a man's back that they wouldn't say to his face." Save sat straight up. "So, nah, I know he's not referencing me."

"Okay then." Terrance saw the set director giving him a ten-second countdown to the number one video. "Well, without further ado, would you please introduce the number one video for the seventeenth consecutive day in a row this time?"

The camera panned straight down on Save as he half read the teleprompter and introduced "It's a Given" with as much swag

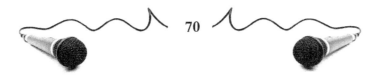

70

as he could muster. As soon as the set ended, everybody was backstage huddled together again. "That was great! Everybody did well. Now listen up. We got things to do still. As soon as we touch back down in ATL we're heading by the studio briefly, then it's off to the taping of the *Monique Show*. Again, we're moving as a unit, so let's get changed into our best and keep it pushing." He watched everybody gather their small belongings as he stepped over to Save and gave him dap. "You did pretty good out there. You speak like you been trained for the cameras."

"Nah, never trained. Just born for it, son." Save smiled.

"That was some slick shit you said too. You stabbin" without stabbin", huh?'

"Nah, that was some slick shit Terrance J came at me with," Save fired back. "I ain't see it coming, and I just responded as casually as I could."

Drip stared at him for a moment. "Just keep it down for now. I got people who wanna help us, so we gone chase our money and not worry about them."

"Yeah, I hear you, but I still feel like we need to let 'em know we got lyrics that kill too. Maybe they'll find somewhere else to play games if they realize this shit ain't just a game."

"Just do as I advise." Drip patted his shoulder and headed over to Blondelle.

*****

After Drako and Diamond had entered Reality Records, they were in a festive mood. All the artists were lounging in the sleep quarters and the conference room. They had all changed into new clothes and were talking about how things went at 106 and Park. They were just as eager to reach the set of the *Monique Show* and hoped to do an even better job. Drako hadn't been to Reality Records but a few times in the last few weeks as he was trying to make special plans that would surprise Diamond for

71

their wedding. He'd found time to send his buddy Deuce, back in Lewisburg, stacks of new pictures and literature he'd been hoping for. And, he had time to research another potential white collar, multimillion dollar scheme.

To say he was pleased with Drip's progression would be the biggest understatement ever! Everybody was taken by storm at how the streets took to Reality's music. Drip used the Internet to spread the brand constantly. Drako looked at Blondelle in her tight white catsuit. He couldn't deny, nor turn away from her statuesque physique. Her wide ass and small waist appeared as if it were possibly molded from clay it was so perfect and came with a camel toe that would have been embarrassing to most. Her skin was almost as light as Diamond's, and her makeup was to perfection. There was no doubt she appeared to be all that. But Drako wasn't convinced with how fast she decided to obviously be regarded as Drip's everything. Of course, he minded his business as he gave Save a pound and his eyes settled on Ebony as she strolled past with a casual wave. She was looking very nice as well in the clingy yellow dress that accented her small waistline. Ebony seemed to be a good fit for Reality Records. When Drako visited by himself she still shot him those enticing looks and her body language still spoke his name. But when Diamond was anywhere near you'd have thought Drako was just another brick in the wall.

"Let me rap to ya" a minute before we dip." Drip glanced at his iced out timepiece. "In your office," Drip added coolly.

"This is what's crackin." Drip wasted no time as they stepped through the door. "The kid, he wants to go at Swirl. He's said it, and I can see it wanting to jump clean out of him. I know it ain't a smart move to fuck with a ship that's anchored the way Wiz holdin" that shit down, but I'm comin" to you 'cause I see somethin" in this boy. I been seen it. He can be a loose cannon. Why you think I told you to record as many verses of his in

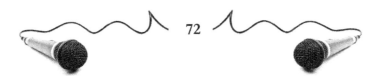

front of green screens? He's on probation already. I don't think he'd ever catch anything more than a skid bid, but he's young. He can't let go. Trust me."

Drako sat down as his mind bounced the thought around. He nodded his head and said, "Straight up, I heard the mixtape. It's really nothing. That silly shit got Wiz written all over it! He's e-mailed me several times and called Diamond whining 'bout my business. I'm tellin" you I know him better than anybody. He wants us to react. We'll make money, but with his distributors and influence over the media and tabloids he'll make three times the pay. This shit—life is just a game to him." Drako's nostrils flared at the thought. "The nigga did some cruddy shit to me. I can't figure out why, nor can I get past it. I'm out here doin' what I need to do to get mine. You know how I get down." Drip just nodded.

"Tell that boy don't bring us no bad press with that. We don't need the Hip-Hop Task Force here yet. Eventually they'll probe us too, but by the time they get here my plan is like always . . . To be done!"

Drip smiled and shook his head. "I got him. I"ma keep a leash on him. I know a few words can't be that serious to him. I"ma watch him grow up in that very booth." Drip winked, knocked on the desk and turned to leave.

"Friday," Drako called out behind him. Drip stopped in his tracks and glanced back.

"You need some special assistance?"

"Nah, nah, not yet anyway. But I do want to move my offshore accounts eventually. I wanna switch about ten big to a place no one knows. I don't want my right hand to be able to keep up with my left." Drako smiled.

"Just let me know," Drip said easily.

"But no, I'm talkin" 'bout the video set Friday. I'm gonna make sure I stop by like I told ya."

"Cool." Drip smiled a little wider. "I thought you'd forgotten. I shoulda' known better. Cats like you always come through."

He gave Drako a cool wink, turned on his heels and headed back to work.

Drako reclined in his comfortable chair, folding his hands behind his head. He was as proud as he'd been in a very long time. He was happy to have Drip on his side and found himself being even more thankful to Toney again.

Toney had not only taught him well, but it was Toney who also pointed him in positive directions, such as in meeting Drip.

Drako knew all he now had, without the help of Wiz, was indeed attributed to all he learned from Toney.

He exhaled a deep sigh, wishing he could talk to Toney and tell him how far he'd come. But Drako felt the time wasn't right just yet. Sitting up straight with his mind made for the moment, he decided to keep doing what he was doing for now. He left the building and headed straight for the post office. Today, he was gonna drop both Toney and Deuce a lump in their accounts. Financially, he was doing well and he was gonna make sure they were doing the same.

Red Rum
Chapter - 12

Swirl stood closest to the huge plasma TV with a blunt dangling from his lips. He'd just made a joke about getting a closer look at Ebony's phat ass when the show returned from commercial break.

"You think that bitch phatter than Nicki Minaj?" Wiz asked Thump, who was leaned over the pool table leveling his stick for the next shot.

"Shit, yaa!" Swirl spoke up. "Titties and all! The bitch might can't spit, but I'll bet yo" ass she can swallow!" The room fell into laughter.

Thump took a long shot down the red felt and slammed the eight ball in the corner pocket. "The chick look just like Mary when she first came out, except she already glammed up." He stood erect and reached for the blunt that had Swirl in a series of hard coughs.

Thump took a long pull and coughs wracked his chest the same way. "Where the fuck you get that from?" Wiz turned to Big Turk who was sitting beside him on the sofa.

"Shawdy, das dat Sour Diesel . . . das all I smoke," he said with his natural mean grit.

"Pass me that shit!" Wiz said, watching Thump tap his chest with the back of his fist as if he could clear it of the strong cannabis effect.

"Okay, okay, shit back on." The room went silent behind Swirl's announcement. Terrance J was sitting on the back of the couch asking Save the last questions of the day, just before the number one video aired.

"No reply," the room heard Save answer with a wave. Swirl crossed his arms over his chest subconsciously, mean mugging the screen with a nod as the Sour Diesel had him feeling invincible. "I mean, he hasn't said my or anybody I'm associated with, name. I take Swirl to very much be a man." Swirl was still nodding, feeling the respect Save knew to throw his way. "Only women go around and whisper or say things behind a man's back that they wouldn't say to his face." He saw Save sit up, and even though Save wore dark shades Swirl still saw that grit he tried to contain behind them. "So nah, I know he's not referencing me."

Swirl's mouth had dropped wide open. And so had everybody else"s.

Swirl and Wiz especially, because they both had a guilty conscience. Any street savvy man knew Save had just called whomever had spoken about him in a whisper or indirectly in any kind of way, a cold bitch!

"Mothafucka!" Big Turk hopped off the couch. "You hear dis pussy ass nigga?" He fumed and Wiz could see sweat popping up on his nose.

He began pacing back and forth in the area just in front of Wiz. "I hate when them soft ass niggaz get outta line!" His big ass fists were bald tightly and his eyes bulged. All eyes now fell on Wiz's newest artist rather than Save as he introduced his number one spot.

"Fuck!" He ripped off his T-shirt so fast his tank top crumpled around his waist. He had what looked like twenty inches of tatted up pythons, and at six four and two fifty plus, he was hulking!

Stalking straight over to the booth, he twisted the handle hard, only to find it locked. He kicked at the door in a rage. "Somebody open up this goddamn booth!" he barked. "I want

this nigga right goddamn now!" He banged a heavy fist on the side of the wall.

"Slow down, slow down, baby!" Wiz hopped to his feet, all smiles. "We gone get to it, just take your time with it. You at the Rum now, baby," Wiz said soothingly.

"Shit!" Big Turk stormed toward the lounge area. "Who da fuck got some blunts?" he shouted, still pissed.

Wiz chuckled proudly. "I like this guy already." He hit the elevator and headed to his office.

*****

Five minutes later, Swirl was pacing the floor in Wiz's office. They had the door shut and Swirl had taken his shirt off. He was fuming!

"See, that's what I'm talkin'' 'bout, my nigga! That shit ain't put together. That nigga called me a hoe."

"Nah, I'm not gone say—" Wiz reared back in his armchair, fumbling with the Red-Rum medallion on his diamond chain.

"Nah my ass! Ain't no way to cover that shit up! He did it real slick and he meant that shit, Wiz!" Swirl huffed in aggravation. He knew Wiz well, and he knew Wiz wasn't feeling his pain. He knew Wiz was happy to have a hair trigger hot head like Big Turk on his team. "You can't identify with this shit. It ain't happen to you." Swirl nodded his head and flopped down in a chair.

"Man, it's just music. No, this is just fun," Wiz reasoned in an easy persuasive tone. He stopped toying with the medallion and gazed at Swirl.

Swirl blinked and paused for a moment.

"Nah, man. I gotta be straight up wit' you. You got Big Turk or whatever his studio gangsta name is. I see right through that shit. The nigga tall and that's all!" Swirl looked at the salty look Wiz tried to hide and knew he was far from convinced of that. "Well, either way he'll do all you need with that. I'm out of it. I

„on give a fuck if I don't make another dime. I won't keep doin"
the back and forth. I'll kill one of them niggaz! Anyone of „em
who run up. I got a set to claim, and I honestly can't take that
part of the game."

"What's the difference in him and—"

"Hey!" Swirl raised his voice. "Fatt Katt knew! This fool
might say anything! I seen it before. I know his type. Just cut
me out „cause I'll make shit ugly!"

Wiz nodded. "You got that, player. You got it! Nothin" but
love." He held out his hand for dap.

"Love back, partna. Love back! —Oh, but one more thing:
keep this Big Turk away from me. I'm not gettin" on shit with
him and I „on wanna do nothin" except find out where he get
dat' Sour Diesel shit from."

"I feel you." Wiz laughed, walking Swirl out the door.

*****

Shortly after Swirl left, Wiz was walking Big Turk through
his expectations at Red Rum and small things in his contract.
Soon they stepped right up to the booth. Wiz turned and looked
up at Big Turk. "I only want you working with certain artists.
No guest appearance unless authorized through the label, and I
especially don't want you working with Swirl. Un-uh. I want to
build your own separate light. I see you at the top of this shit in
no time." Wiz winked, causing Big Turk to smile back.

"I gotta get you some hot jewels too," Wiz said, unlocking
the booth.

"Is that about it? What else do you want me to do?" Big Turk
held the door open as Wiz was about to head over to the mixing
board.

Wiz stopped in his tracks and looked back without a hint of a
smile on his face. "Get at „im. Hit 'im hard!" He turned and
headed for his favorite seat in the building, the one in front of

his mixing board. "And don"t leave shit out" His voice dripped venom.

For the next few hours, Wiz dropped crazy beats and recorded hundreds of bars of music. He was doing what he did best. He had a new toy that was sure to bring starpower back to Red-Rum in a big way. And in Wiz"s mind he didn"t give a fuck! He was ready to wreak havoc on the whole industry, and he was starting with Reality Records!

Drako
Chapter-13

"Come on, Drako," Diamond whined, "you need to pay attention." She peered over her shoulder as Drako lay in bed beside her. He was totally preoccupied with strumming his fingers up and down her spine and kissing her from her shoulder down to her neck, rather than paying attention to the portfolios.

"Unn . . ." she whined, prodding him this time with an elbow. "Seriously, do you like this one or not?"

Drako exhaled, sitting up higher. "It's okay. I mean, it's nice but it looks just like the gown La La married Carmelo in. Baby, I want you to be one of a kind. This wedding planner has given you all these portfolios of celebrity weddings to choose from, which means these themes, schemes, and dresses have all been done," he reasoned as he gently closed the one she was looking at and grabbed another one. "How 'bout this?" he said, opening a Vera Wang catalog Diamond hadn't paid much attention to. "See, I like this. It's contemporary. It"ll fit nicely to accentuate your body and it shows skin." He smiled.

"What about this train?" She took a closer look.

"I love it." He kissed her shoulder again. "It's not too long. It's what's happening now."

"Ten thousand dollars—"

"Ain't no limit, baby. Ain't no roof on this shit, so don't even contemplate it."

"Well, what abou—"

"Damn, you smell so good." He wasn't paying her any attention. His erection swelled underneath the covers.

"Stop Drako . . ." she said this time with a hint of annoyance.

"This is serious. You tell me how much you want it, but I don"t see you helping me plan except whenever I pin you

down." Drako sensed attitude. "But I hear you making arrangements for that silly Floyd Mayweather and Pac-man or whatever his name is, fight." Her cute little nose flared. "You need to stay focused and really pay attention here."

He exhaled again and let her rattle off about flower arrangements and a bunch of shit she was going to take charge of anyway. Drako knew her day would certainly be special. He was in the process of trying to get Jesse Powell to come and sing his classic song "You," which both he and Diamond had always loved. He'd already gotten a commitment from Lloyd. Diamond had always admired his talent and thought the industry had him far underrated. Drip had even said Monica would do something as well, if requested. All this would be a sure surprise to Diamond, and it would all be recorded footage for them to relive forever.

Drako craned his head the other way. He heard his cell phone vibrating. Peeking at the alarm clock beside it, it was almost noon. He reached for it and saw the unavailable number. He knew it was probably Deuce calling to get the 'real'. Drako could imagine how things had been around Lewisburg. Prison speculation was always at an all-time high, and Deuce loved to be the Nigga with the inside scoop! Drako knew Deuce was eager to hear what was up. He hadn't had a chance to catch up with him in weeks! Not since before the raid at Red Rum that the media had blown way out of proportion.

As soon as he heard Deuce state his name, he pressed '5' to accept the call, seeming to forget all he and Dimond were just discussing.

"What up, blood?" Drako greeted.

"Man . . . Good ta hear yo' voice! Dese' fools goin' crazy in here! All kinda' shit flyin"!"

"Like what?" Drako quipped with a curious smile.

Being cautious of the monitored prison phones, Deuce began to speak in code to question Drako about the rumors.

"Two hundred gone to da bad." *(Two hundred pounds had been found.)*

"Shorty left lil homie on stuck. *(Wiz blamed everything on Swirl.)* "And lil homie 'bout ta' change camps and move to da row!" *(Swirl's leaving Red Rum and about to sign with a West Coast Label.)*

Drako stopped him with laughter, reflecting back on his days of prison speculation. "Nah, blood, it ain't like that."

"Homie wrapped red?" *(Is Swirl claiming Bloods now?)*

"Has for a long time now." Drako chuckled. "And sticks alone can't start no fire! They just ain't have nothin" else to say. Believe me that station just fuzzy."

Deuce chuckled this time, quickly deciphering Drako's words. He knew it must've only been a personal amount of weed lying around Red Rum's headquarters—a pound or two, tops! "I knew shorty was smarter than that!"

"Oh yeah, pretty much. You can let that be known."

Deuce's smile spilled through. "A'ight then, now gimme da real. You know I want to lay somethin" hot on that fool, Dub-D." Then before Drako could even respond, he added, "Oh yeah, thanks for the chips and them flicks. Them same old tricks was gettin" old."

"I got you, homie. Shit been busy out here. Life is busy. I ,on got time to sit down and write yo' big ass no love letter, but I always got time to make sure you got paper when it's like this." Deuce nodded his head knowingly on the other end. "Look man, I called ,cause you know the Hip-Hop Awards is next week. You think you can get me some back stage shots?"

Drako pulled the covers back and got out of bed. He didn"t even peep the angry glare Diamond gave when he went into the

den and continued his conversation. "I doubt it, man. I mean, I doubt if I attend, but I'll see what I can get for you," Drako said.

"I took some time off from the Rum," Drako lied. "I'm puttin" together a hell of a wedding for me and Diamond. I got Lloyd to sing, and man, the shit just gone be nice." Drako was beaming. "That's why I don't have much for you today. I'll get back to puttin" you down when things get in order. Now keep this under the hat. I haven't even told Toney yet. I'm gonna send you all some pictures and surprises soon."

"Damn fool, that's what's up! I gotcha. It stays here. Well anyway, I can't believe shorty signed a nigga from Tidewater!" He was referring to Thump.

"Yep, stole him right from under Timbaland's nose."

"Yo', dat fool hot too! But oh, oh!" Deuce's deep voice found even more bass. "You remember Professor, don't you?" He was referring to Drip. "Man, that fool is behind that Reality shit! I fucks wit' the Rum, you know this. But man, that fool droppin" beats and bringin" it! He got a fool called Save! Homie, he a front door nigga!" Deuce swore with excitement.

"Man, you like what you like." Drako smiled. "I heard all they shit. Them boyz bring the real. You know I'm far from a hater." It was killing Drako not to tell Deuce the real. But right now the time wasn't right. He trusted Deuce with everything, but like he always knew, prison gossip spread far beyond its walls and fast! There would be no early tie-ins with him and Drip because of loose lips.

"I can't believe that jailhouse Johnny Cochran . . . Man, I knew it was more to him than that." Deuce ranted on, but made clear he wished Drip only and all the best. Drako and Deuce went on, covering as much as they could in the remainder of the fifteen-minute call. They always brought mutual smiles to each other's faces. Drako was glad to be there for Deuce. He knew he was the only hope Deuce could depend on in the world. And

83

Drako had once felt the same way before about Wiz. So many people turned their backs on a man in prison in due time. Drako planned to never turn his back on Toney or Deuce unless it was covered with dirt!

"Get at me . . . One," Drako said, ending the call shortly after they heard the one minute alert beep.

He walked back into the room. Diamond had put the portfolios up. She had his fresh boxers and sweatpants lying across the now made bed.

"You need to get dressed. The shower's already on," she said dryly, coming out the bathroom adjusting her thick terrycloth robe around her.

"Damn!" Drako huffed. He'd nearly forgotten about the video set he'd assured Drip he'd stop by. "But damn, what about—" Drako licked his lips as his gaze settled on the knot tied in the belt of her robe.

Diamond smacked her lips, not hiding a bit of her attitude now. "You know sometimes I think you really must take me for a joke . . . Yes, you have the money, but you ain't moved a muscle with our wedding arrangements!" She rolled her eyes and slightly bit down on her bottom lip, oblivious to Drako"s surprise he was working on. And as soon as you got that call you forgot all about me. You went to blabbering away about God knows what! And now all you can think about is wetting your dick up! Well, for real Drako, you better think again!" She looked over his big chest and down his chiseled abs knowing normally she"d give in. But this time she turned away and stuck to her word. She also knew Drako had an appointment to make, and more importantly, she wanted to see him make his company successful.

"Come on, ma. Just let me—"

"No, I *said* . . ." She took a step back seeing Drako about to reach for her wrist. She saw the look in his eyes. He knew she

was ass naked underneath that robe and had he gotten a hand on her soft, warm ass he"d have surely taken it. She decided to toss a little more attitude to make her point. "Stop taking me for granted!" She pointed a finger at him. "I keep all your shit together and I go far beyond to make you happy. I"m talking about the things money can"t buy!" Diamond could sense her words had struck a cord in Drako"s mind. Her mind was reeling too. She"d heard about what went down between Drako and Big Turk. She was glad that it didn"t go any further, but she still couldn"t curb the thoughts of if and how another guy would appreciate her.

Diamond shook the vision away. She didn"t mean to harbor it and she knew it wasn"t right, but of course, she was only human. "You need ta get moving, Drako. If you want to see some ass I"m sure it"ll be plenty on the set." She rolled her eyes again.

"Damn . . . it"s like that?" He was taken aback. Diamond hadn"t spoken like this before.

"I"m just saying, Drako. We"re not getting any younger and you need to always be conscious of your priorities."

His oncoming erection deflated as her words resonated with him. "Well, when I get back, I want—"

"I"ll be sound asleep wnen you get back. You can best believe that too." She turned on her bare feet and sauntered her sexy ass out of the room without another word. He knew he wasn"t getting any tonight.

Drako flopped down on the bed feeling like shit. Although he had to hold his wedding surprises, he still realized he"d been overlooking the small things and concentrating only on Reality Records and his list ot schemes. Diamond had been good to him and he knew she was faithful, and that"s the way he wanted to keep it. He had business he had to attend to for now, but he had plans to tighten up his game with Diamond like a boss should. He knew his Diamond was priceless.

Reality Records
Chapter- 14

When Drako arrived at the set, he quickly saw that everything was alive and well for the camp. He drove right past the custom painted tour bus and parked his coupe.

As he approached the set, he first took note of all the props that were set and ready to go. The rented exotic foreign whips were all shined up and ready to dazzle the camera. Drako was further appeased with the tasteful choice of video girls that rounded out the set.

He spotted Drip sitting next to the director's chair, then made out Blondelle propped up right beside him as well. Drako promptly meandered his way through the throngs of models and set assistants, making his way over to Drip. As soon as Drip noticed Drako nearing, he stood to his feet. "What up, man?" he greeted. "I'm really glad you could make it. I just really wanted you to see how hard these guys put it down. We"ve been here since before daybreak for that night scene. Ebony's shoot just wrapped a short while ago. They caught a few moments of rest on the bus and they're all gassed up and ready to knock Save's shoot out today as well."

Drako nodded, then politely spoke to Blondelle, whose glow seemed to brighten more with each passing event.

Drip asked Drako if he cared for any refreshments or anything as Drako took the next wooden stool the set assistant quickly brought over. They began to watch the technicians rearrange the props and ready the makeshift stage for Save's shoot.

Before long, Drako found himself building with Drip for over a half hour. They were now looking at a set that had everything ready to go except Save, who was supposed to be performing his bars.

Drip had told the director's assistant twice that Save would be out in just a short moment as he pulled Drako aside. They stepped out of earshot from Blondelle as Drip gave a cautious glance her way. "Man, I got somethin'' I need to tell you," he said. "Man . . . Blondelle—"

"Don't tell me she pregnant already?" Drako had that gut feeling.

"Nah, man." He waved the thought away easily. "This is much—look man, I'm gonna marry her."

Drako didn't mean for his eyes to bulge so wide, but Drip took him by complete surprise!

"I-I know it seems sudden, but I'm tellin'' ya, Drako." He nodded his head, gazing her way again. "If I'm wrong, I'm just doin'' what my heart tell me to do. Um, um, uh! Look at that woman," he said proudly, turning back to Drako, whose words were still frozen in his throat.

Drako attempted to respond when the director sent the light tech over to tap Drip on the shoulder. "Time''s wasting. Time's your money Benny says."

"Yeah, yeah, yeah. I said he's comin'!" Drip shooed him away, wanting to hear Drako's response.

"Where the hell is Save?" Drako looked around, changing subjects.

"He's in the trailer," Drip said a little too carefree.

"Man, this is business. These people ready to go. They got lives too. What does he think? He Jay-Z already?" Drako looked over Drip's shoulder and the same guy was headed back their way.

"Go ahead and holler at him," Drako said impatiently. "I'll go get Save. Which trailer is it?"

"The first one." He pointed in that direction "But we still need to talk when you get back." Drip went one way; Drako went the other.

* * * * *

When Drako opened the trailer door he expected heavy weed smoke to spew out or to find Save and a couple vixens still spent and lost from the track of time. He never thought he'd be yelling Save's name throughout the virtually empty shell. He tried the first small room to find it unoccupied, and then the second one as well. Drako heard a shuffling sound behind him then a door creaked open. He turned to see Ebony waltzing out the bathroom with a towel wrapped around her.

"What are you doin' here?" She shouldered past him and sashayed straight to the trailer door and locked it.

"I thought Save was in here. It's time for his set," Drako said without a blink.

"Well, ain't no damn Save in here." She smacked her lips with lust burning in her eyes as she stepped back toward Drako. "Ain't nobody on this here stage but me! Me and you!" Her tongue slid to the right crack of her mouth and settled there.

"Chill out, baby girl. I know you got my message. I told you, I „on play wit' Diamond around here like that."

"I „on see no damn Diamond nowhere!" She unloosed the towel and stepped up to Drako, ass naked. "All I see here is Reality's First Lady and the mothafuckin‟ President!" she said huskily, pressing her big firm breasts against Drako's chest while she snaked an arm around his waist. "You „on think I know power when I see it?" She rolled her pussy against his thigh slyly.

Drako swallowed the lump in his throat. "Yeah, maybe . . . and you're exactly right—you're Reality's First Lady emcee, not mine." He didn't hesitate to clarify.

89

"I ain't tryin'' to be your or nobody else's first lady," she countered. "But how about if I just want to be your Monica Lewinsky?" She'd felt Drako began to stiffen and was already tussling a small manicured hand down his sweats.

"Mmmmm! The boss got a big ass dick." She bit down on her lip and dropped to her knees simultaneously.

Drako wanted to stop her. It wasn't like he hadn't gotten head before, but this could be bad for business.

As if it were a magic trick, she smoothly tugged the waistband to his sweats down; his thick dick sprung out like a jack in the box. With a hunger that wouldn't take 'no' for an answer, she began licking and slurping over the head as if it were a lollipop.

"Um-hmm!" she moaned, pulling the dick from her mouth with a popping sound. "Your meat taste fresh. Now I need to taste your cum." She closed her eyes and swallowed over half of Drako's dick in one gulp.

"Mm hmm!" she continued to moan and bob her neck to the same rhythm. She guided Drako to the small bed in the trailer by his dick, then pushed him down. She kneeled between his legs and began to jerk at his huge dick slowly with both hands as her suctioning jaws did way more combinations to the swollen head as he'd ever experienced.

"God damn!" Drako gasped, letting his sounds of satisfaction slip out under the weight of her skills. Drako reasoned that he was only a man, and Ebony would be hard for any man to resist in this predicament. "Make dat' shit bust!" He fumbled on, giving completely in as his dick stood to its full ten-inch potential.

"Where you gone spit dat shit?" he croaked, rocking his pelvis as he felt his urge nearing.

She plopped the dick out again, flicking a pink tongue over the tip. "For you, Mr. President . . . I'ma swallow!'" Her eyes

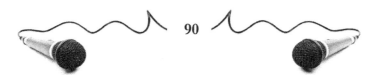

fluttered and closed, and then she swallowed the dick again. This time no hands. She was all neck sucking fast, hard and deliberate. A few moments later, Drako's balls rumbled. His hips lifted off the mattress, his spine arched in the shape of a rainbow and he was feeding her his whole dick and everything that spewed from it. Ebony handled every drop and was loving it until his trembling knees caused his hips to fall back to the mattress. He immediately exhaled a deep breath. He was spent, left staring at the ceiling with his chest heaving up and down. Ebony crawled her sweet smelling body on the small bed and lay beside him. Neither of the two said a word as she reached for his semi hard dick and began to massage both it and his balls. Drako laid there another moment grasping what had just taken place. It was no doubt that the head was incredible. Her oral skills were much more uninhibited than Diamond's. But still, he knew he couldn't start what he was sure to be a fiasco with this woman.

"I wanna feel this meat inside of me, baby." She hissed with another tug as she draped a soft leg over his and kissed his cheek. Drako cleared his throat as he calmly arose from the bed. He reached down, pulled up his sweats and repositioned his dick.

"Nah, ma. It ain't that easy. I „on fuck nobody but Diamond."

"Hmph!" she huffed in defeat and dropped her head back to the pillow, staring off at the ceiling once again.

"Sorry 'bout that. No hard feelings. You know it was cool though."

Drako patted her on the leg. "Play your position." He headed for the door.

"I knew I shouldn't have let you cum." She spoke to his back causing Drako to stop and look back. "So fast." She sat up smiling and rubbed her hand over her fat, shaved coochie. "And just so you know: I'll play my position. I'll suck you until you decide to fuck me. You'll be back. I ain't tryin" to break up no happy home. I just prefer eatin" steak over burgers any day." She bit down on her bottom lip, spread her thighs wider and proceeded to please herself.

Drako shrugged, let out a smile at the thought, and then slipped back out the door.

*****

When Drako stepped back onto the set he must have still had pieces of that guilty look on his face. Drip stepped up, seeming to detect something in Drako's expression. "Don't trip, we found him. He's still on the bus." Drip still didn't seem concerned about how long Save had taken to reach the set. "But like I was sayin", man. I just want us to be like you and Diamond. You feel me? I ain't really tryin" to sort through all these gold diggers and wannabe's. Blondelle's a bright woman, and she's got the potential for a small career in this game." Drako nodded, still feeling the tingling sensation Ebony had left his dick head with. He was just about to respond when Navan came trotting up, sorta winded. "He's coming man, but he's still listening to the dis record Big Turk dropped on him."

"Big Turk?" Drako and Drip seemed to clap off in unison.

"Yeah, Big Turk. He's signed to Red Rum now." Drako and Drip turned to each other with wide eyes.

"Oh shit!" Drip dropped the clipboard he was holding. "Man, this gone be a long fuckin" day!" He turned and darted for the bus.

*****

Drako sat next to Drip and watched Save perform his bars after they finally got him on set. He wasn't able to get all his takes done efficiently and stretched his set on to the next day.

Ebony had traced her lips with a fresh coat of gloss, gotten dressed and was back on the set. She walked up and acted as if she hadn't seen or spoken to Drako in weeks until just that very

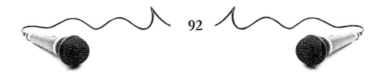

moment. Drako sat around and listened as the camp babbled endlessly about Big Turk running out to New Orleans. Normally, Drako would have had a firm opinion, but today his mind was elsewhere. His thoughts traveled back home to Diamond, but his eyes kept traveling to the tiny shorts every time they seemed to crawl up Ebony's ass. Drako knew he didn't want her, it was just his guilty conscious bothering him for playing that close to home. He thought Drip might have caught him staring at least three times. Finally, he'd taken in enough. It was damn sure after midnight and he was ready to head home. He told himself he'd deal with Wiz and Big Turk another day.

"What's up with you?" Drip gave Drako a funny glare.

"Ain't shit. I told you Wiz ain't nothin" but a prankster." He nodded at him knowingly. "We'll talk about him later. I"ma get on home to Diamond.

"Uh-huh, all right." Drip didn't make much effort to soften his expression. "Yeah, you do that. And don't forget to hit me so we can finish talkin"."

"I gotcha—one!" Drako met his fist with dap and headed to his coupe. He didn't look in Ebony's direction as she passed by on his way out. He made a few steps and glanced back. Drip was standing there with his hands behind his back, watching Drako the whole while.

Fuck no! Drako said to himself.

I can't live paranoid. I 'on eat and shit from the same pot. He made up his mind. He'd keep his dick out of Ebony's addictive grip. She was the true meaning of a pit bull in a skirt.

*****

Drako entered his dark home and quietly slipped into the shower. He scrubbed all traces of deception from his body then slid in bed behind Diamond. She didn't respond much more than a backwards snuggle to feel his warm body near. Hugging her gently, careful not to wake her, he just gazed through darkness with open eyes for a while. There was no doubt about how much he loved Diamond, but tonight he was reminding himself of how much he appreciated her. He felt a twinge of guilt, but knew the only thing he could do was do better next time, he reasoned and closed his eyes.

As if she sensed him about to fall asleep, she nudged at him with her hips.

"What's up, lil momma?" he whispered in the dark and tightened up his embrace a little.

"Unn . . ." she whined, twisting a shoulder this time.

"Huh?"

"Why you ain't made my pussy talk yet?" she pouted, not even looking back.

Drako swallowed what had ailed him. He should have known his ride or die was gonna hold him down. Slightly lifting her leg he slid himself inside her from behind. With just a few strokes of her warmness, Drako realized he was not only giving Diamond what she wanted, he was also reminding himself just why Diamond was the only one for him. He squeezed tighter and pushed himself all the way in, causing Diamond to gush out and cum at the same time. "I love you, ma," he whispered in the dark, feeling her tremble as he promised himself not to slip up with Ebony again.

Reality Records
Chapter- 15

"Don't go against the label's wishes. You don't need a slew of mixtapes or to take every guest appearance to build hype. You're already set on a positive and fast moving path. The game is coming to you; you don't have to go anywhere to find it!"

Save nodded his head, but most of what Drip was preaching meant nothing to him. He was tired of playing the role of Martin Luther King and turning his cheek the other way. He felt more like Malcolm X and had no problem with living by the 'any means necessary' code of honor. But for his label's respect, he chose not to undermine the man who was working even harder than him to bring their futures together.

"I understand," Save said and stepped in front of the full mirror in Drip's office. "So how we gone make our entry tonight?"

Drip smiled at Save's smooth disposition. He was exercising growth by showing this kind of discipline so early in the game. "I'm glad you asked." He shot Save a wink, ready to explain what he thought would be a great look for tonight's taping of the BET Hip-Hop Awards in downtown Atlanta. "Okay, what do you think of this? Me and my lady have a silver Phantom, which is fitting. I have a white Lamborghini Gallardo I think you'd look great zipping up in with Ebony at your side. I figured Navan, Big Jud and Dee-Ruu could all ride together in a Bentley. I'm not sure if it will be gold or silver, but all cars will be delivered here in just moments." Drip glanced at his watch.

"Sounds good to me." He turned from the mirror, concluding his once over glance. "I'ma go put Ebony an nem" down. We'll holla when we're done."

*****

With everybody dressed to the tee and waiting anxiously to head out for the ceremony, Drip stepped into Reality's spacious lounge room. "Y"all look very nice." He began with his last minute and final thoughts of the night. "This is gonna be big. We'll be walking on the red carpet with the best of the best. Just do your best to come across as stars, rather than star struck. All of our work has just recently dropped, so it's expected that we won"t win in any category, but they know we're coming. We will clean up at the next ceremony." He nodded, studying their faces. "Tonight, we're paying homage. We're out to support those who will support us, those who paved the way, and even those who'll one day envy our celebrity." He handed Navan the keys to the gold Bentley Azzure. "Don't matter; it's all in the game. A game we'll be playing till its end!" His eyes trailed over to Ebony, who was wrapped in another amazing, form fitting, Elvira black ensemble. He knew they were ready to represent. "Let's get it." He winked and stepped off.

*****

Downtown Atlanta looked and felt like another warm neon night. A mixture of exotic whips driven by celebrities cruised the streets. The Dope Boyz were out pushing 600 Benzes, tricked out old schools, and it was hard to distinguish one from the other. Save had turned off Peachtree Street and zipped down a side road following Drip"s chauffer driven Phantom. The Phantom trailed Gucci Man's yellow Lamborghini, which was right on the tail of the blue Lambo, manned by Young Jeezy. The entourage came to a slow roll as Atlanta police moved a barricade that blocked the street and only allowed a select celebrity guest list to have access to the ceremony's red carpet entrance.

"We got this, baby girl," Save said with confidence as he glanced over at Ebony after his Gallardo came to a halt and the VIP attendants opened the doors to let them out.

A second later, Save was sinking a crisp Prada sneaker onto the plush red carpet. He adjusted his Gucci frames and tossed his dreads back smoothly as him and Ebony were swarmed by a barrage of camera flashes.

Taking in a deep breath, he felt proud as he watched Ebony strike a pose for the photographer who'd just dropped down on one knee in front of her. He'd watched as his entourage had all pulled up one by one, and now he watched them stroll down the carpet with their own separate swags.

Save had never partaken in anything this big, and the feelings that overcame him were overwhelming! With the treatment he was receiving, he knew he couldn't turn away or let up. He was too close to conquering his biggest dreams.

"Save . . ." The BET personality waltzed up to him breaking his thoughts as she extended the mic his way with a smile. "So, what are you wearing? And who'd you like to see perform tonight?"

Save smiled down on her a bit, and then revealed that his comfortable choice of attire was made by Prada. He answered her questions and several other questions from the select list of columnists who had access to the red carpet entrance.

Ebony was busy doing the same thing and Save had to admit that Ebony was making waves. She had so many curves it was amazing, and her accessories, make-up and hair made her look even more glamorous. She would indeed be regarded as a sex symbol.

They all made it down the carpet, and shortly after, they were in their respective front row seats. The entire auditorium lights went dim. A hissing sound filled the room just before the stage was engulfed with smoke, and a single spotlight shined onto the back of a huge elegant gold throne placed in the middle of the stage.

"What the . . . I know it's not—" Ebony sat up with wide eyes and a smile of anticipation as a Young Money beat pounded through the speakers, causing her to swat Save on the thigh with excitement.

In the next moment, they saw the throne slowly rotate around and when it stopped the whole crowd was on the edge of their seats. Nicki Minaj stood from the throne with her hands on her hips wearing a signature pink wig. She trotted across the stage leading Young Money's camp to open the show with a fury. More lights zipped across the stage, enhancing the sparkling rhinestones of her scanty pink costume and knee-high spiked, pink and white boots. She finished her verse, spun around and the crowd went even crazier, gawking at a backshot of Nicki's behind. She stepped aside, allowing Drake then Tyga to fire up the stage before Lil Wayne popped shirtless onto the set and murdered the crowd like only he could. "Roger that . . . Young Moo-la, baby!" he slurred through a set of gleaming platinum and diamond teeth as he raised his electric guitar in the air.

Lil Wayne, who was a rock star, and arguably the best rapper alive, started the show with a blast and set a tone that would be a hell of a feat to follow.

Comedian Mike Epps wasted no time sliding back on stage to announce Waka Flocka and the Brick Squad's performance next. Everybody took in the show with a lump of pride in their throats. It was surely one of hip-hop"s most coveted events. The Brick Squad put down a hell of a performance and Waka was joined on stage by Gucci Man, where their colored diamond medallions clashed together like a light show under the set's laser beams. As soon as they concluded, Mike Epps was dressed neatly in another suit coat, jeans and sneakers. He had his short, curly fro and that humorous even toothed smile that reminded

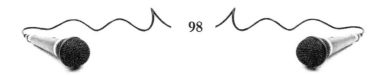

everybody of his famous roll as 'Day-Day' in the movie *Friday*. He told a few jokes that brought laughter across the whole room, then he settled the venue down as the wide screens showed the nominations for the categories of the night. Drake quickly seized Breakthrough Artist of the Year. He trotted back up the steps to claim his victory, while Mike Epps stood there with a silly look on his face that said 'nigga you knew you were gonna win.' Drake gave his thanks to his fans, laughed at Mike and was led backstage. He nearly did a U-turn as Mike promptly announced him as the winner of Collabo of the Year along with TI, who couldn't be there to claim his victory. Drake gave another short thanks and was led away once again.

Drip nodded his head and swallowed a lump. He had a gut feeling as he looked at the huge screens now showing nominations for Producer of the Year. The crowd silenced again as Mike fumbled with the envelope playfully, making them wait with anticipation. "And the Producer of the Year is . . ." He smiled, jumped and sang, "My mothafu—" He cut his curse short. "I can't say that on TV. I'm sorry y"all, but you niggaz know what I'm talkin" „bout. The winner is Wiz, over at Red Rum!" He pointed to Wiz and his camp. "Give it up ladies and gentlemen." He stepped aside holding that huge smile and making room as what looked like all of Red Rum's roster was headed to the stage.

Drip held a knowing smirk from the moment the category was announced. He knew Wiz was gonna bump everybody, but he also believed with his consistent effort that this time next year Wiz would have to work even harder to bump what he had brewing at Reality.

They watched Wiz lead his entourage up to the podium. He held his award up for the fans, then said a few choice words and pointed out a few celebs in the crowd as the trophy was passed behind him for his whole entourage to feel.

The handsome mogul stepped up to the mic and delivered another heart-wrenching, memorable speech with the same poise one would imagine Puffy or Jay-Z to exude. It was undeniable; Wiz was becoming the poster boy for hip-hop.

No sooner than the escorts led them backstage and out to their seats again, Swirl had to climb the stage once more to claim Lyricist of the Year.

"Soou-Woou, baby! I live, breathe, love and die for this shit! Y''all know who I do this for and where this music comes from. Without y''all there would be no me." Swirl choked on his words. He kissed his two fingers and pointed to the sky. "It'll never stop! Red Rum forever, ya heard!" He pumped his award high again and let the flashes erupt all over his brown skin as he shook his neat dreads back behind his shoulders for the cameras. He knew he looked great. He had been prepared because he knew Red Rum was gonna clean up at this year's award ceremony.

The show continued with its impressive light show and swift stage arrangements for each set. Red Rum was nominated in nearly every category. Swirl claimed video of the year for the second year in a row and overall things looked better for Red Rum than it had for any other label tonight.

The crowd was on the edge of their seats itching for the clash of Eminem's alter ego, 'Slim Shady' to meet up with Nicki Minaj's crazy alter ego. The fans went berserk and so did the entire Reality roster. Watching Nicki Minaj transform from a Barbie then perform Roman's Revenge, Ebony couldn't wait for her time to shine. The rest to the camp shared the same high hopes.

"You know it's Lil Wayne," Save whispered flatly to Ebony as Ciara rattled off the nominees for Album of the Year. Silence fell over the auditorium again as Mike turned the other way, handing the envelope to Keyshia Cole to do the honors.

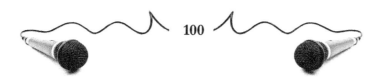

"And the winner for Hip-Hop Album of the Year is . . ." She flipped the card open. "Never Back Down! By Swirl!" She clapped her hands. "Let's give it up for Red Rum tonight." The crowd was in a frenzy, all standing on their feet with applause. Save stood respectfully with the rest of his camp. He didn't clap so much, but not because he was still tripping over Swirl. No, the nasty taste that kept finding its way to the back of his throat was the lingering afterthoughts of the salty glares Big Turk shot at him.

Save found himself with the feeling of subconsciously turning his cheek once again as Big Turk had the balls to accompany Red Rum on stage and throw darts clean in Reality's direction. The show soon concluded without incident. It turned out to be a complete success; another unforgettable moment in time for hip-hop.

Everyone made their way out the same way they'd entered. They'd made it to the red carpet once again and were now standing side bar as Dinella walked up and promptly shoved a mic between Drip and Blondelle. She politely switched the mic from one to the other for their quick responses. She then stepped over to Ebony with the mic while the cameraman panned down her outfit.

Just then, Save noticed Red Rum's entourage gathered up on just the other side of the carpet. Wiz, with his 30-carat pinky rings and enormous diamond earrings, stood in the midst of Big Turk, Barz, and several other guys he didn't recognize. The only thing he was certain of was the way Wiz snickered at Drip and Blondelle and the vicious scowl Big Turk was blatantly throwing his way. Save watched them as Swirl approached the group, listened to a few remarks and then turned and laughed their way as well.

Save didn't realize how tight his jawbone was. He finally realized he must've looked like a pit ready to strike when Drip tapped his arm, breaking his trance. "Come on, man. We talked about that. Don't even trip." Drip took a smooth step in front of him, somewhat blocking his view. "I see that shit. Just be patient, I got somethin" for you in due time, but that time is not here yet."

He reached for Save's arm and urged him down the carpet.

*****

As the Phantom slowed to a halt, the back window slid down simultaneously. "Everybody good?" Drip asked as he tilted his head out the window as his Phantom had the Lambo and Bentley blocked in.

"It was great," Ebony spoke first. "What's next for you?"

"Not too much tonight." He glanced at the crew as they stood outside the cars still talking about the ceremony. "We got a heavy day tomorrow, so y"all try to catch a couple of z"s tonight." He looked back at Blondelle who was reclined back lazily already. "We headin" on in. I'll get wit' y"all tomorrow." He leered back and his window rolled up as the Phantom sailed away.

Save tossed Ebony the Lambo keys. "Take it. You good. I'll holla at you tomorrow. I"ma dip out wit' Navan and nem"." He stepped off with a smirk on his face and hopped in the Azzure.

*****

While the Lambo and the Phantom pulled up and parked at a nearby luxurious hotel where Drip had reserved suites for the camp, Save instructed Navan to drive straight back to his tour bus. All he could envision was the look on Big Turk and Red Rum's face. He still felt their laughter poking him in the back when Drip led him down the carpet, and as far as he was concerned, this was it! "Yo, fuck the label. Ain't nothin" in my contract that say I can't do this," Save assured himself. "And right now, I don't give a fuck if it is!" He clicked on the lights to the bus"s recording booth.

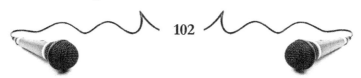

"Well, what the fuck you gone do?" Navan asked, sitting down as he watched Save flipping switches and getting everything ready.

"I"ma fuckin" kill „em'!" Save dripped his words venomously. "They gone wish they never spoke the God's name!"

"You gotta do somethin" big. Somethin" that ain't been done before," Navan suggested. "You know Game dropped 300 bars at Fitty once."

"Good!" Save said without a mere blink. "Then I"ma drop 400!" He put the headsets on and readied himself for a mic check. "And I"ma call it „400 Degreez Again"!"

Navan smiled. "I"m wit' it. I'll hook wherever you need me." From just after that moment and into the light of day, Save unleashed a fury that only a true battle rapper could deliver.

Never had he caused Reality Record's regular booth to tremble with such fury. And never would Big Turk or anybody at Red Rum be prepared for the bomb heading their way.

Drako
Chapter -16

Drako had pondered his scheme the whole time he was in flight. He was now satisfied and assured that his plan had been well thought through. It was the 28th, and the deadline to make it work had to be executed precisely. He wanted to bring Diamond, but she was busy trying to get her vocals acquainted with Reality's booth and Drip behind the keyboard.

The moment Drako got off the plane at Bradley International, he moved on schedule to Avis car rental, where he slid behind the wheel of a pearl white STS Cadillac and headed for the Westin Hotel in downtown Stradford, Connecticut.

After a quick shower and his normal routine adjustments, he was now fancying his reflection in the mirror. His horn rimmed Malcolm X glasses, fake beard and the kufi were all in place.

He'd pulled out the eight cashier's checks totaling seventy-five thousand from the garment bag Diamond had packed for this caper. He slipped them into his leather bank deposit pouch, and then slipped the wallet with all his phony credentials out from the same pouch. He stayed consistent with his schedule as he slid the wallet into his inside breast pocket and straightened the lapels on his gray Hugo Boss suit.

Drako nodded his head confidently as he turned and headed for UBS Warburgh Bank to meet with Charles, the bank manager, for the last time.

*****

At around 10 a.m., Drako entered the bank as usual. In a few moments he was seated at the desk engaged in another personal conversation fueled by mutual admiration. Drako felt compelled

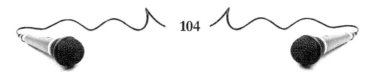

104

to chat even further today. He sorta liked Charles. But it was just too bad that the scheme had to play out right under his nose. Within fifteen minutes the checks were deposited and Drako had accidently told the bank manager he had been contemplating moving all of his interests to one bank.

Their conversation soon ended with a laugh and another firm shake. Charles was certainly ready to do business with Mr. Smith, and he meant to make sure that the wealthy contractor continued all his future banking with UBS.

Drako had exited the bank feeling confident about his final interview with the banker as he stopped at a Subway drive-thru. He copped two subs, a large iced tea, and tipped the cute cashier with a smile of anticipated success. He then drove straight back to the Westin where he texted Diamond to let her know that it was all good and he'd be flying back home soon. He then caught up on a little sleep, but by 4:30 p.m. sharp he was back up, fully alert, and ready to execute his final step.

*****

"BOP Financial Division," a customer service agent answered.

"Yes, this is Mr. Scott Smith of S&S Contracting Incorporated. I'm calling in regards to the payment that will be due on my account on November first."

Drako provided her with the account number and all the correct security information.

"I'd just like to have those funds rerouted to my other account," he said. "I'm currently working to meet deadlines on an enormous contract and my interests will be focused here in Connecticut for the next few months."

"I need to know the number of the account you wish to transfer payment to."

"Oh sure," Drako politely said before reciting the number. "I hope this isn't too much trouble on such short notice. I'm pretty

105

sure you guys are swamped with work this time of the month, just as we are."

"Yes, we are," the woman said and laughed in agreement.

"Right. Now, here's the number where I can be reached." He gave it to her. "Call anytime."

"I'm gonna have to get verification, and I'll call you back to let you know that the routing account number has been updated."

"All right, thanks so much."

"Thank you, sir, and if I can receive verification tomorrow, I can make sure our files are updated myself before I leave."

"That would be tremendously appreciated."

"I'll try."

"Thank you again. Take care."

Drako lay back on the king-sized bed and hoped for the best. He knew that all the financial division could do was call the UBS Warburgh Bank and seek verification of the account holder's identity. For such a personal inquiry and large wire transaction, the bank would direct the call to the senior bank manager, Charles.

Drako knew Charles would positively identify him as the account holder and be satisfied at having gained the full trust of another filthy rich customer.

He thought deeper into his plot; it was just after 5 p.m., which meant Charles had left the bank, and BOP wouldn't catch him until the next day. This wouldn't come across as suspicious to the banker, as he would be secretly relishing in the victory about the full partnership he'd just won over.

Drako needed those funds to be transferred on the first, because he'd been informed that Charles would be on vacation that week. As soon as Charles went on vacation, Drako was simply going to call and get the next available banker to transfer the funds to his offshore account number.

With this scheme, Drako felt he would at least have a few days without suspicion, because government checks were notorious for being three or four days late. He'd let the money lay for a day, let Diamond call on the third to make sure Charles was gone, and then call right back and proceed in his first successful multimillion dollar wire fraud scam!

Drako was filled with happiness. He knew if he jumped through this window of opportunity on time, there would be nothing for Mr. Smith to do except take it up with the government. He'd be feeling the same way as Mary Williams in a couple of months when he stopped paying the mortgage on the bank fraud scheme Diamond pulled off and the bank finally sought to seize her properties.

In both cases, he'd be long gone with all the money before the victims finally realized that someone had stolen their identities.

Tired of wishing that Diamond could've made the trip with him to help celebrate his long deserved money, Drako called and confirmed his flight back to Atlanta which was scheduled for departure in just a few hours.

Wiz

Chapter - 17

When Wiz awoke, his personal butler had just delivered his breakfast plate, glasses of chilled orange juice, his copy of the *Miami Herald* and this week's *Hip-Hop Weekly*, right to his bedside.

Wiz took a moment to clear some of the fog from his head from the two-day romp he'd been the guest of honor to. He sat up, first reaching for the replenishing glass of orange juice. He took a nice gulp and set it down and picked up the *Hip-Hop Weekly* next.

His focus cleared in a matter of seconds as he saw Drip and Blondelle splashed across the cover. *Get the fuck outta here!* he thought to himself. *What fool would red carpet that tramp?* He chuckled, further dropping his focus to the lines printed below. 'Is Drip the next Super Producer to grace the throne of the South?' Wiz laughed the ridiculous assumption away as he turned the page to see pictures of the couple at, at least two red carpet events. He tossed the tabloid fodder publication to the floor and reached for his *Miami Herald*. He flipped straight to the entertainment section and staring at him was an even bigger photo of Drip taking Blondelle's hand and curtly helping her out of the silver Phantom and onto the red carpet. The same carpet that Red Rum"s entire roster had walked before going on to win more nominations than any other label that night! Wiz further reasoned as something awkward pricked at his conscious and caused him to turn warm.

'The next Kanye West and Amber Rose have just arrived' the journalist wrote. "Amber Rose?" Wiz couldn't believe the comparison. "Kanye West!" He didn't realize he was talking to himself until Jayonna rubbed a smooth hand across his stomach and snuggled closer. "Umm," she moaned, "Kanye's good. Is he coming over to party with us?" She kissed Wiz's bare chest.

For some reason Wiz just felt irritated. He snatched the covers back, prematurely ending his fantasy to be with twins.

"Get y"all asses up!" he growled.

"What's the matter? I thought—"

"Get y"all asses outta here!" He pointed to the door. "Go find another room. I „on feel like bein' bothered wit' yo whining ass today!" His tone straight spooked Joyanna. She turned over and nudged her identical friend Jayonna, awake. They scurried out of the bed and he watched the two petite, white girls with pretty blonde hair streaming down their backs hurry their buck naked asses down the hallway.

"Shit!" he yelled, balling up the newspaper in a rage and hurling it at the door behind them. He flopped back down on the pillow, staring now at the chandelier over his bed. At first he hadn't recognized the emotion that pinched him, but at this moment he could no longer deny the first twinges of jealousy. How could the industry compare an unproven producer to Kanye over him? He'd just won producer of the year so he really didn't understand how Drip could be sharing any part of his light. Then the worst part of all was that he was sharing the light with a trick Wiz had smutted out so many times it was uncountable. *Fuck it. Let 'im get fifteen minutes of fame*, Wiz reasoned. He curbed his temper, got out of bed, smoked a blunt and readied himself for a new day.

*****

A few hours later when Wiz entered his entertainment room, everybody glanced his way and an awkward silence permeated the room. "What the hell is goin' on?" Wiz didn't hesitate stepping over to Damien first. Damien didn't respond, his eyes only trailed to the iPad on the bar in front of him. Wiz's eyes

109

bounced around the room. He saw the mean look painted on Big Turk''s face and an almost twin expression on Swirl''s face. The two girls Swirl had perched on two barstools got up and pranced out of the room with one mean look and a nod in their direction from Swirl.

"Damien, I asked you a question," Wiz spoke louder seeing that no one was speaking up.

"It's not good," Damien said. "This kid Save. He—he dropped like a four hundred bar diss song and slammed it right through our front door."

"So what the fuck? Let Big Turk fire right back!" Wiz gave the order.

"Well, of course, you should do that because Big Turk is who it's mainly aimed at. He's made up all kinds of bullshit. He says he stomped . . . well, put feet all over Big—"

"Ay, yo', shorty. I'm tellin'' you, cool it wit' da lip! That fuckin'' fake ass prophet don't even know me like that, yo!" Turk hopped to his feet.

"Hold up your attitude, Big Turk." Wiz stepped in. "We're on the same team and my advisor just tells what he sees or hears, ya dig?"

"Yeah, yeah I'm just sayin'' though. That fake, confused, righteous lil'' pussy asked me to do somethin'' a while back. I refused the offer ,,cause I ,,on step in the booth with no soft ass . . . Man, I'm tellin you, I'm damn near two seventy!" He added ten or fifteen pounds to himself. "I'd crush that pussy wit' one hand!" Turk made good sense.

"At the end of the day you'll soon understand. It's just music," Wiz reasoned, staring at Turk. "Just cool your jets and focus on making better music than him. It's that simple."

"Really on this one, maybe not," Damien cut in candidly. "This shit this fool has tossed out for free! It's all over the net. I mean any and everywhere. The bars are so long they''re

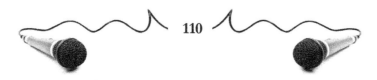

breaking the song down into as many as four parts. It comes along with a trailer of him actually performing most of his bars on a tour bus. I can't say it any other way. It really does feel like 400 degreez again. The idea is definitely working," Damien confirmed.

"Pussy mothafuckas!" Big Turk stormed out of the room.

Wiz looked at Damien and then to Swirl as he stood to his feet. "He's your project, homie. This y"all lil fight. I'm sure you'll figure it out." Swirl made clear he wouldn't be the one to respond.

"I gotcha." Wiz tried to seem unfazed. "Can you believe this clown ass nigga got Blondelle on his arm?" Wiz chuckled, changing topics.

"Red carpet and all." Swirl nodded his head in disbelief. "There is a sucker born every day." He capped on. "Let lil sis milk that trick!" Swirl laughed, heading out the room.

"Get Diablo for me. I want my hands freshened up," Wiz called after him.

"I gotcha." Swirl disappeared down the hall.

Wiz turned to Damien and continued to chat as Damien toyed with the iPad again.

"Fuck them fools; their light won"t burn long. I've seen these indies come and go with a bright flash all in the blink of an eye." Wiz smiled, but saw Damien still had a serious face.

Finally Damien said, "I understand, but I'm just not sure if this is a fleeting moment." He turned the screen to Wiz. Blondelle was splashed on the cover of at least three hot publications and Drip had nearly three times as many.

"They love this woman's look. If nothing else she's gonna be a fashionista in the world of couture. Now that has nothing to do with music, but together their star power will be a lot for the media to want to capture on film. They'll be acquainted with TMZ in no time."

"Yeah, well, we'll see,'" Wiz said with a trace of defeat in his voice.

"That, we sure will," Damien said with certainty as he left Wiz with his own thoughts and vanished from the room.

Wiz let out another exasperated sigh. As he slumped even deeper in his thoughts, his heart began to pound faster. The emotion that constantly poked at him had festered its way out of jealousy and straight to fear! Not a fear of physical pain, but the fear of losing his status! There was no way he was gonna share his light at the height of his career with a man who hadn't earned his stripes, such as Drip. Drip's stripes were surely a given. Wiz chuckled to himself because he knew if he had anything to do with it, he was definitely gonna try to take them! Just then, a bright, bright light flashed on in Wiz's mind. His feet moved with a mind of their own until he was bent over in the secret cabinet in his room. He was searching through hundreds of hours of video footage in hopes of finding what he needed. It took nearly two hours to locate the exact thing he looked for, but once he did he felt that wonderful feeling of victory again.

"Nobody can outthink the genius." He smiled, making a b-line back to Damien.

*****

As soon as Damien pulled his little dick from Jayonna's mouth and slipped on some pants, Wiz was closing the door to his entertainment room behind them this time.

"I think I'ma need to dim those lights for a while," he whispered deviously, causing Damien to look totally baffled.

"How so?" He spoke hesitantly.

"I just need a lil help from you," he said, watching Damien's expression, who failed to respond.

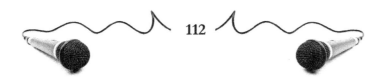

112

"See if you can make this the second shit to go viral this week?" He pulled a disc from his pocket and handed it to Damien.

Damien smiled and nodded his head. "You are a fuckin" genius!"

He couldn"t wait to see the reaction from this one.

Drako
Chapter - 18

Drako had to be in one of the best moods he'd been in, in quite a long time. Just this morning he'd gotten off the phone with Jesse Powell, who assured he'd love to perform at Drako's wedding. Diamond was especially happy about her position in life as well.

"Really baby, I like the sound Drip has for me," she said, wiggling her hips into a tight pair of Seven jeans. "He's not as good as Wiz but he's perpetual. He's definitely gonna get there." She turned, trying to snap the button.

"I just told him I don't want to be in competition with that girl. I'm not really hung up over that First Lady shit anyway. I mean, if you're not the face of it, who really cares?" She shrugged. "I told him to refer to her as the First Lady emcee and me as the First Lady of R&B, or just give her the title all together. I think the girl seems cool and she'll handle it well." She looked to Drako for a response.

"I-I „on know." He fumbled. "I ain't paid that much thought, but I'm sure you're right either way." He tried to pass it over easily. A conversation regarding Ebony wasn't about to happen and ruin his good mood. Today marked two days since Drako received the call back from the Bureau of Prison's Finance Division. The woman had called and was happy to inform 'Mr. Smith' that she had received verification, and the routing address had been updated in their system as of October 31st.

Drako was ecstatic about the news and he'd told Diamond immediately. And now he was about to play the biggest joke that UBS had ever seen. First, he called the bank's automated service to check his balance. It was $4,260,000, which

confirmed a payment of $3,940,000 had been deposited on top of the $320,000 that was already lying in the account.

He and Diamond had a brief discussion, concluding that there was no need to wait another day. Drako called the bank and asked for Charles, who he knew was away on vacation. He then politely asked the next manager in charge, which was the junior manager, to transfer nearly four million dollars to his offshore account. Drako tried to sound a little distraught as he informed him that he and Charles had previous conversations about this and that Charles had promised to help him whenever he needed. To Drako's good fortune, the junior manager was well aware of Mr. Smith and was eager to please him. He and Drako ran down a list of the same basic questions with the call ending with the promise of a call back to let Drako know the transaction was complete.

As usual, it took less than an hour to receive that call which verified the transaction would be completed in four to six hours. Drako thanked the manager again for the free money. He disconnected the call and was filled with a sharp tingly sensation. To say he was proud was surely not enough. Drako was overwhelmed! He was so happy and proud of himself. A once young kid raised in the streets of Charlotte, North Carolina had just gotten away with a multi-million dollar heist! He felt exhilarated as he hugged Diamond, kissed all over her and squeezed her ass. Drako was adding numbers up in his head. He knew in just a few hours his offshore account balance would be a staggering ten million dollars plus!

"Goddamn, we did it!" His voice was choked with cheer. "We „bout to have over ten million dollars of our own money, ma!" He popped her ass firmly this time. "Come here, ma. I'm ready to celebrate."

Diamond pecked his lips and pulled herself away from the erection she felt pressed against her leg. "I am too, baby. But

MIKE JEFFERIES

did you just forget we got the caterers waitin" for us, and we're gonna stop by and decide on our theme for the layer cake?" Her pretty eyes brought Drako back to reality.

"Damn, I almost forgot." His hand automatically repositioned his dick. "But you can bet your ass I'ma tear that pussy up when we get back. I'ma knock this dick all the way to the back of that pussy real good, ma."

"Umm, just how I like it." She bit her lip and cooed. "Don't play wit' me tonight. Fuck me like you're the 10 million dollar man." She winked and switched her sexy hips out the door. Drako grabbed his keys off the dresser and trailed her ass all the way to his coupe.

116

Wiz
Chapter - 19

Wiz was on his knees in front of her when he crisscrossed her feet, just at the ankles. He laid them on his left shoulder then smoothly rolled to his right to lie on the mattress beside her with her feet still draped over his outer shoulder. One of his arms wrapped around her legs, while the other snaked around her side until they met. He clutched her firmly in place and his big dick never slipped out. Now, closely facing her, he began to pound at her wetness all over again.

"Oh, shit, yes . . . um, shit!" She gushed out, sending gobs of white cream down Wiz's dick as he drove deeper and deeper into her center.

"Yeah! . . . Fuck me, da-da—Oh shit, fuu-huck ma-mi!" she begged as the x-pills caused Wiz to pound at her forcefully for the next few minutes.

"Ooh, God yeah!" she moaned a few moments later, just before Wiz eased his throbbing dick out.

He got to his knees just as Swirl's weight settled down behind her on the mattress.

"Uh-huh! Let's go!" she gasped, letting her head fall back in pleasure as Swirl lifted her leg and slid his condom covered pole right back inside her from behind.

"Um . . . uh . . . Oh, shit, um, um!" she began to whimper as Swirl began to pound her just as hard and deep, causing her juicy ass to make clapping sounds and her perfect, yellow titties to bounce wildly. Wiz made his way up the bed, repositioning himself and shoved his throbbing dick that was covered in her juices right into her pretty mouth.

In seconds, she was howling out and convulsing at the wake of an intense orgasm, clearly from the euphoric thought of being pleasured by two men.

Just then Drip leaned over and snatched the plug out of his computer. "I ,,on wanna see no more of that shit!" he told himself through a cracked voice and held back the tears of rage.

Drip was now sitting in a dark room all by himself. He had no idea what to do next. His mind was still in a whirl. By the time he received a text that there may have been a celebrity sex tape on-line which claimed to be Wiz, Blondelle, and Swirl, the download was already a viral disaster.

Everyone he could possibly think of had seen the tape and now shared a piece of everything he'd just thought was so special just moments ago. On one hand, he was ashamed and hurt with disappointment, but on the other hand, he was wracked with a ton of pain and confusion for Blondelle. There was no denying if it was her or not. The hidden cameras in the room were of the highest quality around. But from the way he saw this woman bawl over the situation, it was heart-wrenching. He really didn't know what to think anymore. He didn't know if she was still the same woman he'd wanted to care for so badly. All he did know was that she didn't leak the tape, and it was the last thing she ever would've imagined at this point in her career. She knew she'd just gotten completely knocked off the fast track of Couture and Europe's runways. But she more so admitted it was even more than that. It was the deception of someone she once trusted and had obviously did special favors for.

Drip was now further disappointed with himself as his pride allowed him to watch her pack up her things and leave. Her eyes were puffy and red and she was unstable. There was no telling what she could do to herself, and there was no reason for him to give a fuck! But he did. One other thing he knew for sure; he had fallen in love with Blondelle.

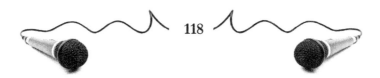

118

Drip caught himself as he felt the tear slip down his cheek. He wiped it away and sucked in a deep breath as he manned up.

He'd made up his mind. He was his own man. Made his own decisions and he didn't have a spotless past his damn self. After he talked to Drako he was going to find Blondelle. Even if she felt best to stay out of the limelight, she was still his bitch and he'd foot the bill. When and wherever he found the party who leaked the tape, he had all the plans in the world to turn their life just as upside down as they carelessly did his. They were gonna get dealt with . . . and that was for certain.

*****

When Drako looked across the desk, he saw the hollow look in Drip's eyes. He could only imagine how this man felt.

"Yo, man, I can't say I know how you feel. I just know that shit is fucked up."

"You . . . you saw the tape?" Drip asked evenly.

"Hell naw!" Drako reared back and lied, trying not to swipe over his dick, still envisioning the images of Blondelle"s banging naked body. "You know I „on indulge in no silly games."

Drip stood to his feet and began a slow pace. "But see, man, that's just it. This shit ain't no game!" He looked at Drako and stopped. "You wouldn't say no shit like that if you saw the tears that woman spilled." He nodded his head and paced on. "Man, I did some coward shit! . . . I watched a woman, a real woman, cry her heart out, then I watched her leave my crib, man." He balled up his fist, his eyes looking deranged. "Man, don't no real man watch a woman cry. I can't ignore that shit. And if that nigga Wiz did that shit, he a straight childish pussy, man!" He swiped his fist through the air. "Only a kid go like that! Regardless of what nigga, if you respect da game then you see what I'm doin. Blondelle my bitch now! I got a plan for her!" He pointed a trembling finger at his chest. "And when a nigga

119

consciously know that and violate he could end up getting dealt with!"

"So, hold up." Drako sat up and leaned forward with a squint in his eyes. "So you tellin" me you 'bout to deal with Wiz?"

Drip turned his glare from Drako and thought for a moment.

"Nah I-I ain't sayin" that." He choked on his words. "I can't say for sure Wiz did that. I don't even know where they are. The footage was zoomed in only on the bed." He nodded his head. "But that don't matter anyway. And truthfully, I can get past them niggaz fuckin" before my time. I'm only worried about my watch. Feel me?" He sat back down calmly. "But if I knew he did that, me and you would have our differences," he said calmly. "Man, you can't undo what just happened. The problem I got is this ain't music, I can deal with the diss records. But this ain't that! This is my pride, my reputation, and my woman's heart! Straight up, man."

Drako nodded. "I see what you're sayin", but like I told you from day one, let me deal with Wiz."

"No, you told me whatever fall between you and Wiz, stay out of it. I've never questioned you. I'm sayin" now if Wiz did this it involves me, and I'd have to say he just crossed the line."

"Well, we don't know if Wiz did this. Now, I know Wiz and he loves money and the light. I honestly don't see a payday from this. I"m telling you, he'd have to get paid to give that tape up. He don't know the meaning of „leak". Now, maybe someone near him is responsible. I'm sure of that, but I don't know who. All I know if it's not about the money, he's not in cahoots." Drako's stare was unbreakable and he hoped convincing because he honestly wasn't sure himself.

"Real talk, I ain't want to speak with him anytime soon, but on the real gimme some time. I"ma get at him before this shit spill outside these booths."

Drip nodded and stood to his feet. "You do that. Meanwhile, I'm goin' to find Blondelle and the first cat pop off, I'm cashin' in on his bitch ass!" Drip turned and walked out the door. Drako took note of the plastic Glock in the small of his back. Drako nodded his head and flopped back. He knew someone had pushed Drip off his square. He just hoped that that someone wasn't silly enough to be Wiz.

*****

It was several hours later and everybody other than Save and Drip had long left Reality Records. Drip had been locked away in his office. He'd texted and e-mailed Blondelle furiously, but never received a response. His mind was now tossing so many crazy thoughts around and he knew he was no longer thinking rationally.

Eventually, he stepped out of his office and into the cockpit where he signaled Save to come out of the booth. He looked Save up and down and Save returned the same glare. Save knew that today something different, an entirely different hunger, lurked in Drip's eyes. He too had seen the footage but declined to comment on it.

"What"s up, son?" he asked behind raised brows.

"Remember I told you I had somethin" for you?" He had a distant look in his eyes. "The time has arrived." He handed Save a disc and nodded toward the monitor and screen in his office.

Save took the disc and slid it in the DVD player. A minute later, he nodded his head knowingly.

"Yo, tomorrow, son. The God got you." He gave Drip a pound.

Drip walked back into his dark office trying to figure out what to do next. He now understood all the things Save was feeling when he'd gotten on him earlier in the week for going against the label's wishes with his cowboyish attempts. Drip could now identify with the wrath against someone trying to destroy all you had worked so hard for. He hoped Drako was right about someone else being responsible for leaking that tape because otherwise it made no sense. In no way would Red Rum have to put Reality's light out in order for theirs to still shine.

Drako and Wiz
Chapter - 20

Wiz happened to be sitting in his big armchair. He'd just gotten a call from Adam & Eve Adult Entertainment. They were trying to strike a deal with the mogul to direct or perhaps produce another sex tape involving himself. Wiz had toyed with them for a while, trying to see if he could get an offer bigger than Ray J to show his dick on screen again. Eventually Wiz hung up, letting them know clearly that for now he wasn't interested and that the footage had to have been stolen. He never once attempted to deny his astounding swordsmanship skills on screen.

He was taken by surprise when he saw Drako's number pop up on his caller ID next. Lowering his feet from the ledge of his desk, he sat straight up when he tried to remain calm and answer the call. "Red Rum, what's happenin'?" Wiz answered as if he hadn't peeped the caller ID.

"Nigga, you know who the fuck this is! Stop playin" games!" Drako growled.

"Hold up, man. Slow down. Now, the last time we spoke you talked to me in a bad tone and you ain't 'bout to keep handlin" me like I'm no hoe, man." Wiz's voice cracked.

"Nigga, this ain't „bout that. That shit I tossed you I meant! You needed to hear that shit for the—look, that's neither here nor there," Drako reasoned, not wanting to rehash those thoughts. "I'm callin" you now „cause the shit. . . . the games you playin" can get ugly. Real talk, man. You play so much you got people that would really hurt you if given the opportunity."

"Yo man, it's just music. It's entertainment, that's all it is," Wiz countered.

"Nah, fuck naw, man! We been through that part too!"

"Well, why do you even care? I been tryin" to call you. I know you saw my text and read my e-mails. I thought you ain't got shit to do with Reality Records," Wiz said sarcastically.

"Why the fuck would you make any assumption on me? I ain't tell you shit. Which that alone oughta tell you to mind yo" business! You ain't stupid. You ain't gave me shit! I'm out here doin" what I gotta, and all you do is keep finding an incessant need to bring them fuckin" people to our doorstep. Man, I'm tellin" you to make money before you either get yo'self fucked up or have us both where we can't get a dime without the IRS countin" it first!"

"Hmph . . ." Wiz huffed knowingly and sucked diamonds again. "Well, like I said. Since everybody in this business without being in this business, they just need to know if you in the water with a shark like me eventually you gone get bit!"

"Man, who in the fuck do you think you talkin" to wit' them slick rhymes?" Drako barked, making Wiz pipe down. "Nigga, I called you to tell you somethin" good. Now play all you want. You know me, and you know I ain't the one to be doin" all the explaining. On the strength of me and you and the strength of another friend, I made a decision to call you."

"Oh, so you called behind somebody else, ha?"

"Look man!" Drako said heatedly.

"It, it's just music, man," Wiz said sort of weakly.

"Nigga, that shit with that man's woman ain't got a damn thing to do with music! Her career is dead! Emotionally, she's torn! That was that man's heart and you had—"

"Is that what this is about!" Wiz snapped hard this time. "You think I stooped that low, man?" He hopped to his feet and banged his fist on his desk.

"Fuck that funky ass bitch! I didn't want anybody to know I'd ever touched her! Blondelle is a prostitute, man. Get it—

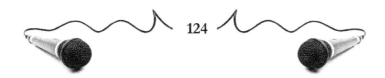

124

prostitute! She ran with Chilli, Cherry, and Bubbles and all them N.O. bitches! She ain't nothin" but a dime a dozen Creole bitch who found her muddy glass slippers on a red carpet!" Wiz was seething. "Man, somebody stole that goddamn tape. You know how I live it. If it don't make dollars it don't make sense! I ain't had shit to do with that, I swear!"

Drako heard Wiz clearly. He knew he was responsible for the diss songs, but certainly not Blondelle.

"I'll let him know—"

"You'll let him know?" Wiz was still heated. "Man, you fucks with that no beat makin" chump over ya boy now?"

"We on somethin" else right now—"

"Man, I „on give a fuck! You tell that pussy nigga if he ever accuse me of somethin" like that I'll put—"

"Come on, playboy. Don't run that shit through me. You a businessman. A pretty good one at that, but you ain't no gangsta. If you ain't ready to pack up and die, I suggest you leave a nigga like Drip be. Let him try to piece this shit back together and hope the finger don't point back to you."

"See, you really think I'm pussy, don't ya? I may not have walked all your paths, Drako, but I'm tellin" you if a nigga like that sucka run up, nigga, it's—"

"Don't you dare claim soou-woou!" Drako cut him off.

"Man, fuck that nigga! Just tell him that!" Wiz ended the call and slang the phone against the wall, shattering it to pieces.

He was glad Drako had called, but he was further jealous of Drip. He knew how loyal Drako was to his friends. He couldn't figure out what the hell had found its way between the two. All he knew was what was once so easy seemed as though the wires had been crossed up in every way. Wiz was gonna call Drako back as soon as he calmed down. He knew damn well he couldn't keep talking to Drako like this and hope for things to ever piece together again.

*****

Drako heard the phone click in his ear. He knew Wiz could be childish. He also knew Wiz was just mad because he had nothing to do with what Drako had accomplished at Reality Records. He also knew that Wiz was pissed about the friendship he felt Drip had forged along the way. He chalked the thought up to „shit happens‟ and had Wiz given him some real paper just maybe he wouldn't have been out there taking penitentiary chances to get what he deserved. He meant to speak further about Wiz cooling the wax war aimed at Reality Records, but he'd got lost on the most important part and that was finding he had nothing to do with Blondelle so he could tell Drip. He would eventually call Wiz back, but for the moment he was sure Wiz heard him, and when he came to his senses, he was sure that Wiz too would soon cool his jets.

Drako stood up feeling slightly relieved. He was headed to tell Drip exactly what Wiz told him had to have happened. Hopefully, this would clear Wiz‟s name, because if Drip and Wiz were to ever face off, Drako would have to choose sides with a deadly, irreversible decision.

Las Vegas, Nevada
Chapter- 21

As dusk began to settle over the dry Nevada desert, all the celebrities and ballers scurried up and down the busy Las Vegas strip. Stretch limousines of all sorts aligned the entrances to the grand hotels and every exotic car from Ferrari to Lambo to Rolls Royce convertibles cruised the strip in anticipation of the Floyd Mayweather vs. Pacquio extravaganza.

Big Turk sat behind dark tinted windows on the passenger's side of the blacked out Hummer as he, Barz and Jay-Poon pulled out of the MGM Grand and onto Vegas Boulevard.

"Yo, real talk. When we touch down after this I got to see that nigga. I „on know how they did that shit. It must be Photoshop or they found a nigga that look like me but yo, dat shit ain't me!" Big Turk held his usual mean grit, but on the inside he was totally demolished. The diss song Save shot at him was called "God U Now" and it had become another viral tsunami on YouTube. This time its effects proved to be even more damaging because it came attached with a trailer that showed footage of Save stomping footprints all over a man's back, just like he claimed on his "400 Degreez Again" bomb! The footage showed a clear image of Save profusely stomping a man that looked just like Big Turk, until another distorted image of a man came on the camera and began dragging the man away. Of course, Big Turk was sticking to his story and not letting up, but denial was eating at him bad! He really couldn't wait to get back and get his hands on Save once and for all. Save had truly embarrassed him in front of the whole world, and in his mind the shit was now on and off wax. He didn't care how it was brought. All he knew was that no more rules applied!

"Man, don't stud that shit! Just ignore niggaz when they look at you funny," Barz said easily which made Big Turk feel even worse. Now he felt that everyone was gonna look at him sideways, and it was a positive indication that even Barz might not have been sold on his story.

"Pull over right here and go buy some blunts, nigga!" he barked, resorting back to his alter ego. He was felling like: Fuck it! If Barz and Jay-Poon didn't believe him, they were damn sure gonna act like they did. He tightened down on his usual wolf game and decided to make the best of the trip. "And hurry the fuck up, nigga! I ain't blazed since this morning!"

*****

Skating down the other side of the famous Vegas strip in a shiny black Maserati Quattroporte, Save felt like he had the world at his fingertips! He was feeling all the opposite effects of what Big Turk heard from "God U Now" buzz. He bobbed his head as the track began, and a moment later he was performing the bars to his own lyrics.

Heart bleedin' fake niggaz cause treason/
But that's just part of the reason/
I put it to his head and start squeezin/

He was hyped and proud as his song got blasted over Las Vegas' airwaves. Save leaned over and turned it down as he looked over and saw his new acquaintance smiling. Even she was exceptionally happy to be riding on the arm of a young artist as hot as Save. He pulled out of the Bellagio where he and Africa, along with Drip and Blondelle, were staying in luxurious five star suites. He zipped down to the MGM Grand and was about to go in and toss some craps with her on his side.

128

Africa had a beautiful healthy, dark afrocentric complexion and neat dreadlocks with gold tips hanging down her back and her hard body was enough to stop traffic!

Not feeling the vibe after his track came to an end, he decided to skip over to Ceasar's Palace instead. He cruised back onto Vegas Boulevard. His only flaw was that he never spotted the blacked out Hummer that trailed him.

*****

"Nigga, that is that pussy boy!" Big Turk barked. "I said slow the fuck down!" He pounded the dashboard feeling like Christmas was just two minutes away. "Man, I don't give a fuck when that car stops, you just pull up right beside him!" Big Turk reached over and hit Barz on his shoulder a little too hard.

"Aw, man!" Barz winced for at least the fifth or sixth time. "Stop talkin" wit' yo' heavy ass hands!" he complained again.

"My bad, man. Sometimes I don't realize my strength," Big Turk admitted.

"What you want us to do?" Bass had found its way back into Barz"s voice again.

"Nigga, this ain't shit!" Big Turk cracked his knuckles. "I'm 'bout to get my face back. I"ma straight run up and put hands all over this pussy nigga! I don't give a fuck if I go to jail. I"ma let the whole world see he was telling a fuckin" lie the whole goddamn time!" Big Turk pledged.

"Okay, okay that's it." He swatted at Barz"s leg anxiously. "He's pullin" in, nigga! Don't let him get away!"

*****

When Save pulled up in front of Ceasar's Palace, he gave Africa a moment to do a glance over in the mirror. He was just about to lose the nine millimeter from his waist and tuck it under the seat when intuition caused him to spot a dark Hummer creeping up slow in his side view mirror. In seemingly the next instant, the Hummer lurched forward then came to a

129

screeching halt. In a panic, Save tried to pounce out the Quattroporte at the same time as Big Turk spilled from the SUV.

"Shit!" Save snapped with disappointment. He had only one foot on the pavement and Big Turk was stalking straight at him.

"What up now, pussy boy!" Turk shouted viciously. "Get yo" bitch ass out the car and put feet on me now, you lyin' soft ass bitch!" He was right up in Save's face. Save couldn't believe he allowed him room to step out of the car. Just then, Barz, with a nasty visage on his face slid from behind the driver's wheel and ran around the truck as Jay-Poon hopped out the backseat as well.

"Slap that chump!" Barz yelled out.

Save took a few safe steps back trying to get clear of Big Turk's reach.

"Ay yo", son." Save looked Big Turk straight in his eyes. "You disrespected me, son, and that's it." He managed another step back, watching Barz in his peripheral and taking note of Jay-Poon's position as well. "Now, I'm tellin" you kid, you niggaz ain't in no booth. Shit is real over here, so just back up out the God's space," he warned.

"Man, beat dat nigga ass!" He heard Jay-poon order just as Big Turk flung a heavy wild right at him. Save weaved away from the punch and found two more yards of space between them. Big Turk's face grew angrier as he turned to lunge again and simultaneously caught a glimpse of the steel Save yanked from under his shirt. Things started to move so fast that all he saw next were two quick flashes before God slammed thunder through his thigh.

"Oh shh—" Big Turk's eyes widened in terror as his words froze in his throat.

"Boom!" Another bolt slammed through his shoulder and knocked him clean off his feet.

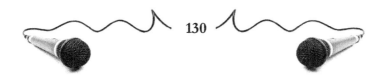

Save quickly turned to see Barz with his mouth hung wide open. He was so paralyzed with fear that he never got a chance to run. "You too, bitch!" Save dumped two hot rocks into his stomach crumpling him to the ground instantly.

Jay-Poon tried to quickly turn and run back to the Hummer, but Save was dead on his heels.

"Boca, boca, boca!'

The final two slugs caught him in the ass and his lower back splattering him against the Hummer before he fell face first to the hot asphalt pavement.

Save was engulfed in a blind fury at the thought of Turk and his two dummies nearly beating him down and stomping him out.

Save trotted over and hopped back in the Quattroporte and peeled off, burning pure rubber down Vegas Boulevard. He turned off on the first side street to his right and tossed the gun out the window at the sound of sirens in the distance. As soon as he made the next sharp left, two police cruisers fell on his bumper. Save stomped the accelerator harder as Africa screamed in hysteria. He looked in the distance ahead as two more cruisers came into view. They kissed bumper to bumper and the two cops sprang from behind the wheels as they successfully set up the roadblock. "You don't know shit, and you just met me tonight!" He schooled Africa, slammed on the brakes and yanked the steering wheel left causing the Maserati to slide sideways to a halt. He stepped out of the car, placed his hands atop of his head and kneeled down on the pavement in surrender to the authorities. He didn't even look up at Africa as he still heard her cries. Next, he heard the helicopter land right on top of the scene as the Las Vegas police cuffed him and brought him to his feet. He kept his head hung low with shame. All he could envision was Drip telling him to be careful before he'd left the hotel. There would be no prizefight for him to attend tonight. Save was about to duck his head in the backseat of a police cruiser when two special agents approached him.

"Jeffrey Morgan, is it?" The short relatively young looking agent spoke up first.

"Who are y"all? What branch do you work for?" Save looked at them suspiciously. The black agent looked familiar.

"You could just say we're very special—" The agent was smiling when Save cut him off rudely.

"Ay yo", fuck y"all! I ain't speakin" to nobody till I talk to my lawyer!" He knew they had to be Hip-Hop Task Force.

"We're only here to—"

"Just gone and book me!" Save disregarded them rudely and sat himself down in the back of the cruiser.

Once the officer closed the door, he lay his head back.

Heart bleedin' fake niggaz cause treason/
But that's just part of the reason/
I put it to his head and start squeezin'/

He began to hear his lyrics pound through his head again. He knew not only was it gonna be a long night, but also a hard road ahead. He closed his eyes as the cruiser pulled away and "God U Now" continued to play.

He'd forgotten his lies/
I felt a rush of honorable pride/
When as he replied/
I saw the fear of God in his eyes merged with the shame/
Some is forged and some is burnt in the flame/
He called out my name/
I cocked back put his brains on the floor no remorse/
All I gave 'im was a look of disdain.
Live by the code/
or God a come reclaiming ya' soul/
Ashamed of myself/

132

A LIFE FOR A LIFE II

Hell nah/
But sometimes I'm even scared of myself.

Thump
Chapter - 22

Meanwhile, back on the East Coast, the non-stop money-making wheels of Red Rum were at full speed. Wiz was marketing Thump tremendously! His latest star hit the couch on 106 and Park, Vibe's 'Next,' Source's 'On the Verge' put him on their new artist lists and his anticipated debut buzz on the street was absurd.

Thump was as street-savvy and marketable as Swirl. He was ready to be embraced by mainstream, but the first place he wanted more love in was his home state of Virginia.

The Virginia Beach Amphitheater was doing it big! Wiz Khalifa was definitely in the house with Corey Gunz backing up his set. But the emcee requested by the sponsors was none other than the brown-skinned nightmare of all wack emcee's—known as 'Thump!'

Thump was ready to blaze the stage; he was in a damn good mood, and even better, Wiz and Swirl were both coming out to show their support. To Wiz, it was great marketing, a way of solidifying to his home state that it was official. Thump was indeed a lyrical assassin, inked as a Red Rum soldier. Wiz felt it let the fans know that Red Rum was going to be hands-on with Thump 100 percent.

The highly sought after $250,000 beats Wiz rarely sold would now be at the disposal in unlimited supply to Thump. Wiz also knew this meant a definite lyrical threat for breakthrough artists on every coast! The show took off with a blast! Thump hit the stage with the energy of a seasoned vet. He had a minimal movement, heavy lyrical delivery styled air that was very reminiscent of Jay-Z. The fans flocked to his style with loud applause that begged for another song, and surprised

Wiz and Swirl much more than they anticipated, as they looked on the packed amphitheater from the curtain backstage.

Thump concluded his hot 30-minute set and got out of the way for Corey Gunz. Afterwards, the crowd, as well as Wiz and Swirl, enjoyed the rest of the concert.

Once the show was over, Wiz shook hands and socialized with all the people who made it possible. He toyed with all the beautiful girls who were lucky enough to make it backstage, and he did it all with Thump and Swirl at his side.

"Man, you already got this state on lock!" Wiz said to Thump. "Now I want you in the studio gettin' your next project completed as soon as possible."

"I got over 500 songs in my head. I'ma be the next Seven-Day Theory, the closest shit you eva' seen to 'Pac!" Thump bragged, making Wiz flash those diamond encrusted teeth.

"I want you workin' with him every day to get this done," Wiz said to Swirl.

They continued fraternizing and having a few small laughs. "I wanna show y'all how we ball out here on Virginia Beach before we leave for New Orleans tomorrow," Thump said to everyone.

"Well, let's see what kinda love they givin' up in VA," Swirl replied.

Wiz signaled his two bodyguards and the entourage departed the amphitheater.

They had been standing near the side entrance door for celebrities when they were bombarded with showers of unwanted attention. The greeting from the sudden rush of fans was led by loud cracking sounds, followed by bright lights, as every shot popped from the barrels of four unmasked gunmen who were running straight at Red Rum's small entourage.

In a fraction of a second, everything changed for Wiz; all he could hear were voices screaming.

"Get down! Get down!" Came from every direction.

He heard stampeding and screams of patrons trying their best to run for cover. Then, suddenly, his body turned warm as the first bullet ripped through his thigh.

"Arghh!" Wiz yelped out in pain, just before he felt the next bullet explode through his shoulder and twist his body in a mind-boggling circle. Wiz saw his security man hit the ground on instinct, as if he were taking cover from the threat headed their way. The gunfire shook everyone as they all fell to the ground to seek cover, while the advancing assailants let off shot after shot.

"Take dat' fa" Fatt Katt, mothafuckas!" one yelled.

The all too familiar sounds of gunplay fell upon deaf ears to Swirl; the only thing he'd heard was 'take dat' fa' Fatt Katt!' as he watched another bullet slam into Wiz's gut. The impact tossed Wiz backward into Thump's chest. Swirl was already ripping the Desert Eagle .44 caliber concealed on his side as he simultaneously watched over Wiz.

Swirl stood straight up and clicked off the safety in the same motion. "Bitch! What's happenin'!" he shouted in anger as he aimed the pistol and popped off. No other sounds were audible to Swirl as he fearlessly ran toward the gunmen. He fired rapidly, with no regard for his own life.

The first two gunmen tried to shoot, but their guns clicked, indicating they were out of bullets. As they turned to run, one of Swirl's bullets nailed the first target in his back, knocking him to the pavement. The other three men were still running, and only one of them returned fire.

Swirl only had three shots left. He set his sights on the man with the gun. With the next squeeze of his trigger, the man's neck jerked the other way as the bullet ripped through his throat.

Swirl kept chasing the other two assailants, popping off his last two shots, which failed to strike their marks. Stopping at the clicking sound of his pistol, he watched the two other men vanish into the crowd, which was now in a complete uproar.

"Mothafucka, y'all dead!" Swirl swore, clenching his gun tighter. He turned and saw all the people from their entourage surrounding Wiz as he lay sprawled out in a puddle of blood. Swirl ran back over, staring down at Wiz clutching the gaping hole in his stomach.

Tears of anger and loss were already flowing from his eyes at the sight of Wiz. One of the bodyguards was ripping Wiz's shirt from his body when Swirl approached.

"A paramedic is on the way. Please get back, I have everything under control here," the man announced.

"Shut the fuck up and get yo' bitch ass out the way!" Swirl barked as he shoved the man away from Wiz.

The man looked confused. "What the hell is—"

The rest of his words were met by Swirl's hard fist in his mouth before he fell to the ground. "Yo' punk ass gettin' paid fa' nothin'! If I had another clip, I'd load it up and shoot yo' bitch ass too, ya heard!"

"Swirl, don't do it like that," Thump spoke coolly. "I know how you feel, but you gotta lose that gun. You gotta get the fuck outta here and figure out a way to clean this up later. Stay focused, man."

Swirl looked down at Wiz, whose eyes were still open as he struggled to speak.

"Be still, homie, and keep quiet! Stop moving fo' you make the bullet travel," Swirl coached as Wiz gripped his arm desperately.

"Hold on, partna! You gonna make it! Don't worry 'bout nothin'! I'ma give it to dem niggaz Third Ward style! Ya heard me!"

Wiz's eyes were glassy and complete confusion had overtaken his face. His whole life and everything he loved had just flashed before his very eyes in a matter of seconds.

Swirl was not listening, nor did he even feel Thump pulling on his shoulder in an effort to pry him away from Wiz as he encouraged him to leave the scene. The sound of sirens grew closer and closer as Swirl locked eyes with Wiz.

Wiz coughed up blood and tears ran from his eyes as he struggled to speak to Swirl. "Puh-please . . . Go man—please!" Swirl saw the pain in his eyes, but knew he had to take heed to what might be his mentor's last advice.

Swirl looked at the bodyguard. "This gun is clean. Yo' bitch ass took this shot, or you'll be takin' the next one when I catch up with ya, ya heard? If you didn't do yo' job then it's best you act like you did."

He just stared into Swirl's eyes and saw the promise of death behind them, making him nod his head in agreement.

Swirl stood as Thump yelled, "Let's go, bruh."

The two disappeared into the crowd just as police began to arrive. Thump immediately recognized some Bloods he knew, and they helped the rappers escape.

The paramedics arrived with the cops and rushed Wiz to the Trauma Center at Sentara General. He was reported to be in critical condition.

Every news station from CNN to Fox broadcasted reports about the shooting. So far, the bodyguard was pinned with the rap as the shooter. But the authorities suspected foul play behind the unlikely confession he'd offered up.

Swirl was now on the move with nothing more than murder on his mind. He didn't know whom to turn to or what would be his own fate. All he saw was everything he'd worked for and everything he loved vanishing right before his eyes, as Wiz lay bleeding on the hard asphalt.

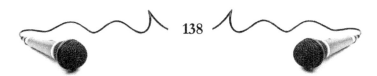

138

The only thing Swirl was now sure of was that behind this, somebody else was definitely going to bleed!

Drako
Chapter - 23

"Man this can't be so! . . ." Drako huffed angrily into his iPhone, still stunned with disbelief. He stepped back into his closet where he kept an assortment of handguns. "Dame, I want you to hit me up with every fuckin" thing you hear!" he growled. Drako tried to keep his voice down in hopes of not upsetting Diamond, whom he"d left in the living room, anymore than she already was.

"Of course I"m going to do that," Damien replied solemnly at the thought of how the devastating news he immediately rushed to Drako had crushed him. "And please Drako, don"t make any rash decisions until we know something solid. If we"re able to make a move I"d like get to the bottom at our first attempt." Damien knew the news had knocked Drako back into the dark place he"d only witnessed him in once before with the Pazzo"s, a place he hoped he"d never see him in again.

"Just stay on top of it and do like I asked you to. I got this!" Drako snapped, but knew he had to take hold of himself and not let his emotions lead his thought process.

"I"ll call back soon." Damien ended the call.

Drako placed the .40 cal he was clenching back on the shelf. He looked in his full-length mirror, his chest still heaved and his shirtless body dripped with sweat at the thoughts of vengeance.

I gotta get this shit together, he thought to himself, drying his face and body with a thick, soft towel. "But them bitches gone pay!" he swore further, tossing the towel to the floor and quickly grabbing a fresh T-shirt to slip on. Drako knew more than anything he had to lead those around him by example.

A few moments later, he still had that „all fall down" feeling churning in his gut, but he went to check on Diamond and keep her strong. He held her in his arms, doing his best to console her. She had lost all forms of restraint. Her uncontrollable tears for Wiz came from the bottom of her heart. She'd known and loved Wiz from childhood, and if he passed it would surely be a long road to recovery for Diamond's mind.

A short while later, Drako realized that bad news traveled fast and tragedy always brought loved ones together. He was just as surprised as he was appreciative when just past noon he received a text from none other than Swirl. It wasn't as though he and Swirl had love for one another, but the one common interest that neither could deny was the unconditional love they both shared for Wiz. No matter what, Swirl knew he had to find Drako.

Leading Diamond to the couch, Drako handed her some more Kleenex as she sat down and gathered some strands of composure, while he dialed Swirl at the number he texted to him.

Naturally, the two gangsters laid their egos aside, proving that realness does recognize realness. Drako was the first person Swirl reached out to. He recalled the incident as best he could, and then went on to tell Drako about the rift between Wiz and Bless, all the way down to the prank calls and what Wiz perceived to be a pail of empty threats.

"How could he underestimate a nigga who knows he bleeds just like him?" Drako countered with a nod. He was still stumped as the two went back and forth about how Wiz had traveled so far out of bounds without the proper security blanket. Drako let Swirl know that he felt because of Wiz's antics he should never take any threat as an empty one.

For the moment the two gangsters saw eye to eye.

"Somethin" just ain't felt right in a long time, man," Swirl admitted. "I'm there for Wiz, he my folk too. But like I tell him, y"all got somethin" way fo' my time. All I pray is he pull through this." Swirl choked a bit. ""Cause if he don't somethin" gone die behind this one, ya heard?" Drako heard him sniffle.

"Shit don't need to be said." Drako tried to slow Swirl's loose lips. "If it ain't his time he won"t go nowhere, feel me?"

"Yeah, yeah . . . I gotcha." Swirl sniffled, knowing that what was understood didn"t need to be discussed.

Drako reached for his other vibrating cell phone from the table. He saw Damien's number. "Look, I got all my eyes and ears tryin" to get to the bottom of this. You need to do what you can too. Let me take this call, but I'll keep you posted."

"Yeah, man," Swirl said with a drag. "You need to get us in that hospital, man. He gone need you there." Swirl spoke sincerely.

"I"ma be there. I"ma see him through," Drako pledged.

""Preciate it, my nigga." Swirl cleared his throat.

"I'll get back at you. One."

"Soou!" Swirl disconnected the call.

Drako picked up the line and replayed everything right back to Damien. Drako and Damien had launched probes with all their connections hours ago. They'd watched the news and tracked the net closely, and as soon as the two wounded gunmen's names were released, they ran a background check on them. They were definitely from Marcy projects but in no way tied to Take Money. Take Money had went into full defense mode over the net and to the media, trying swiftly to sever its name from any negative allegations. So far for Bless' sake, his alibi had checked out. And now Damien was calling to reaffirm the ongoing consensus that the gunmen were a couple of random hip-hop junkies who just had mad love for Fat Katt and tried to big-up their burrough in a senseless way over the fake

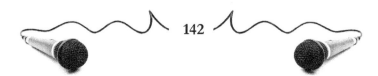

beef Wiz once had with Fatt Katt. They were now both reported to be in critical condition, but expected to survive.

Meanwhile, Wiz lay unconscious under heavy sedation, registered under an assumed name without a clue as to why his whole world had faded to black.

Drako ended his call with Damien. He reclined on the couch, resting his head on the cushion as he closed his eyes and gently massaged his temples. Quietly, Diamond lay sprawled across the couch with her head on his lap for a lingering moment.

"It's gone be all right," Drako said, gently strumming slow fingers through her hair.

"I know it, baby. I know it," she said weakly as they prepared to wait patiently for Drip to call back with news about Save.

*****

The next day just past noon Drako received the unexpected call from Dale Cissaro. Drako was a bit surprised when Dale told him Wiz had listed him as his immediate contact person if any life-threatening or grave mistakes befell him.

"Wait . . . hold on a moment," Drako said as he pulled Diamond closer to his side and that queasy feeling settled in again.

"His initial will was prepared several years ago," Dale said. "Then he added you as the contact six months ago. He—"

"I'm not interested in a will right now." Drako sounded defeated for the first time. "I-I just want to know what the fuck happened at that hospital!"

Dale grew quiet a moment, and then realized Drako's misconception. "Oh, no, no, sir. I'm not calling you with that kind of news. I'm calling to inform you that he's now been moved from critical to stable condition. He's still not responsive, but you are now allowed to visit him."

143

"He's okay, baby." Drako smiled down on Diamond. "He gone be a"ight."

A breath of fresh air seemed to surge through Drako's body. "We'll be there as soon as possible. Thanks." Drako ended the call and promptly called Swirl and Damien with the good news.

Drako proceeded to make all the necessary travel arrangements and Diamond began to pack their bags.

*****

Ten hours later, Drako was walking through the emergency room entrance at Sentara General Hospital in Virginia, with Diamond right on his heels. As soon as they received clearance from the nurse's station, they were promptly ascending on an elevator that would deliver them to Wiz's recovery room.

Once they got off the elevator and made their way up to the observation window, Drako was instantly wracked with a series of emotions he hadn't dealt with for as long as he could remember.

Drako realized just how bad he would've felt, regardless of how things were going between him and Wiz if something so senseless would've claimed his life. Wiz was now lying out on a hospital bed. He no longer was draped in rose gold, ten-karat studs or the latest urban apparel. He was now draped in a paisley, blue hospital gown. Two plastic tubes were pushed deep into his nostrils and the I.V. bag to the left of him dripped what everyone prayed to be a lifesaving solution.

Drako now understood why these suppressed emotions overcame him. The Wiz he was now looking at was the Wiz he knew as a kid. For a moment in time, Wiz had returned to his essence. No signs of the scheming midget he'd grown to become had shown through. Wiz now lay peacefully in as close as he'd ever been to the realm of spirits.

Drako looked up and saw Swirl making his way toward him. As soon as Swirl got close enough Drako extended a hand. The two hands met, then Swirl truced into a small embrace.

"It"s all good." Swirl looked up at Drako, breaking the fleeting hug.

"Yeah, man. We"re just hopin" for another day," Drako said.

Swirl spoke to Diamond, then they all turned back to Wiz, still resting in that peaceful realm and began what would be the start of a patient wait for the same common interest—Wiz's next chance at life.

Sentara General
Chapter- 24

Damien had called every few hours since Drako arrived to get an update. It had taken a little over forty-eight hours before Wiz showed any signs of consciousness, and when he did he found himself surrounded by friends. From that moment on, his will to live grew more and more with each passing hour. Soon, the tubes were removed from his nose and they were allowed in his room for bedside visitation. He was speaking in a low but audible tone as his body slowly adjusted to the heavy sedatives for the pain in his stomach.

After a few moments, Wiz tried to feel for his legs, and then swiped at his crotch to make sure his dick was still in place.

Being that it was, he made a feeble effort to smile. "I'm glad y'all were here." His weak voice cracked and his eyes trailed to Drako.

Drako didn't respond as he glared back at him.

"Well, you should have known you ain't got to ever worry about that." Diamond stepped closest to the bed. "You just get better. We're gonna be here till this is done." She smiled warmly, causing a tear to trickle down Wiz's face.

"I owe you one, partna," he croaked, staring in Swirl's direction.

Swirl smiled. "Man, all you need to do is get out that bed good. You „on owe me nothin". You know dis' shit real." Swirl's voice was firm. Drako remained quiet for the most part. For the next short while, most of his words were short. They were still warm, but Drako still found himself looking for the things that had grown in Wiz now that he was conscious again. Drako had never gotten past what Wiz had first done to him, and even now

Wiz continued to make bad decisions. Things the true Wiz that Drako knew would never do.

Drako looked as hard as he could, but no matter what, he still couldn't pinpoint, nor did he still see the friend he nearly wanted to kill just a few months ago.

Obviously, Wiz must've sensed the awkwardness between them as well. He seemed to find a reserve of energy and pointed in Swirl and Diamond's direction. "Lemme speak to Drako alone," Wiz said.

"Sure," Diamond said, quickly getting to her feet. "Come on." She swatted Swirl lightly across his shoulder and they quickly departed the room.

"Wha-what happened wit" us, man?" Wiz asked sincerely.

Drako cracked his knuckles gently and gazed at Wiz for a moment. "Man, it's you. All these dumb ass decisions you makin"."

"Drako, don't start wit' all them riddles and shit. Just be straight forward; what's really up with you, man?"

"See, that's what I'm saying. This ain't no riddle or no game. Look at you now. Probably still sayin" in your head „It's just music!""

"Look man, I got caught slippin". I made a mistake. But this? You been on some other shit long before this, and as far as my decisions, I'm grown. I'm a man! My decisions made me rich!"

"Yeah, well look where they got you now. You supposed to be a goddamn genius, but you way out of bounds without proper security with all this in the air."

Wiz thought about explaining why he'd chosen to only have two security men on duty in Virginia, but the thought of how Drako spoke to him made him choose otherwise.

"Man, I would'a had security if you hadn't turned your back on me and went— Look man, I can't believe how you tried to

147

handle me like that on the phone. And then I come to realize it was all about money!"

"All about money!" Wiz pricked him with that remark. "And you gone lay there and say I turned my . . . I tried to handle you? Man, you can't be serious!" Drako hissed heat from his nostrils as he stumbled out his words.

"Well, it's the truth. You tried to squeeze me for more money and I'd already told you all you had to do was ask."

"That's what I'm sayin", nigga! I shouldn't have to squeeze or ask no other man for shit! Especially when I'm supposed to have friends like you. I helped you put in place the first major block to this shit! Why da" fuck I ain't got five or ten million dollars wit' all this goddamn paper layin" around?" Drako stood and stepped closer to the bed, barely able to control his loud tone. "Nigga, you was spendin" money on cars that you never got to drive. You was the biggest ten thousand dollar tossing trick in the whole state of Louisiana! Man, that was just money to burn! You could"a gave me that and not even missed it, but you wouldn't even do that! How long was I supposed to wait!"

After pricking Drako, Wiz held his tongue purposely, allowing Drako's angry tongue to slip.

"Damn, man," he said with a voice filled with disappointment. "I ain't know you felt that way. We way bigger than that, you heard? All you needed to do was talk to me like you talkin" to me now. I admit I've made some bad choices— some you know about and some you don't—but in your case you gotta believe me. I never wanted to see you broke. I love to see you wit' it."

Drako studied Wiz's expression hard as he tried to cover up his faults.

"Yo, man. It's like our wires is crossed up bad, in every way. I thought giving you pocket change and the crib was doin' you a favor. I was just gonna wait and see what you like to do, other

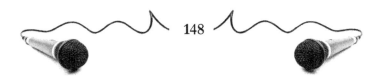

148

than push coke like we used to, then help you get set up in maybe a year after you had a moment to enjoy yourself. I spoke to Dame about it, and we both figured that giving you or any nigga that kind of money comin" off a ten-year bid could cause problems. Homie, the streets done changed, and I just didn't want you back in „em. After a while, I knew you were up to somethin", but I just couldn't finger it." He looked at Drako knowingly.

Drako fought as hard as he could to see through Wiz's bullshit, but he had to admit he couldn't. "How da fuck you gone let somebody tell you somethin" about me, you goddamn genius? I know the streets have changed. But so have I, in ways you can't imagine." Drako wouldn't let up.

"Look man, somebody gotta be big about this lil shit, arguing like kids ain't makin" it no better either. All I want you to know is that me nor Dame meant you no harm, okay? We just made a bad decision together. I see how you movin" now, but at that time I had no one to confide in." Wiz paused, allowing Drako to take it all in.

"Dame has never given me bad advice before. Look around Red Rum's office. Look at my mansion. Hell, look at ya" own shit." He reasoned. "And like now, I shouldn't be laying up in this state trying to prove myself to my best friend. Nigga, I'll bleed for you too; best believe that!" Inside, Wiz's gut churned violently with guilt. He'd meant what he was telling Drako, but he knew the drugs and all the bling had caused him to take too long to do what he'd always intended for Drako.

Drako still had no response. He just nodded his head in deep thought.

"Look man, we can find a way to make this shit work out eventually. We ain't got to be at odds on this. I mean, do yo' thang over there. I"ma do my thing where I'm at. All I'm sayin" is at the end of the day, if and when we get together we make these labels work good together, feel me?"

Drako squinted at him with an even more serious glare. "Man, this been a long road and things done got complicated," he replied sternly. "We'd really have to take it slow, 'cause for real, man, you ,,on ever put all your cards on the table. And plus, you got the whole world keepin" their eyes on yo' every move." He emphasized. "I can't live like that."

"I hear you this time and I ain't gone lie. I been dirty, but not that kinda dirty. We gone get 'round that shit. But like you say, we can take one day at a time. Them niggaz caught me slippin", and I see now it don't take but one slip to cost you a hell of a trip!"

He decided to tell Drako his silly reasoning for only having two bodyguards in Virginia. Then he went on to confess almost everything. They talked first about how the Hip-Hop Task Force had been following him around, and then about Bless' so called empty threats. He even told him about his unsuccessful 'Goon Squad' team he tried to organize, and he finally confessed to the bootleg scheme. He assured Drako he didn't need the money. He just wanted to see if he could get away with it.

Wiz poured out everything except his heavy use of x-pills, the secret feelings he'd had for Myria, and of course, the shameful mistake of leaking Blondelle's sex tape. He told himself he'd take that one to his grave.

"Damn, bruh, you mean it take me to get shot for us to laugh like old times?"

"It ain't back to old times just yet, but don't trip. This time I"ma make sure we a"ight!" Drako finally gave him a smile.

Just then, the doctor, followed close by Diamond and Swirl entered the room. He checked Wiz's vital signs, and then read over the chart on the clipboard placed at the foot of his bed. A moment later, the doctor announced that he'd be detained a

minimum of ten days, but they'd do all they could to make his stay as comfy as possible.

With that prognosis, it was quickly agreed that at all times one of the three would remain by his side. Drako then summoned for some reliable security men he knew. He placed two in the lobby and another outside of Wiz's door and set them on a 24-hour rotation schedule.

Drako soon kissed Diamond and was first to depart. He had high hopes for Wiz"s recovery and was now 100% commited to keeping Wiz safe. But for now he had big business of his own to attend to. Drako was desperate to get some answers. His thoughts were already on the westcoast, just where his feet would be in a few hours. Once that was concluded, Drako planned to return to Wiz"s side as soon as possible.

Drako
Chapter- 25

When the charter jet landed on the private airfield in Nevada, Drako was immediately met by a white super stretch limousine. He stepped off the plane and walked right up to the back door that was held open by a white gloved chauffeur.

Drako slipped inside to see Drip seated to his right and two clean cut black men seated side by side in front of him.

"Barron Brown," said the closest man as he reached a long slender hand to introduce himself. He had a clean-shaven head, which appeared huge for his one hundred fifty pound frame, and the thick glasses he wore didn't brighten his appearance one bit.

"Drako . . . good to meet you." He met his grip with a nod.

"William Oliver," said the much cleaner cut African American, super power attorney as he introduced himself. William Oliver, as in 'Oliver and Associates', needed no introduction. His reputation in the courtroom preceded him wherever he went. First, for winning multiple high profile corporate cases that had reportedly settled in the billions, before he went on to become one of the country's most sought out criminal attorneys and celebrity shields from the law.

"A pleasure to meet you as well," Drako said with gratitude as the limo cleared the landing field.

Drako noticed that instead of the limo cruising back toward the never sleeping lights of the Vegas Strip, the limo was heading West, further into the Nevada desert.

"So, what do we have here?" Drako wasted no time asking William about Save's options.

"There are only two simple choices here. We either deal this way or deal with Nevada's guidelines."

152

"How quickly can we start this game?"

"Well, so far I've snipped all media outlets in Las Vegas from reporting anything further. Other than the tabloid fodder that got out before Barron summoned your importance to my attention, the only thing that'll be left will probably be Twitter chat, but it'll dissipate in time," he said, glancing at his watch easily. "Now, I can have him back on the streets as early as this time tomorrow."

"Well. After that, what other guarantees can you give me? I know for such a favor it won't be as simple as in most cases."

"But you can bet it'll be well worth it." William sat up straight and began to stroke his dark chin. "I can guarantee you as long as this case is in Nevada, it can be bought. I'll put it off and put it off until it's virtually forgotten by the public. At that point, it may end with a slap on the wrist. Perhaps, a small term of probation and possibly a few hours of community service."

Drako had no response. He pondered with a nod.

William sensed that Drako was still indecisive. He leaned up a bit, looking directly in Drako's eyes. "Please do not let my dark skin fool you. I am as close as you can get to those who built this city. I have represented them well in numerous cases, and I have 'em all on speed dial, in which I'll be sure to use if we proceed. Believe me, my voice will be heard."

Drako liked what he heard. "How much we talkin" about?" Drako asked as the limo topped a steep incline and came to a halt. They were now on the property of a small mansion perched high in the hills of the Nevada desert. Drako gazed out at the twinkling lights of the Vegas Strip in the far distance below.

"Well, with him being a celebrity, and this case getting tossed to the public so fast, and well, frankly, with you being who you are, I couldn't see doing it for anything less than two million dollars." He casually tossed the heavy number in

Drako's lap and tried to read the pain it brought to his face at the same time. But it was to no avail. Drako had to have the best poker face in all of Vegas.

"I got plenty of palms to grease on this one. Italians eat a lot of pasta. My judges golf on only the finest of turf, then everybody visits the Bunny Ranch every so often." He smiled to soften the blow.

Drako simply nodded and took another moment before responding. "How 'bout we toss you two and a half. I want the charge to disappear completely. Put it off till it ends that way. He doesn't need the scar on his record later. This man is gonna eventually travel abroad on the regular, and we don't want any reason for him not to be able to obtain a passport."

"Hmm . . ." William smiled proudly, stroking his chin again. "Indeed, a man who knows how to spend his money," he said. "It can be cleaned up and smoothed over. It'll be done." He reached for Drako's hand again. "Welcome to Las Vegas, I forgot to tell you." He winked.

"Don't forget these." Drip passed the documents to William.

"Wise decision. I'm impressed with this, and when I get done talking to him I'm sure he'll agree," William stated. "I hope we continue to do great business." He tapped on the partition so the chauffeur could open the door. He grabbed his briefcase and he and Barron exited the limo.

*****

Drako and Drip cruised back toward the city lights, filled with hope of much better days ahead. Drako understood that the papers Drip passed to the attorney was an agreement stating that in order for Save to get out of jail and for his case to disappear, he had to first sign a new contract locking him into a three album deal that placed perimeters on the music he released and the people he recorded with.

Save was definitely an asset. A likable one at that, but to allow him to spread his lyrical corruption so freely would no longer be a good business choice. Drip had washed tons of money for Barron years ago, and he knew just who to call to get close to William Oliver.

Drako told Drip about everything going on with Wiz's situation and recovery. He reassured him that Wiz was indeed upset about someone stealing and releasing the sex tape. He even told him at some point he hope Reality could find a way to work with Red Rum.

"You know the only problem I foresee with this case is even if it goes away in court, Big Turk and those guys could still make a rift," Drip said with a nod. "I'd have never imagined the kid knocking Big Turk out of his Timbs like that."

"Yeah, I thought about it. I'm gonna talk to Wiz. He's gonna have to speak with his own people. I warned him. I guess now they realize everything ain't what it seems." Drako gazed at the huge fountain of shimmering water as the limo pulled into the Bellagio.

"Let's roll a few craps for old times, tonight," Drip suggested.

"Nah, not tonight. I got a few things still on my mind, and I want to get back to Wiz on the first jet out tomorrow."

"I understand." Drip nodded. "Well I"ma lay out here and do me while I wait on 'em to spring my boy."

Drako was about to get out the limo, but paused for a moment. "When can you move this other paper for me? I'm liking the security you spoke about in Bermuda." He held onto the door handle.

Drip smiled. "Don't even trip. Next week I'll get everything in order."

The two slipped out the limo and headed to their suites. Drip dressed comfortably and headed right back out to the crap tables. He tossed dice and raked five thousand dollar chips up with Blondelle right on his arm.

Drako went to his suite and stretched out across his bed. Diamond was first to call him. They spoke for a few moments, and then Damien called to check on Wiz and report what he'd heard.

"So you got no better leads yet?" Drako asked.

"None at all. Everything checks out and I can't honestly find a viable reason to point a finger at Bless," Damien admitted.

"Well, I'm not convinced. I just ain't feelin that shit Bless or none of ‚em screamin'," Drako said heatedly.

"Well, how's Wiz coming along?" Damien's voice dripped with concern.

"He's doin' okay. He's steady. The surgery to his intestines has gone well so far. They're just holding him to monitor for internal bleeding, intestinal poisoning, all that kinda stuff. He can live with the shoulder and the flesh wound to his leg."

Damien sounded relieved. "God, I hope he stabilizes fast."

"Oh, he's gonna stabilize, and I‟ma be here this time till this shit is over!" Drako's tone was a forceful one.

"I—I just can't see him looking like that. I know Wiz is in shambles."

"I can understand. Believe me, it was a Wiz you‟ve never seen." Drako spoke honestly.

"Well, how 'bout you? Things movin‟ along pretty well?" Damien tried to change topics.

Drako sat up and twisted his neck a bit. "I'm good. . . . I'm good. I think I‟ma cool it down for a while and see what me and Wiz can do. I just wish you‟da had more confidence in me from the start though." Drako couldn't resist letting him know he'd spoken to Wiz about the bad decision they made together.

"What are you—"

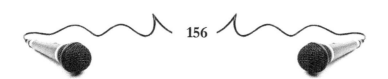

"Don't even trip it. It's neither here nor there. This is where we are now." Drako nipped it in the bud and left Damien with his own thoughts on the matter. "I"ma skate for now, but I'll keep you posted."

"All right then." Damien sounded sullen.

"A'ight—one." Drako ended the call and sat up on the edge of the bed, still processing his thoughts. He decided to drop the next fraud scheme brewing in his head. With all the paper he'd already gotten away with, and the endless potential he foresaw at Reality Records, he knew this was a wise decision. His plan was to get back and await Wiz's recovery. Drako felt that if Wiz pulled through and started making better decisions, there was no limit to where their lives could be. His last hope was that Save would agree to the contract and things would soon get back to normal.

Wiz
Chapter- 26

At Sentara General, everyone was in good spirits with Wiz improving more and more each day, and Wiz was glad to be surrounded by Swirl, Diamond, and his old friend Drako, who had gotten back and made certain that the security guards were doing their jobs to the utmost. Damien had called and said he'd checked out Red Rum Headquarters and Wiz's mansion as added safety precautions.

It was now the second day since Drako's return and five since the shooting.

Wiz was just starting to wake up. The morphine blurred his vision at first, but after a few blinks, he recognized Drako sitting in a chair near the door.

Before either could say a word, Wiz's doctor walked in the room and informed Wiz that he might be able to go home in three more days, his eighth day, but he suggested five more to make a full ten. That was fine by the mogul, as long as he had his friends to keep him in good spirits.

After the doctor left, Drako tossed him a paper with an article about the shooting.

> *The hip-hop mogul is in critical*
> *condition after a hail of gunfire left*
> *his perforated body sprawled in a ...'*

Wiz didn't read another word, discarding the overbearing article that made his recovery sound as if only a miracle would save his life. He decided to cut off all tabloid gossip, headlines, and even radio broadcasts. His health came first and foremost, and he was now truly appreciating it with his closest friends supporting him. The only other concern for Wiz was the probe

Red Rum had launched to seek information on the gunmen responsible for pulling the trigger on him.

Finally, on the eighth day, everyone was sitting in the recovery room with Wiz. The group laughed and joked, reminiscing on old times back in Charlotte and back at Red Rum's Headquarters, when the doctor strolled into the room.

He did his normal routine of checking Wiz's vital signs and so forth, and then picked up Wiz's chart. "You seem to be doing fine. It is good that we got you into surgery so fast." Everyone sat in silence as he briefly paused to further study the chart. "I don't see any signs of intestinal problems or internal bleeding. You seem to be recovering just fine."

"I want to remind you, though, that it's only been eight days.

Your condition has stabilized enough to release you, but I would advise you to stay and let us keep an eye on you a little longer."

Wiz looked at the doctor with that full platinum smile. "So you telling me I'm free to leave?"

"If you'd like to, sir, but I—"

"Doc, don't even waste your good breath," Wiz interrupted. "I know how you feel, but these folks right *cheer'* will do all the observatin' I need." He pointed to Swirl and Drako.

"You did your part, and I thank you. We all thank you, and you'll be gettin' a blessin" from Red Rum fa' keepin' these guts together, ya dig?"

Wiz's slang confused the doctor. "He thanks you and wants to pay you with a personal check," Diamond interpreted. The doctor smiled again and jotted his name and address on a piece of hospital stationery that Diamond handed him.

*****

Once the release papers had been signed, Wiz and the crew prepared to ride out to Norfolk International, where a chartered jet awaited them, ready to fly to Miami. Wiz had been lifted

159

from the recovery bed, bathed, dressed and placed in his wheelchair.

Diamond quickly braided four large cornrows on his head, and Wiz was ready to bounce.

"How do I look?" Wiz questioned as he looked up at Swirl.

"You look even shorter," Swirl joked.

"Stop playin', man. Seriously, how I look?"

"Player, you gone always look like cash money!" Everybody laughed with Wiz.

"Say bruh, I got somethin' for you," Swirl said. "I brought your Cartiers with the burgundy lenses. I left 'em in the car."

"Go get 'em, man," Wiz ordered with a smile. Wiz's signature frames would complete his attire as he ventured back into the world.

Diamond chatted with Wiz while Drako gave orders to his trusted men. Suddenly, Drako's attention was diverted. He heard a loud voice that sounded like Dale Cissaro. He looked in the direction of the door and saw Dale following two plain-clothes agents.

They were trailed by two more uniformed officers and heading directly toward Wiz's room.

"Wiz, we got company," Drako announced. When Wiz looked up, the two agents were entering the door.

"Wiz, you don't have to answer any questions," Dale said before the agents could utter a word. "You don't even have to allow them to stay here. They don't have any warrants; they're just looking for information about you and Swirl."

Wiz was shocked; he recognized the agents immediately. They were the same two agents that had been following his path for months. He quickly gathered some traces of composure as he glanced at Dale.

"I ain't worried about them! Swirl ain't did shit, and I ain't either! Hell, I'm the one who almost got killed! Don't they nosey asses read the paper?"

"We haven't said you've done shit," the first agent, a white man, replied. "And for your information, we've apprehended one of the other gunmen who was previously at large."

"Good, so what the fuck you want cheer'?"

"Yeah, well maybe it's good for you, but it ain't so good for Swirl," the black agent said. He briefly paused to lend a confident glare at the other agent. "The gunman is cooperating with authorities. We knew that bullshit your bodyguard gave the cops wasn't gonna hold up."

"Man, what the hell you talkin' bout?"

"We know he didn't—take those shots—Swirl did!"

Wiz's eyes lit up. He tried to stay calm, but the agents picked up on his expression and smiled.

"We're helping prosecutors pull enough evidence together to get your artist indicted on felony possession of a firearm in the Commonwealth of Virginia," the first agent said. "Swirl will be looking at least ten years on that alone. Not to mention the 922(g), which could get him another fifteen."

The agents laughed at the brave front Wiz was trying to hold. "Oh, and don't let him die," the other spoke again. "If we don't get murder one, we'll at least get manslaughter!"

The agents laughed again. Wiz's mind was discombobulated as reality struck. He wondered how in the hell someone could try to kill him, and the Feds only concern was with a felon who possessed a firearm? Wiz thought about Swirl, whom he knew was indeed a convicted felon, and the Commonwealth alone would burn him. A Federal sentence would be even worse.

Swirl had really grown on Wiz; he was almost like a little brother to him. He thought back to when he was lying on the hard asphalt, drenched in blood, his life fading away. Swirl was right there, trying to save his life by chasing down the bastard gunmen, and then he ran back to hold Wiz in his arms for what could've been his last breath.

Sorrow, hurt, and pain instantly gripped Wiz's heart at the thought of losing Swirl. Swirl would be regarded as a fallen soldier, and once again, the media would have a field day, hyping up the downfall of yet another rapper.

A small tear escaped Wiz's eye. He raised his head. When he looked up, he saw Swirl coming back to the recovery room.

The smile painted on Swirl's face sent volts of pain through Wiz's already wretched body. He thought deeper for any way he could help Swirl, and still couldn't find another one of his schemes to fit the bill. When Swirl got about fifteen feet from the door, Wiz's only choice nailed him in the head. He knew it was his turn to man up!

"Swirl didn't take the shot. I did!"

Confusion clenched the agent's faces as they looked back and forth at one another.

"What?" they yelled in unison.

"I took the shots before the last guy shot me." Wiz briefly paused as his scheming mind concocted the story. "I ,,on even understand why y'all here. They shot first. They were tryin' to kill me, and I protected my life! What? Do y'all think I go around killing fans? They're the people who feed me!"

The white agent was fuming. "You lying piece of—"

"Fuck you! I ain't gotta lie! I just wanna live! What would you have done? Don't you want to live? If it were you, I'd have wished you'd done the same, so how can you be mad at me?" Wiz banged a fist on the arm of the wheelchair and shifted, causing it to roll a bit before Dale could reach for the handle and hold it still.

"Wiz, that bullshit is not gonna fly! Your fancy lawyer can't save Swirl or you if we pin the gun on you."

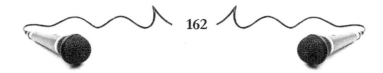

162

Dale quickly interrupted. "Pin a gun? There will be no such thing! My client admitted he took those shots, so Swirl will not be charged. Second of all, my client is not a convicted felon, so he is allowed to bear arms to protect himself."

"Bullshit! We're gonna have our day in court!" the agent yelled.

"I think it would be great! But only to see you there in a better choice of attire, because the charges you're aiming for have absolutely no merit! I would actually enjoy watching a judge shred them in court," Dale stated with confidence.

The agents stared at Wiz with faces full of anger.

"You know what, Wiz?" the black agent said. "You're a tiny piece of shit! You run around with all this bling bling shit and sit in that headquarters and call shots! We may miss you on this one, but we'll get you one way or another. I'm going to be on your ass like paparazzi! We know you marked the hit on Fatt Katt, and the day that we get enough evidence, I'll watch you crumble! We'll be back, and I won't be buying another Keyser Soze story again!"

Wiz laughed blatantly this time. "You know what? Do what you gotta do."

"Wiz, you don't have to say a word," Dale assured.

"Yeah, I do. I need to enlighten these guys. Y"all are the biggest idiots I've ever met! First off, I ain't kill Fatt Katt! I'm a businessman, not a murderer! In Virginia Beach, I only shot in self-defense. As far as Fatt Katt, I shouldn't be a suspect in that case. I wasn't there, but evidently, y'all were, just like I've seen y'all everywhere else!"

"What do you mean, 'we were there'? You—"

"The road manager said he only saw the blood burgundy masks. He was unconscious when they fled the scene, but yet you know the color of the Yukon they used to get away?" Wiz barked. "I saw the footage; it was filmed in black and white!

Looks to me like somebody had to be following Fatt Katt too, but I guess you don't want to apprehend them! It wouldn't make a dent in hip-hop, being that they have no influence or money to seize."

"You don't know what we know—"

"Shut up wit' the bullshit! What I do know is that y'all are afraid of what y'all have no control over, and I know that y'all spend millions of taxpayers" hard-earned dollars a year on this hip-hop task force bullshit!"

Wiz paused a moment to let his words sink in. "Y'all spend millions and do so much dirt to prove you don't exist, yet y"all follow rappers all the time, some twenty-four hours, only to keep comin' up empty—a bag of weed here and there, a bullshit gun charge, even though you know a nigga from the streets need a gun if he's a multi-million dollar star. You mothafuckas ain't got nothin' better to do than decipher lyrics all day in hopes of solving criminal investigations." Wiz briefly paused to catch his voice as he saw he had the agent's attention.

"Lemme enlighten yo" dumb asses some more . . . ain't no real nigga dumb enough to confess what he gon' do over no damn track! If his dumb ass does, then he ought a go to jail! We got sense! Hip-hop is art, it"s poetry, timeless writings—they have college courses to break down the art of our culture. This is my culture! Maybe you should take the class and try to understand it before you pass judgment on an entire genre!"

Feeling Dale"s grip tighten on the wheelchair"s handle as if he was about to move him, Wiz raised a hand to stop him because he wasn"t done. "Rock and Roll music has been accused of making children kill their entire family, but I ain't ever heard about you deciphering their lyrics! Do y'all spend millions of dollars to follow Marilyn Manson? What about Black Sabbath?" Wiz paused at the dumb looks on the agents" faces as they failed to respond. "I thought not! But I see yo' asses won't leave me alone, not even at a time like this."

One agent cleared his throat before he spoke. "I'm not here to face the whole hip-hop genre; I'm here to face you, and right now you're a suspect, and if you're innocent, you should help us."

"I ain't a homicide investigator. I'm CEO of Red Rum Records, a legitimate business, so I won't be helping with shit!"

Wiz turned his attention to Dale, but was still speaking for the detectives to hear. "Matter of fact, Dale, the charges filed on the guys who shot me . . . I want them dropped!"

"What?" Dale swallowed in disbelief.

"I want them dropped! I ain't helping these rotten mothafuckas with shit! They can do whatever they want, but I won't be there! I don't believe Take Money had anything to do with this. Hip-hop had nothing to do with this. Hip-hop is not responsible for all the crimes that take place in the hip-hop community. Those broke-ass street thugs acted out on their own; they caught me slippin' and tried to catch the juice at my expense. I believe in karma—they'll get theirs."

"Uh, are you sure?" Dale asked as he cleared his throat.

"I'm sure," Wiz stated firmly as he directed his attention to Swirl. "Gimme my glasses, partna."

Swirl smiled, handing Wiz his Cartier frames. Wiz placed them on his face as he turned back to the detectives.

"I ain't got nothin' for y'all today, and the next time I catch up with y'all, maybe y'all will have found either that warrant or some dignity, ya dig?"

Wiz paused, noticing the anger and defeat etched on their faces. "Hold up fo' you blow up!" He pointed to the black agent. "I do have a statement you can leak to the press . . . Tell 'em I'm innocent. I'm a law-abiding citizen of America, and when I leave this hospital, I'm gonna buy even more guns, beef the hell outta my security, and Red Rum 'bout to make even better music." Wiz snickered, clutching his bandaged wound. "Now, could y'all wenches please get out of my room? I've got a studio appointment and plane to catch to get there."

"You little no good mu—" the small white agent shouted.

"Sir, sir, that will not be necessary. By the way, I did not get your names or badge numbers?" Dale stepped a foot closer to the black cop and whipped out his notepad.

"It's okay. We'll see you around," the agent growled, turned and stalked out the door.

As soon as the others trailed him out, Swirl leaned over and hugged Wiz. "Goddamn, you let 'em have it, man."

"If don't nobody start standin' up for hip-hop, we just gon' continue to fall for anything, ya dig?"

"I feel ya, dog, I feel ya." Swirl gazed at Wiz and let him go. "I appreciate that other thing."

"Don't even kick it; ain't nothin' new to me, either. I could've laid a lil' while too," Wiz spoke easily.

Diamond stepped up, "Wiz, you crazy! Telling that man you 'bout to go straight to the studio!" Her bright smile was warm.

"Shit, I am!" Wiz snapped, trying to sound serious, but everyone knew he was joking as he glanced at Drako. "Hey, man, don't get it twisted! I'm hurtin' now, but this is still business! I may not be dissin' nobody else, but I just took five wit' a smile! Y'all crazy as hell if y'all thinkin' the genius ain't 'bout to grace covers and straight bubble off dat' shit!"

Red Rum exited the hospital safely. They boarded the jet and stayed together until Wiz was safe within the confines of his mansion in Miami. They all stayed over the first night, and Drako had his team surround the home.

Drako and Diamond flew back to ATL the following day. Swirl stayed another day to confide in Wiz, and then he flew

back to New Orleans, knowing that in just a matter of time, their world would once again soon be life inside of Red Rum!

Myria
Chapter- 27

For the past few nights, Myria had lain sulking in bed, a bed she shared with Damien in his home. She'd been at his home lately because she felt it was the one place she could get the best news about Wiz's health and the future of Red Rum, which the media reported would be crumbling soon.

She spent much of last night sobbing. Damien thought they were tears of joy, attributed to his endowment and undying love at his hands. But truthfully, she was crying because there really were no feelings; her pussy couldn't get wet. She felt similar to Julia Roberts in *Sleeping with the Enemy*, only nobody forced her.

The video vixen had temporarily become a product of her environment. There was a plethora of negativity circulating in her life, and pressed against the fact that it had been two weeks since Wiz's mishap, and nobody, not even Diane the fucking hairdresser, had even attempted to call her about Wiz's condition.

Although she knew how Wiz felt, she still wanted to tell him how bad she felt for him at a time like this. She thought about Damien when he'd gotten out of bed last night; she remembered all the red welt marks she'd left on his flat ass when they played their S&M games. She wondered how she let herself stoop so low to get ahead. Truthfully, the work had not gotten any better in quality or quantity.

She'd booked a shoot with a new artist named Killer, who was supposed to be big. Myria had flown out to L.A. to do the video, but when she got there, it was some corny black rapper.

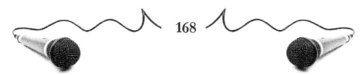

The set was surrounded by lily-white, flat-assed models. All the director wanted from Myria was a close-up booty shot of a phat-assed black girl in a thong; he didn't even want to shoot her face.

And Damien was another matter; she felt like he didn't truly show any real genuine concern about Wiz. She hated it when he cried out "buena-panocha, negra puta" (good pussy, black bitch!) when they had sex. She felt totally disrespected and would spank Damien's ass even harder when he spoke his supposedly sexy bedroom dialect, which seemed to heighten his pleasure.

Damien didn't know anything about Myria. If he had taken time to know her, he'd have known about her Puerto Rican roots and that she spoke fluent Spanish. He would've known her favorite color was red, like Wiz did when he used to send her roses and sexy lingerie. He would've known her favorite songs, where she was from—hell, he didn't even ask her age. Damien was so shallow he just thought that he and Myria were meant to be. All Damien truly knew was that Myria was beautiful and had good black pussy!

Myria began to feel queasy, momentarily disgusted by the mere thought of Damien. She rolled over and tried to think about something else. She replayed Drako's words: "Until you find Mr. Right, charge the hell out of Mr. Right Now! Find your morals and stand on top of them."

She thought she'd used his advice right, but there was clearly not enough money or lack of self-respect in her heart to continue enduring these long nights. Myria realized she'd made a huge mistake hooking up with Damien. The tears started to flow again.

"Oh, God, gurl, you can't live like this," she softly told herself between sobs. Myria pulled the covers over her head to conceal her face as she wept, telling herself that when she got up, she was leaving with the small strands of dignity she had left. Realizing that this was her first mistake of the sort, she promised herself it would be her last!

*****

Myria was still whimpering lightly underneath the covers when Damien entered the room talking on the phone about something in Spanish. He peeked over at the bed and took note of Myria; she appeared to be sound asleep beneath the satin sheets. He strolled about the room briefly, and then went back toward his office.

Myria had just wiped the last traces of tears away when Damien's voice re-entered the room. "They won't have a problem finding a thing."

Myria began translating his words into English.

"After the ballistics match up, this will be all over." Her ears instantly pricked up to hear him even better. "Relax. I have it all, and nobody is seeing a thing until the deal is in writing."

Damien's voice faded as he walked out the room again.

Myria began to replay his words in her head. She had always known that Damien had some sort of hidden agenda. So many things intrigued her about him, but they intrigued her in a suspicious way.

Damien re-entered the room. "Just be glad the black piece of shit didn't die. This is perfect timing, we have a whole week left before the shit goes public. I told you to relax! Now I have to go. I have pussy begging for my attention." Damien continued in Spanish.

He ended the call then promptly woke Myria up with a light tap to her ass. "Wake up, beautiful," he said as Myria pretended to awaken. "Get yourself together so I can get you home. I have quite a few appointments to meet today."

Myria's well-practiced, sexy morning voice whined, "Morning baby. I can't hardly move . . . you wore me out last

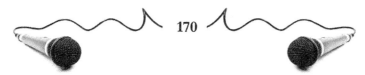

170

night." She grabbed his hand and whipped up the best bedroom eyes she could find. "Can't I just lay here for a while? I'd rather just shower, rest, and wait on you to get back," she lied, then faked a half-smile as she rose up and pecked his cheek.

Damien felt warm and fuzzy all over as he watched her lie back down and pull the satin sheets back up over her naked body.

He gently squeezed her ass through the thin material, and then leaned over and planted a kiss on her forehead. "Just relax, baby. Your lover will be back to please you in a couple of hours." She smiled appreciatively, closed her eyes, and drifted away.

Myria lay there as she listened to Damien quickly get dressed. He gathered his cell phone, iPad, and keys before he pecked her forehead again. Then he was out the door.

The minute Myria heard the sound of the garage door closing, she was out of the bed and on her feet. She hastily began to search for clues.

For twenty minutes, she checked the bottom dresser drawers in his room and the closet. She went underneath the mattress— still nothing. Finally, she checked the nightstand, where she found two small identical keys. She tried to think of what they went to as she sat on the bed replaying the pieces of his telephone conversation in her mind. Then she thought to go to where he always went—into his makeshift office.

She whisked through the papers on his desk, but found nothing suspicious. Myria then moved to the closet, where she found three athletic bags; one with several handguns, another with cash, and the last with two cameras and what appeared to be a small recording device. She left everything in place and went to the two tall filing cabinets and tried the keys. No dice.

Myria couldn't put it together, but she felt leery of Damien. Finally, she concluded the search as she closed the closet door.

Then she noticed the gold keyhole on the large drawer at the bottom of the wooden office desk. She quickly pushed the key in, and it unlocked the drawer. She pulled it open and saw two large Ziploc bags filled with yellow Ecstasy pills.

Myria saw the black briefcase, which she knew had to be filled with money. She pulled it out and placed it on top of the desk, then popped the two gold buttons to unlock it.

The sight of the bloody hunting knife in a plastic Ziploc bag caused her to gasp. She picked the bag up and discovered stacks of pictures, papers, and audiotapes underneath. Myria set the bag aside and began rifling through the papers.

The first was a list of various twelve-digit numbers. She had no idea what they pertained to and set it aside. The next sheet, though, got her full attention; it was a hand-drawn map of the interior of Wiz's Miami mansion.

She quickly began rifling through the rest of the papers. There were names of banks and a list of dates. She realized then that, the twelve-digit numbers must've been account numbers and cell phone numbers, none of which she recognized. Then there was also a list of popular record stores, all in New York, and scribbled at the top of one of the random pages was a number that Myria surely recognized—it was the private number that White Chocolate had used to reach Bless!

Myria dropped the papers as anger and disappointment washed over her. She began to look through the large pile of photos. All sorts of pictures of Drako and Wiz were taken, including shots of Wiz at his Source Awards after-party, standing next to Damien's Latino friend.

She viewed photos of Drako's 760 Li in a parking lot and a white woman handing him a large manila envelope, and more of the same white woman entering and exiting a Hertz and driving a Toyota Camry. The angles proved that the snapshots had been secretly taken.

Myria had no idea what to do next, but she was pretty sure that Damien had some sort of hidden agenda, and maybe even malice in his heart for Wiz or Drako. She was also almost certain that he had been the one to tip Bless to Wiz's bootleg scheme. She figured it was Damien's way of getting her out of Wiz's arms.

Taking a piece of paper, she carefully jotted down the account numbers, along with Bless' private number and the spots in New York where the bootlegs were sold. She stole two pictures—one of Drako and the white girl, and one of Wiz partying. Double-checking the office before retracing her steps back to the bedroom, she hid the items in her overnight bag. Nervously, she got back in bed and tried to make sense of all she had just seen.

Lewisburg Penitentiary
Chapter - 28

Back at Lewisburg Penitentiary, it was a day filled with hope for every solid convict on the yard! The United States Supreme Court had only three days ago ruled nearly unanimously on two cases, Booker and Fanfan, which provided hope for the inmates who constantly stayed in the law library fighting their life sentences.

Toney had been up since the cell doors cracked open. His henchmen had been there to hold post as he showered. Today, he had on his shiniest steel-toed boots and best prison fit. The word was out on the underground buzz—Toney was one of the very few men that the cases might apply to, and everyone hoped that he'd found a loophole, thus opening doors for other deserving convicts to follow.

Toney sat at his cell door at 7:30 a.m. work call, when all the other inmates passed by and wished him luck. He held a proud smile that hardly ever crossed one's face at Lewisburg, but every inmate knew it was rare when the government ruled in favor of inmates, so today, a smile was almost mandatory if you fit the bill.

"Inmate Toney Domacio, number 11262-056, report to visitation."

Toney stood, tucked his shirt back neatly over his slightly protruding belly, and gave his soldiers firm handshakes.

"Good luck, Toney," one said. "Find out all you can."

"My lawyers are the best money can buy! If this case can help me, I'm gonna get back in court. I'm gonna open a floodgate for a lot of cases," he replied.

Toney was led into the visiting room. This day wasn't a regular inmate visitation day; it was a Tuesday, and today,

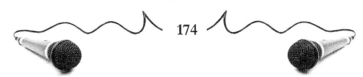

Toney would be led into the smaller, private room where attorneys met with inmates. He walked in the door, and his two lawyers immediately ordered the guards to uncuff him and dismiss themselves from the room.

Toney smiled proudly at the gesture of power. The visit was real, the Booker and Fanfan cases were real, but the two men left in the room with Toney weren't criminal defense attorneys; they were United States prosecutors, and here to seek Toney's cooperation in a highly-anticipated criminal case.

"Mr. Domacio, I'm Jason Dawkins." He reached over to shake Toney's hand. "I head the U.S. Attorney's Office in New Orleans."

Toney returned the gesture and looked at David Altman, who needed no introduction; Toney recognized him as New York's U.S. Attorney.

"Sit down, Mr. Domacio, or may I call you Toney?" Dawkins began as he crossed his legs and reclined in his chair. "Make yourself comfortable and tell me what it is you think we'd be interested in knowing."

Toney sat down and got straight to the point with a dead serious stare. "Listen, Mr. Dawkins. I didn't call you here for bullshit or your long, drawn-out interrogations! What I have is what your resources can't seem to get!"

"And what might that be?" Altman snapped.

"Altman, I've dealt with you for years!"

"That's right, Toney. And you played both sides of the fence. Face it, your time was up and Pazzo just beat you to the punch." The prosecutor snickered.

"Yeah, well now the ball is in my court! I'm no dummy. We're gonna play my way, or we don't play at all!"

"Tell us what it is that you want," Dawkins said, interceding to head off any confrontation.

"I want my sentence vacated! I want immediate release, and I want an agreement in writing signed by all parties granting immunity to the person who helped me on the outside!"

Altman chuckled at Toney's request. "You're asking a lot, and you've told us nothing."

Toney grinned confidently. "You want something? How about I can give you Red Rum on a fucking platter!"

"Red Rum?" Dawkins blurted with desperation in his voice.

"That's right, Red Rum, and I don't mean a few artists and a few trumped up charges. I mean solid, fool-proof convictions starting with the head—Wiz!"

Dawkins sat straight up in his chair. He was at full attention and jittering involuntarily. It was as if Wiz's name alone made his entire ass itch. "How are you gonna do that? I mean, how can you assure us it"s solid?"

Altman still wasn't moved. "Toney, you're asking for a lot just to help build this case."

"A lot? I haven't asked for enough! What I have to give will send Red Rum crashing! I know where the murder weapon is that was used to kill a rival gangster rapper named Fatt Katt. I know the whereabouts of two other undiscovered bodies and the weapon that killed them. I have audio tapes, pictures, and hidden bank accounts. I have proof that the label deals in ecstasy pills, working with the Velasquez Organization. I got it all!" Toney yelled.

"Bullshit! How you gonna deliver on that?" Altman asked.

"What"s bullshit is, you got a bunch a black gangsters posing as some kind of music artists. They seem to have a license to sell dope, not report revenue, and put out mob-style hits! Their black asses are worth well over $100,000,000 and growing! They employ new gangsters all the time. In fact, I know the head of security is Wiz's personal assassin."

"How do you know—"

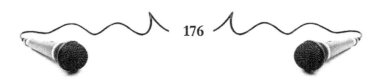

"I know what I know! And what I know now is solving Fatt Katt's murder would look good on your resume," Toney stated as he glared at Altman. "Taking down the seemingly untouchable Wiz would look good on Dawkin's resume, and bringing down Red Rum will look good to the government!"

The prosecutors pondered the possibilities. "I can try—"

"Ain't gonna be no goddamn trying! I'm Toney Domacio, and I know what can be done! This case involves DEA, FBI, ATF, and maybe even Customs on just the ecstasy! I know damn well you can cut a deal!"

Toney slammed his open palms on the table. "You have one week to draw it up. When I see the agreement, I'll use your cell right here, call my contact, and your contact can look over everything. If you can't do it, the deal is OFF!"

Toney was an excellent judge of character and knew the prosecutors had bit. "Oh, yeah, I almost forgot. The day you lock Wiz up, I want to be moved to protective custody. And when I'm released, I want witness protection as an option."

"An option? Witness pro—"

"This meeting is over! I've told you enough for now. Draw the papers up and contact my attorney."

Toney rose to leave, now confident that his plan had worked. He knocked on the door to gain the guard's attention, indicating his visitation had ended.

Toney was escorted from visitation and led back out on the compound. He still held a proud smile of hope on his face. Many inmates approached him with the same greeting and questions.

"Good luck, Toney."

"I heard you flew your lawyers in. What did they say about the case applying to us?"

"Who can it help? How much can we possibly give these bastards back?" They questioned Toney, who knew jack shit about the mechanics of the new cases, but pretended he did.

"I've thought about each and every one of you in this struggle," he lied. "My team of attorneys is drawing up a complete brief of the details, explicitly outlining our avenues. I should have it in seven to ten days, and I'm going to share it with everyone."

Toney sold hope and bought himself time in the same breath.

He shrugged off all the other questions and told everyone he needed time to think alone and to write his family about the good news.

Toney returned to his cell and closed the cell door. He stripped down to his boxers and lay back with his hands folded behind his head. There was no way he could remove the smile from his face as he stared at the ceiling.

He felt so fucking proud of what he imagined was the most ingenious plan anyone could've come up with to get out of prison. He even named the scheme, calling it 'A Life 4 A Life.' It had taken him over a decade to bring it to fruition, but he'd seen the greed in the prosecutor's face, and knew his day of freedom was approaching. After all, he had Damien anonymously provide fictitious tips to the Feds and Toney put the hit out on Fatt Katt, which was part of the final phase of his plan to bring down Red Rum and get him out of Lewisburg.

Reflecting back to how it all began, he remembered exhausting all of his appeals to no avail. The restless nights, the migraine headaches he got trying to devise a plan, whether it be a legal loophole or well-planned escape. He watched TV and kept up with the headlines and he saw exactly what the government targeted publicly.

Secretly, he hated the arrogant, flamboyant black race. He toyed with the imaginations of trading places with one just as

178

Vinny Pazzo had traded him out, and then the idea hit him like a ton of bricks—what better way than to build a target of his own? He'd enjoyed taking Drako in and befriending him. His complex, psychologically advanced mind overpowered Drako's and kept him in awe. He'd quickly realized that Drako was a power freak. He had the heart to kill, and he was loyal to anyone that showed genuine love to him.

Drako thought he was smart, but to Toney, he was so smart he was dumb—a 'smart-dumb nigga', as they call them. He listened to Drako sing along to rap music and read all the magazines about the business, and when Drako confided in him about Wiz struggling with an independent label, he helped him build one.

Toney couldn't help but laugh aloud. *I built Red Rum just to watch it fall! I'm the goddamn puppet master, even from here!*

He had surely played puppet master to both Drako and Damien right from his prison cell. "As long as you keep the greedy nigger broke, he'll do whatever it takes to get his own money," Toney remembered telling Damien about Drako. And now with Red Rum constantly feuding with Reality Records it was even more controversy in the public eye.

He brought Drako in with motive. He knew the day Drako fell under his wing was the day this whole setup began. *I'm a fuckin' genius, the best that's ever done it!* he thought as he noticed his erection, which had grown in the midst of his excitement. *It won't be long before I'll be using this again!*

He squeezed it and fell asleep, enjoying the most peaceful slumber he'd had in over ten years! Not once did the fate of Drako cross his mind.

Reality
Chapter - 29

After the black chauffeur-driven Town Car Drip was riding in came to a halt at the private airfield, it took only moments for him to spot the white Rolls Royce Silver Spur pull up close to the hangar and park.

"Gimme a second," he said with a huge smile. He didn't even wait for the chauffeur to open the door this time.

Before he had time to give another thought, he'd hopped out of the Town Car and was almost at the Rolls Royce's door. His smile bloomed even wider the moment he saw the Spur's door kick open and Save's shoe hit the pavement, just before he stood his full six foot frame on free land again.

"What tha'' fuck . . . man!" Drip's voice was full of excitement as he dapped Save up and they shared a short man hug.

"A yo', son . . . my bad . . . You know shit just happens," Save said sincerely as they broke their embrace. He glared at Drip and tossed his dreads back over his shoulders. "I felt threatened. The kid was all up in my space, then he sparked them bustas up to try and jump me, yo." He shook his head with a disgusted look in his eyes.

"I understand that some things just have to happen." Drip spoke with a nod of his own. "And like myself, you have to understand and go out of your way lots of times to avoid them." Drip's focus shifted to William, who was about to get out the Spur and head their way. He stepped a foot closer to Save with a stern look on his face and lowered his tone a bit.

"On some real shit. You're lucky." He sniffed with another sure nod. "Big Turk was hit pretty bad. He'll probably get off

180

with no more than a limp. Jay-Poon can live with his wounds as well. But the kid Barz? . . . You fucked over him pretty bad. He's now been moved from critical to stable condition, and the surgeons say he's gonna make it, but from my understanding you've got him being custom fit for a colostomy bag as we speak." Drip stared at Save as he awaited his response.

Save didn't utter a word. He just spit to the ground, sucked his teeth and gazed the other way. Drip didn"t see a drop of remorse in his eyes.

"So . . ." Drip spoke hesitantly. "What do you plan—"

"Look man"—Save cut in forcefully—"It's like this. His God forgives. This one don't! This God give a life, just like he take a life. Son was 'bout ta" do me. It was me or him. That's it, that's word, son." He huffed hot air from his nostrils, seeing William waltzing right up to them. "Next time maybe it'll be different. I „on know. Maybe that shit bag won"t be forever. I „on know. All I do know is they had a choice, they made it, and the God resolved it." He licked his lips and ran his hand across his dry mouth. "I got you though. Trust man, you can trust," he said in an assuring tone.

Just then, Drip gave a final nod and extended his hand to the attorney. "Thanks for springin' „im. We appreciate all."

William smiled proudly, accepting his shake. "I told you, it could all be fixed. Just give things time to play out." He turned to Save and laid a firm hand on his shoulder. "I made sure we're clearly understood on everything." Save's smile somewhat melted. He knew Mr. Oliver, or 'Will' as he told Save to call him, was referring to the contract he had to sign in order to get out.

"This kid is worth millions!" William said with a sneaky cackle and a strong pat to Save's shoulder. "You need to make sure you protect your investments." His hand slipped from Save's shoulder and so did the smile from his face.

He turned his focus back to Drip. "Anything you need I'm at your disposal." He passed Drip a card with his private number scripted on it. "My jet will have you guys back in Atlanta in just a few hours." He glanced up at the gold stripe on his white custom JetStream he'd arranged to get them back ASAP. "You delivered . . . now I'm delivering," he said, smiling again as he and everybody's attention was taken the moment Blondelle decided to step out of the car and come give Save a hug.

"Glad ta" have you back," she said with her beautiful white smile. "And this time you better stay out!" She playfully gave a shove to his chest as soon as she let him go.

"You can bet on that," he said, trying not to look her up and down in the tight, pussy pink, nearly transparent body suit she was wearing. "And that's the realest shit I ever spoke!" Save smiled, trying to keep his cool.

William shook his head, staring at Blondelle's cleavage. "Y"all get on out of here. I'll be around." He headed back over to his Rolls Royce and soon pulled away.

Save nodded again. He was glad to be out for certain. And he also knew 'Will' was the 'crooked' cream of the crop, and Reality Records had just tossed major gwap for his freedom. There was no doubt he was playing in the big leagues; he liked Drip's display of power, and he'd decided to play the game until its end.

"Yo son, I'm just happy to be the fuck up out that place. It is what it is wit' me. The God ready to get it in and make it all back. That's my word, son." He pounded a fist to his chest emphasizing his pledge.

"Just do what you do." Drip winked and gave him another pound, and then turned to Blondelle. "Let's get movin", baby. They'll grab your purse." He snaked an arm around her waist and smoothly nudged her toward the steps leading up to the jet.

"Okay baby." She leaned forward and kissed Drip on his lips. He popped her on the ass just as she sauntered away.

They both stared as Blondelle clicked away in her matching four-inch peep toe pumps and climbed the steps. She looked amazing and Save could no longer hold it in. He turned to Drip. "A yo, man . . . what the fuck does she have on?" He gazed her way again.

Drip smiled like a kid in the candy store thinking about the nearly painted on body suit and heels she wore. "Man I „on give a fuck! That's my lady, and if she like it you best believe I"ma learn to love it!" Drip's voice was filled with confidence again. "I went and found her, and this time I"ma finish what I started." He knew Blondelle was in love with him.

"Cool," Save said, watching the luggage handlers load the last of the luggage onto the plane. "That's all that matters. She's yours now and she make you happy."

"All mine." Drip made clear. "And if a nigga try to change it, that'll be the realest shit I ever spoke." They exchanged that knowing smile and stepped toward the plane.

"Let's get to ATL, get you cleaned up and back in that booth."We'll talk business later," Drip said, feeling just as happy as Save felt at the moment he sniffed freedom again. They boarded the jet with nothing but high hopes for their futures at Reality Records.

Neither of them had a clue that in just a few days there could be something so evil lurking, that it could crush Reality Records and make Save's problems look like peanuts!

Myria
Chapter - 30

Myria lay in Damien's bed, trying to steady her nerves. She had spent the better part of an hour trying to figure out Damien's motive. She checked the caller ID for suspicious calls, or maybe even Bless' number. All she found were incoming calls that mostly read 'out of area.' Myria often recalled Damien pressing the select key to accept the charges and figured most of the 'out of area' calls were from his friend in prison. Trying to place a name with the conversations she had overheard, she recalled Damien saying Toney.

But Myria still couldn't put it together. As she continued to ponder over her assumptions, the thought of something happening to Wiz began to weigh heavier and heavier on her conscience. She thought about the mysterious Drako; she knew he'd been in prison. He was street savvy and above all, real! Maybe if she could talk to Drako just once more, she could alert him to Damien's dealings.

For a brief moment, her mind replayed the images of the bloody knife, the pictures and audiotapes. She remembered all the ecstasy pills, the guns, and the money. She became even more nervous, realizing that this was entirely too much, and she wanted no part.

"Drako can get the word to Wiz," she reasoned aloud.

The last place she saw Drako was in the parking lot of an office building in downtown ATL. Myria never forgot the grateful feelings she felt when she'd gotten home and realized there was nearly twenty grand in that bag of money he had given her.

Drako had told her not to come back, and she respected his wishes, but Myria knew Drako was doing something in that building. She had passed it several nights on her way to bartend at the strip club. She had observed his cars and Diamond's red Lexus a few times and there was always lots of activity going on. Yes, she had respected Drako's wishes. Until now!

Myria jumped out of bed in hopes of going there and catching him at the mysterious building. It was time to get clarity, and Drako was the only person affiliated with Red Rum who might listen.

She packed an overnight bag and slid into the tight, cheesy L.A. Lakers jersey dress Damien bought her. Quickly, she splashed water on her face and brushed her teeth while trying to ignore the image of her now tainted reflection in Damien's mirror for the last time.

Myria then left Damien's house without even locking the door. She jumped in her Honda and prayed to God that she would find Drako, and even more that he'd listen to her.

*****

Today, Drako and Diamond were the only two to occupy the walls inside of Reality Records. Save had been released two days ago, and Drip had texted Drako their plans and the camp was right back to work. They were now all on the tour bus headed to Memphis, Tennessee to do a concert at the FedEx Forum. From there, they were set for Little Rock, Arkansas.

Drako had every reason to have his feet kicked up on his desk with things now moving in the direction they were. Just moments earlier, he'd gotten off the phone with the automated customer service to his offshore account. And with the nearly $4,000,000 his last wire fraud scheme netted, now placed on top of the $4,950,000 that was already there. Drako had an astonishing balance of $8,850,000 in that one account. Drip had bounced the $2.5 million from the account he'd stashed Pazzo's money in, with ease. Drako knew he'd made good use of it springing Save from jail and it finally came in handy.

He looked over at Diamond who was leaned over, peering through the glass of the huge 200-gallon salt water aquarium she'd had put in his office. She wore another pair of those juicy sweat pants he liked to see her ass in so much. Tomorrow they were to round out their guest list and send out all the invitations. The wedding ceremony was set to take place in Miami at Wiz's waterfront mansion.

Drako nodded his head appreciatively and rolled his chair back. Because right now he was about to have kinky, rough sex with Diamond on top of his desk. That was one of the things he loved most; even after all this time, they constantly switched up, trying new and wild things. Her flexibility kept their love and sex life fresh and his eyes only for her.

"Come here, boo," he called out in a husky tone.

She looked back over her shoulder and smiled. She saw that mischievous look on his face and knew just what he had in mind. She smacked her tongue and stood up with a hand on her hip. "You so durn nasty." She smiled, bit down on her bottom lip and strutted toward him with her nipples already straining against the fabric.

The thought of sinning and winning at the same time was the motivation behind Drako's smile as Diamond stepped close enough to cradle her soft ass cheeks through the thin fabric with both hands.

This time Drako was totally oblivious; he didn't get a chance to peep any marked cards. Toney was now the unseen dealer and had done his best to deal Drako the silent hand of death!

*****

Today Wiz was locked inside his master suite all by himself. He used a walker to help him get around as he began to

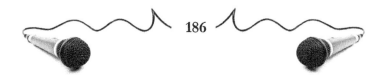

186

convalesce himself back to health. A few hours ago, he'd opened the doors to his balcony and let the warm breeze in.

He'd now been sitting in front of his secret cabinet reflecting back on his fast life. In lots of ways he felt terrible about the choices he'd made. And so many things Drako said to him in that hospital bed rang much clearer now. Wiz had hours and hours of footage he was destroying. No one ever knew that Wiz had the best covert cameras money could buy installed in every bedroom in his mansion. He had footage of Swirl, Damien, himself and anybody else who'd ever had a romp on the estate. It no longer felt slick to him. He realized it wasn't cool. It was calculated and conniving. He watched on and saw how not only did the ecstasy pills take over his libido, they also took over his mind. The things Wiz had the women do to him, each other, or whomever he invited to share his bed was often totally degrading.

He also realized when he leaked the sex tape it was just in a fit of rage. He'd been geeked up on X for three whole days, and the powerful drug just intensified his hate and jealousy for something that didn't even exist. He made up his mind to destroy the footage and never use the cameras again unless by consent.

Yep, looking back over his life he'd made several dumb and rash decisions. And staring at Myria's beautiful, sexy, bare body on the screen he knew tossing the black ball card at her had been his biggest mistake of all!

All the other women fucked the mogul well, but Myria made love with him. She was by far the best. She was the sincerest, and Wiz now regretted it. He thought about all the women he went after just because they resembled Myria. But still, none turned out to be anything close to her, and now he realized just how long his brain had been fried.

There would be no more Myria in his life, just like there would be no more X-pills or bad choices. This time he'd stick it out. He'd take on a twelve-step program to kick it if he had to, and this time him and Drako would remain closer than ever.

Wiz watched the screen as something pricked his attention, badly! Shortly after Myria had gotten out of a bed in one of his guest rooms, he saw Damien come into view. Damien's face had a terribly suspicious look. He glanced right, then left, then he peeled the covers back and sniffed at the mattress like a wild blood hound searching for the spot where Myria had just lain. He did it for a long moment and when he was done and stood with his hand stuffed down the front of his slacks. He was surely masturbating.

Wiz began to speed through more and more footage, now searching for Damien. He soon spotted him come into view again. This time Damien laid his briefcase on the bed as he peered around suspiciously. When he popped the briefcase, Wiz's mouth dropped wide open. Damien slipped on a pair of latex gloves then retrieved two large Ziploc bags filled with x-pills and sat them aside. Next, he held up another plastic bag, but this one held a semi-automatic handgun!

Damien slipped off his shoes, removed the lamp from the nightstand and pushed it over a couple of feet before he climbed on top of it and removed the screwdriver from his pocket. Wiz watched the footage a few more minutes before he added it to the pile to destroy, and then made his way downstairs as quickly as he could.

*****

"Just yank the damn thing down!" Wiz huffed, looking up as Swirl stood on the same nightstand and was trying to unscrew the bolts from the vent.

"Just gimme a minute; if somethin" was there it'll still be here." Swirl tried to keep things cool.

A moment later, the grate was off. Swirl reached inside with a handkerchief and pulled out a loaded .44 caliber semi-automatic Smith and Wesson. He laid it down carefully on the nightstand, and then retrieved both bags of pills.

Wiz nodded his head presumptuously. "Son of a bitch!" His voice trailed in disbelief, but this time he wouldn't make any bad or rash decisions. He was gonna take this news to Drako and not over the phone. "Get Corwin on the line. I want an emergency charter to Atlanta."

He glanced his watch. "We can have feet on the ground in an hour and a half!" He nodded.

"Tell 'im he better make it happen!" Wiz turned away, dialing Drako's number.

Myria
Chapter - 31

Myria could feel the slippery sweat her nervous palms left on the steering wheel as she whisked her Honda through the busy lunch hour traffic.

From the moment she'd left Damien's house, she'd thought about what she'd do if Drako decided not to listen to her. She considered just driving away from it all, but quickly realized that neither her curiosity nor her conscience would allow her that option.

When Myria turned down Forsyth, the butterflies began to flutter even worse from anticipation. She spotted the snow-white BMW parked beside a fire red Lexus Coupe. *Fuck it! Talkin' to Drako's the only hope I have left. I ain't got nothin' left to lose!* She steered into the lot and quickly parked.

She went into her overnight bag and retrieved the items she'd stolen from Damien before exiting the car and making her way to the front door. Readjusting the tight fitted dress and eyeing her reflection in the glass door, she tried to rake her out of control hair back in place. She then gathered her last bit of composure and began ringing the bell.

*****

Diamond straddled Drako's lap and he couldn't resist her sensual touches. He'd just successfully rid her of her halter-top when he heard his doorbell.

"Dammit!" he huffed, letting her tittie plop from his mouth. Diamond sighed as she hopped up on the desk. Drako pecked her lips and assured her that whoever it was he'd be right back.

Approximately fifty paces later, Drako had adjusted his erection as best he could to keep it from showing through his sweats. He had just turned down the corridor leading to the front entrance when he recognized the last person he thought he'd ever see ringing the bell at Reality Records.

A feeling of pure annoyance overcame him as he got closer to the door. He looked at Myria wearing a knockoff jersey dress that had to be two sizes too small. He could clearly see that her figure was still intact, but the short, cheap ensemble showed no hint of class compared to the Myria he once knew. Her hair and the look on her face made her look more like hot trash as he got closer to the door.

Drako further realized that he'd made a mistake by giving her money, and she damn sure wasn't about to become a stray cat around Reality Records. He knew it was time to nip Myria's ass in the bud before Diamond nipped it her way.

The anger on his face was evident as he unlocked the door. He didn't give her time to speak. "Didn't I tell you not to come back? You gon" make Diamond whip some sense into yo' hard-headed ass?"

"No, wait Drako! It's about Wiz! Somethin' ain't right. I got somethin'. . ."

"Why you tellin' me? This ain't no goddamn clinic, and I ain't no fuckin' doctor! Look at yourself! You ain't listen to a fuckin' word I told you. Myria, this is the last time I'ma—"

"Is that what the hell y'all think of me now? I ain't got nothin' like that! This is what I found, dammit!" Myria shouted as she unfolded the paper and quickly held the two pictures up for Drako to see as his harsh words made tears slip down her cheeks.

Complete confusion overcame Drako as he recognized himself in his BMW and Diamond handing him an envelope.

He snatched the pictures with one hand and Myria with the other.

"Where the fuck did you get this?" he asked hard enough to make Myria tremble at the tight grip he had on her arm.

"Damien, Drako, Damien!"

"Damien?"

"Yes, Damien!" she blurted as even more tears and confusion soaked her face.

Drako paused, not wanting to believe the thoughts resonating in his mind.

"Drako, I heard every word you told me. I shouldn't have gotten with Damien, but that's over now. I need you to listen to me. I don"t know exactly what's going on, but I think Damien tipped Bless to Wiz doing them bootlegs."

"What the fuck are you talking about?" Drako barked, not realizing his grip had gotten even tighter as he pulled her inside and pinned her small body against the wall.

"What do you think of this, Drako?" she asked, shoving him the papers with Bless' cell number and the list of sequenced numbers she'd jotted down.

Drako released his grip as he took the papers and studied them. It only took a second for jolts of hot flashes to shoot through his body. It spooked him to see all of his old fictitious bank account numbers staring back at him. Immediately, he recognized the number to his offshore account, which Damien wasn't even supposed to know about.

Drako didn't give Myria an answer as he continued to look over the paper and pictures. Myria continued on with caution.

"Drako, I heard Damien on the telephone saying things that I thought weren't right, so when he left this morning, I started to go through his things. He had a briefcase with stacks of pictures of that white girl you creeping with. There was a bloody hunting knife and a lot of other suspicious things."

192

Myria realized she had gained Drako's full attention as he stared directly into her eyes and demanded to know all she'd seen and heard.

She started from the top with the overheard telephone conversations, all the way to what she found inside of Damien's study. Drako never stopped her once as she recounted everything. He was so hurt from the betrayal and infiltration that a single tear of anger slipped from his eye.

From all the information he'd just gathered, Drako knew that Toney must have had some knowledge of Damien's actions. Drako no longer possessed the ability to mask his emotions. He held his gaze to the floor as disappointment wracked his brain like never before.

Myria continued babbling about telling Wiz that it was never her that crossed him. Drako barely paid any attention to her small thoughts; he realized that Myria was blind to the true picture. She had no idea as to the impact that this information had on him. He never thought that she would ever be the bearer of news that could turn his life and the lives of everyone he loved upside down!

All the happiness he was enjoying just moments ago had instantly vanished. All the love and trust he held in his heart for Toney was now hate! It was hard to even fathom Toney having a motive or harboring any ill will, but either way, the unwritten rule of the game applied—Toney had sent Damien, so Toney was now responsible and should be held accountable for Damien's actions.

Myria picked up on the angry, perplexed look on Drako's face. She knew there was more to what she'd found. She slowly reached out and held his arm in a comforting manner as she attempted to seek closure.

"Drako, please tell me what's really goin' on. I promise you can trust me."

Drako was looking down in Myria's face from the moment she held his arm. The lie he was about to pacify Myria with was abruptly cut short, when Drako heard Diamond's voice.

"What the hell is this? I know this dirty ass bitch ain't had the nerve to come up in here!" Diamond's small nostrils flared with disgust as she approached.

Drako knew that Diamond misinterpreted the situation.

"Hold up, ma. It ain't what you think." He turned and stepped into Diamond's path.

Myria quickly did her best to get out of harm's way as she stepped behind Drako. Drako caught Diamond by her arm and shoved the two pictures right up to her face.

"Someone is tryin' to tag me or Wiz, and Myria brought it to my attention!"

"Somebody what!" Diamond gasped, recognizing her image in the photo, dressed in the white girl costume. Her hands covered her mouth in disbelief. "What the hell is going on?" she asked again, feeling like she was near fainting.

"I ,,on really know yet, but I'ma figure it out. Right now, all I know is Myria is here to help, and I think you need to be listening!"

Diamond looked at him and Myria, and then held the picture in her hand. She was trying to stop the room from spinning.

"Do you know her?" Myria asked her.

"I-I know that's our car," Diamond managed to stutter out a lie.

Drako knew he had to quickly gather his composure and try to make a move himself. He interrupted in an effort to steer Myria away from asking the wrong questions and to gain her confidence.

"It's gon' be okay, ma," he first stated to Diamond, and then turned to Myria. "Myria, we need to talk. I want you to tell

Diamond what you know, and we need to find a way to save Wiz and tell him that you never tried to hurt him."

"Save him from what?" Her face squinted with a look that was totally baffled.

Drako was at a loss for a solid explanation, but he knew Myria's focus was on the bootleg, and she was too naive to see the rest of Damien's scheme.

"Myria, it's some things about Dame and Wiz you don't understand. Dame is tryin' to secretly harm Wiz, based on false pretenses. I'm sure."

Myria's eyes sparked with interest.

Drako didn't give her a chance to respond. "We'll all have to try and figure this out, then fix things, and we need to come together and do it fast! I'm glad you made the right decision and brought this to me. I want you to stay with us 'til I make things right."

Myria watched Drako's dark eyes as he spoke. She could still feel the mysterious energy radiating off him that first made her confide in him, and now she wanted to trust in his words so badly. She happily agreed to stay and vowed she'd help to save Wiz's name in any way.

Drako held Diamond's trembling hand on his left side and held Myria around her shoulder and guided them to his office.

"Make yourself comfortable," he suggested to her as he held the office door open to let her in. "Diamond, unlock the safe," he said next, sending Diamond into another room in the building.

After seeing Myria seated comfortably, he promptly caught up with Diamond in the other room. Her face was already soaked with tears as he assumed they'd be the moment they were alone.

"Baby, this ain't no time to cry, okay? I need you to help me think." He held her in an effort to console her. "Damien is up to some shiesty shit, but I'll die before I let that rat get away with it!"

Diamond sniffled as she looked up at Drako. "How could this happen? You „on know what else he might have! Our wedding is a fuckin' fairy tale, and I'm the one going back to prison dammit!"

Drako knew how Diamond felt; he knew that neither of them thought that someone trailing them was even a possibility. "I'ma catch Damien and I'ma—"

"Damien?" She snatched away from his embrace. "He ain't the only one! You know damn well Damien ain't gone make a move without Toney knowing about it! Why hasn't he opened his mouth to tell you Damien's no longer any good?" She folded her arms across her chest, awaiting Drako's response.

Drako dropped his gaze to the floor, defeated. He and his woman had that mutual gut feeling. The thought of Toney's betrayal crushed Drako's heart and hurt more and more as he watched Diamond cry over the thought of losing all she'd ever had.

"Listen, ma. I hold Toney responsible too, but right now I can't touch him—I have to start with Damien, and Myria is all we got right now."

He held Diamond's chin up to look in her eyes. "Get yourself together and let's try to clean this up. I ain't lettin' you go back to prison—I'd rather die first!"

"Let's just clean the account out and go, baby," Diamond suggested.

"Diamond, there are other things you need to hear. I think we could stop Damien if I figure out a way to catch him right. Ain't nobody moved on us yet, so we may have a small window. We have to be patient. Myria is only worried about Wiz. She can't see nothin' else. Just help me play her for all I can. Her nosiness may be what saves our lives or at least gives us the opportunity to vanish."

Diamond nodded as she tried to compose herself. In a few minutes, Drako had cleaned her face and calmed her down, and they rejoined Myria in his office.

Drako began with confessing to Diamond that it was Myria he was speaking with the night she'd pulled up and saw the female pulling away. He told her that he had always believed that Myria was innocent, and about all of the attributes he realized Myria embodied after they'd spoken. He admitted these things in an effort to create a comfort zone between the women and to make Myria more relaxed so that she could speak and think clearly.

He listened attentively as Myria replayed the whole story for Diamond. He had hoped that her words were on point. She recalled Damien saying that it would be another week before things went public, and that everything was in his possession. All Drako needed now was to figure out a way to catch up with him.

Drako continued to comfort Myria as he silently pondered a way to stop Damien in his tracks. He had listened as she described the hunting knife, and he knew for sure it had to be the knife he'd used to kill the Pazzos. He never imagined that Damien would double back and pull the knife from Mrs. Pazzo's corpse.

Drako sat on the couch in a trance as he realized that Damien possessed the resources to cage Diamond up, implicate Wiz, and send him headfirst into the gas chamber!

The vibration of his cell phone brought him out of his meditation. He saw the hope in Myria's eyes; she must've thought it was Wiz. Drako knew it probably was; he'd ignored several of his calls, because now wasn't a good time. He wanted to try and get at Damien first.

Drako got his cell phone, glanced at the caller ID. It was certainly not Wiz; it read 'out of area.' Drako knew it had to be Toney; he hadn't phoned in a couple of weeks, and a talk was overdue.

Phony, cruddy bastard! Drako thought to himself, but he decided not to reveal his hand to Toney until he caught up with Damien. He tried his best to hold his anger in check as he paced the floor.

"You gonna answer it, Drako?" Myria asked.

"It's Domacio," Drako stated to Diamond, ignoring Myria altogether. Diamond nodded and instructed Myria to stay quiet as Drako took the call.

The automated prison call came through, and when the machine instructed the inmate to say his name, Drako heard Deuce's voice boom through the line. Relieved, he accepted the charges and excused himself from the office.

"What's good, homie?" Deuce asked happily.

"Looks like I gotta keep it movin', blood. Ain't nothin' good 'round here, not even a diamond." Drako briefly paused to take a deep breath. "One of our own switched teams, so I may have to switch coasts (I'm about to be on the run, and Diamond has been implicated too. Someone close to me has turned into an informant.)."

"What!" Deuce huffed angrily after easily deciphering Drako's words.

Drako continued to confide to Deuce in code as best he could. He always felt Deuce's true gangsta, which compelled him to elaborate further. He vented with full emotion, and Deuce felt the anger and pain in every word. Not once in all the years of Drako's incarceration had Deuce heard Drako speak with such rage. Deuce knew that Drako was doing his best not to break down.

198

As Drako went on, it didn't take long for Deuce to figure out that the informant was Toney.

"Enough said, lil homie! Them fools oughta" realize what goes around comes around! All I'm tellin' you is keep it movin' if ya wanna keep ya head above water, feel me?"

"I feel ya, blood. Just keep it to ya self and stay real."

"Always, fool, always!"

They ended the call after Drako told Deuce he was going to chip his inmate account up in a big way. They both knew that Drako would surely hold court in the streets before he would return to prison. This time, the two gangsters said their goodbyes with lumps of sorrow in their throats, because they both knew the code of the streets, and this would probably be the last time they would speak.

Drako fought as hard as he could to conceal the death in his eyes when he re-entered his office and saw Myria and Diamond babbling on about Wiz and Damien.

Myria tried to offer more help. "I could go back and lay up for a few more days. I could gather more information or maybe try and get him to tell me something," she offered.

He heard the sincerity in Myria's voice. He realized he'd sold her on the idea that Wiz was the focus of all this. Her last ironic suggestion matched his revengeful thought pattern. He pulled a chair up right in front of hers. "Nah, Myria. I'm gon' be the nigga waitin' on Damien when he returns."

Myria smiled, misconstruing his remark as a suggestion rather than the pain-stricken fact that it would have become had she not complied.

She began to listen as Drako convinced her that it was best that he talk to Damien, and as soon as possible. He began asking her for a detailed synopsis of his house. Myria eagerly complied and gave Drako directions.

He picked up Myria's car keys and told them that he'd be driving her Honda back, so that Damien wouldn't suspect anything out of the ordinary. "I'ma fix this shit, ma, and Myria, you gon' be a"ight. After Damien hears what I have to say, all of our problems will go away." He further instructed Myria to get as comfortable as she liked. He nodded for Diamond to follow him as he went back into the other room that held the closet safe. This time Drako opened up the safe, allowing him full access to a small arsenal of handguns.

She watched as he slipped his shoulder holster over his white T-shirt before securing the plastic Glock .40 into it. He reached back into the safe and retrieved a nine-millimeter Ruger.

Diamond saw the promise of death in her man's eyes as he gave her a final nod of approval before he stuffed the Ruger into his waistline.

"Baby, I'm scared!" she confessed as she watched him put on his butter leather coat to conceal the guns.

"Come on, ma, I got this, a"ight? Come here." He held her and they locked eyes. "If we run, the problem still gonna be chasin' us. I gotta do it this way. I'ma stay rich, and I ain't gonna die tryin'."

Diamond gave no response because she knew there were no words to change his mind, nor was there any other solution to the problem.

"I'ma call you back and keep you posted. All I need you to do is make sure Myria don't leave until I get back. Can you handle that?"

"I got my end; you just do what it takes and get back."

"Just believe in me, baby," he replied as he quickly grabbed four extra clips from the safe. He shoved the loaded clips into his pockets before rushing Diamond back to the office.

Before leaving, he reassured the girls that everything would soon be okay. Diamond handed him his cell phone,

emphasizing that she'd be standing by. He kissed her soft lips once more, assured her of the call back, and headed for Myria's Honda Accord.

By the time Drako pulled the small Honda back onto Forsyth Street, his blackened heart was filled with the hope that Myria had been Damien's one false move. He knew with certainty that if he was one-step ahead, Damien's ass was dead.

Drako

Chapter - 32

Twenty minutes later, Drako had easily located the modest neighborhood. He'd turned onto Damien's street with caution, and then quickly absorbed the first feeling of close redemption when he didn't spot Damien's SUV in the driveway.

Drako parked in front of the right port of the two-car garage, just as Myria had told him she did. He peeked through the windows of the garage to make sure it was empty before he approached the front door. He found it unlocked just as Myria said she'd left it.

Casually, Drako entered the home, gently closing the door behind him as if he'd lived there for years. Yet, the second he locked the door, he pulled the black Ruger from his waist and held it firmly in his right hand. His back was flushed against each wall as he combed the entire home for anything in human form.

After concluding nobody was home, he proceeded with his mission and retraced his steps back to the master bedroom. Everything in there was just as Myria described. He turned and looked at the adjacent room. He saw a couch with a glass table in front of it, an office desk and chair on the far wall with a mini bar and large file cabinets, confirming that this was Damien's private study.

He wasted no time moving to the nightstand where Myria said she'd returned the spare keys fitting the desk drawer.

"Bingo!" Drako sang as he picked up the two small keys. Drako could feel the happiness all attributed to his vantage point: being one step ahead of Damien. "I got yo' bitch ass now."

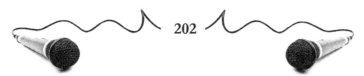

Drako's first thought was to go straight to the desk drawer. *Nah, nah, slow down gangsta"*, his better judgment encouraged. So far, everything that Myria said had checked out, but he still felt that she was naive, and he couldn't underestimate Damien's return based on her shallow presumptions.

He slowed as he spotted a small stereo system in the room. He turned the CD player on and adjusted the volume to a modest pitch. His next move was to turn on the shower and leave the bathroom door slightly ajar. He added these safety precautions as a ploy, just in case his ambush took place in the bedroom. After feeling more in control, he moved on course to Damien's study.

The weight of curiosity sent him straight to the desk drawer. He pushed the key inside, and immediately heard the clicking sound as it unlocked the drawer. He pulled the deep drawer open and saw two large Ziploc bags filled with ecstasy pills. The drugs didn't concern him though; he pulled out the black briefcase underneath and carefully placed it on top of the desk.

Using both thumbs, he simultaneously snapped the automatic locks. He inhaled sharply as he braced himself to see what his mind had fought to conjure ever since he'd visualized all Myria had told him.

Anger immediately washed over his body at the first sight. Right before his eyes was the hunting knife he'd handled so fiercely when he'd sliced Vinny Pazzo's throat. The hope he'd once held somewhere in the back of his mind that Myria could've been wrong had just been crushed!

Moving the knife aside, he was even more shocked at the hoard of pictures piled in the briefcase. He began sifting through them and saw himself parked in Harper's restaurant parking lot on the day he got Diamond from the cab after she escaped the authorities at Hertz. He saw another picture of Diamond getting out of the cab and into his BMW.

Drako spotted her in at least twenty pictures. He also saw several snapshots of Wiz and Damien's so-called ecstasy dealing friend socializing. All the pictures were clearly taken from covert surveillance angles.

"Dirty, snitchin" mothafucker!" Drako huffed, shoving the pictures back into the briefcase and picking up a stack of papers held together by a single paperclip.

He whisked through the entire stack. He saw bank account numbers, his old cell numbers, and updated numbers belonging to both him and Wiz. Then he saw a hand drawn map, and upon further study, he realized the map was to Wiz's mansion.

Drako had subconsciously lost track of time as the reality of Damien's intentions captured him. His mind raced with curiosity as to what was recorded on the audiotapes lying in the briefcase.

Drako knew that assumptions were one thing, but this case was much more than just a paper trail leading up to circumstantial evidence—it was a certain life (if not death) sentence for him!

There was only one solution for Damien. The picture being painted in Drako's mind left no room for remorse, snitches, or potential witnesses! He decided to camp out and wait on Damien for now. He closed the briefcase and went into the closet where Myria said she'd found the gym bags. He dragged them out and examined the contents: the cash, the guns and the electronics. He picked up the bags and carried them to the desk with the briefcase. Then he sat in Damien's chair as he further contemplated the best way to ambush him and the best way to get rid of Myria. He didn't want to have to do her in, but he had no choice. She knew too much.

He settled on an idea. As soon as Damien came in the door and waltzed into his bedroom, he was going to catch two to the

dome! No need for words or wasted opportunities to beg for his life while offering up pathetic excuses.

Drako stood back up, hoisted two bags over his left shoulder, and the bag of cash over his right shoulder. He firmly gripped the Ruger in his right hand and the briefcase in the left as he proceeded to move his attack post into the living room.

He was approaching the hallway leading back to the front entrance when he heard the garage door opening.

Drako raced back to the master bedroom, his heart pounding with anticipation. He realized quickly there was no place to hide in there. Then he remembered the closet in the study that he'd just come out of. With the speed of an Olympian, Drako ran straight in, briefcase, money and all, and closed the doors behind him. He kneeled and grew still as he waited for his mark to appear.

*****

A few moments earlier, Damien was relishing one of the best days he'd had in a while. He was steering the rented black Yukon into his modest community as he concluded his call with Toney.

"Well, I suggest you get all the rest you can. I'm sure that in a few weeks, Red Rum is gonna take you to places you've always dreamed of. Their controversy has freedom written all over it!"

They both chuckled before ending the call as Damien turned on his street. He smiled when he saw Myria's Honda still parked in the driveway. The thought of finally conquering Myria's heart and having constant access to her Grade A pussy filled him with joy.

Pressing the remote, he opted to pull the SUV inside the garage. He was horny as all hell and planned to spend the next few hours butt naked on top of Myria. He pulled in and hit the switch once more to close the garage door while leaning over to retrieve the briefcase lying on the passenger seat. After exiting the Yukon, he entered his home once again.

The first room Damien came to was the kitchen, where he hoped he'd find Myria preparing a romantic dinner for the two of them. He felt a twinge of disappointment when he saw the room was empty and headed on to the bedroom, where he could hear the sound of Myria's Jill Scott CD softly playing as he neared.

When he reached the room, his disappointment vanished; the bed wasn't made yet, so he figured Myria's only plans were to get back in it. He also heard the shower running.

His smile grew larger as he set the briefcase down, preparing to strip and join her. *Better yet, let me add a little spice to make sure everything's right.* Picking the briefcase back up, he waltzed out of the room and into his study to the bar.

Drako watched Damien enter the room. He went straight to his bar, where he sat his briefcase down and grabbed one of the many bottles of liquor. He reached for a shot glass, and then retrieved a canister of ice from the small freezer and dropped two cubes in the glass before he poured his first double shot of what appeared to be Hennessy.

Drako slowly stood from his crouched position, certain that Damien was oblivious to his presence.

Damien turned the shot glass up and emptied its contents in a single gulp. He quickly refilled the glass, smirking all the while, without any idea how close he was to death.

Drako gripped the Ruger tighter as he saw Damien turn to open the briefcase. He watched him pull a small pill bottle out and twist the cap off. After popping two pills into his mouth, he chased them down with his second shot.

"Ahh," he grunted with satisfaction. "I'm gonna wear some black pussy out tonight!"

Drako took note of Damien for what he knew would be the last time as Damien milled around the small area of the mini bar. The mere smile that Damien held was now irritating Drako. He thought back to the day he first met him; the neatly trimmed hair that always stayed slicked back, the tailored linen suits and fine jewels, his eloquent speaking voice and demeanor. Drako realized that it was all part of Damien's deceitful nature; his slicked back hair now made him resemble a human rat—a rat he was about to exterminate.

He watched as Damien returned what had to be Viagra pills to the briefcase, and then secured it. *Burn this trash and keep it movin'*, Drako's voice of reason told him as Damien turned his back to him. All he had to do was open the doors and take the shot.

But in the flash of the next second, that window of opportunity closed. Damien was again facing Drako with another irritating smirk, as he seemed be be fondling himself through his linen pants. *Hell, no! Shootin' this bitch ain't good enough! He thought Mrs. Pazzo was somethin' . . . I'ma make sure this mothafucka feel me!*

Just then, Damien turned and walked over to his office desk. He pulled the large ring of keys from his pocket.

Drako thought, *This is it . . .*

*****

When Damien unlocked the drawer in search of the ecstasy pills, his whole body went numb! He too felt jolts of hot flashes; every nerve in his body stood at high alert. *What the fuck? She took the briefcase!* It felt as if hot ants were crawling all over him as he gasped in confusion. He clumsily stumbled forward, leaning into the drawer as if he could reach deeper and make the briefcase reappear like a magician. His natural instincts made him pull the small, two-shot .357 Derringer that he kept concealed in his front pocket.

"Myria! Myria!" Damien shouted his first thought.

*****

At that moment, Drako dropped the briefcase with a thud and burst through the closet doors. He made four quick steps and leaped over the couch with the Ruger in his right hand and the promise of death in his eyes.

Damien quickly turned around, his eyes widened with fear. He let out a horrific scream of terror, gasping at the scariest sight he'd ever seen: Drako was leaping over the couch; his arms spread wide like an angel of death swooping down upon him. His trembling legs gave way to the fear that now controlled his body. He closed his eyes and nervously squeezed the trigger, collapsing to the floor and dropping the gun in the process.

*****

As soon as Drako's feet hit the ground, he realized that Damien was holding a small Derringer. Drako raised his Ruger to fire at Damien when something with incredible force slammed into his abdomen.

The impact lifted Drako off his feet and twisted him into a backwards somersault, landing him back on the other side of the couch.

*****

Damien was still trembling as he quickly hopped back on his feet. He nervously swatted a hand to his chest and couldn't believe that he hadn't been hit. He had been a split second away from death, and somehow he was unscathed.

As his panic-filled eyes searched the room, he saw the gun Drako once held lying on the carpet. He dove in the gun's direction in desperation, fumbled with it nervously until he gripped the handle tightly.

Drako wailed out in agony as Damien extended the gun and strolled around the couch to see Drako face down, clutching

208

himself. He spotted the closet door standing open and the missing briefcase lying in plain view. He was instantly infuriated and he didn't have time to wonder how Drako found out. He was just glad that his lucky shot had put him back in control of the situation. Damien knew all too well that any man could lose; it was all about who squeezed first. And this time, he was the grand prize winner!

"Look at you now, you dumb ass nigger!" Damien yelled. "Turn yo" ass over and look at me!"

Drako only moaned as Damien watched him struggling to hold his wound.

"I said turn over, you bastard!" Damien shouted again.

Drako rolled over slightly on his side, but he did so silently. He had to know his death was assured, but he refused to beg for his life. This seemed to irk Damien even more.

Damien also knew that he hadn't consciously pulled the trigger; pure fear was what triggered it, and pure fear was what had saved his life. But could he just aim the gun and purposely kill Drako? He felt he had a point to prove, not just to Drako, but also to himself. He had ordered many murders, but not once had he had the courage to personally kill anyone.

He trotted over to the closet and picked up the briefcase. "Is this what you came for, you stupid fuck? Huh?"

Drako lay there wheezing and bleeding out.

"It was Myria, wasn't it? That fucking whore!" he stated furiously.

Still no response from Drako.

"Okay, Drako. Congratulations. I fucked up. I made the mistake of thinking with my dick. But you know something else?" He raised the Ruger and pointed it at Drako.

"I made an even bigger mistake by not killing you sooner! I should've had you killed instead of Fatt Katt!" Damien's laugh was sinister. He was doing all he could to get something out of Drako. But Drako still said nothing.

"Look at big bad ass Drako now? You shit talkin" punk! You ain"t so bad now, are you?"

Silence.

"You've accomplished nothing! Wiz is still going down! The gun that killed Fatt Katt is hidden in his mansion and believe me, the Feds won't have a problem finding it. You wanna know your problem? It's greed. All your dumb ass could see was the money, but me, I see power! Power and victory. I'm the winner! I am the best!" Damien taunted with a victorious smirk.

"Oh yeah, you do have one other flaw . . . that pretty bitch of yours. But you ain't gotta worry about her. She'll be in good hands . . . my hands!" He laughed again. "After I erase Myria, I'm going to fuck the life out of Diamond—literally! Can't you imagine that, Drako?" He snickered on at the thought of his perverted threat, only to see Drako struggle with his side.

"Didn't I tell you to turn over?" He strolled over and kicked Drako in the ribs, causing him to scream in pain.

"You don't think I can kill?" Damien asked to build up his own courage. "Answer me, dammit!" He viciously stomped Drako's head into the carpet with the heel of his expensive alligator slippers.

Drako's face was smashed into the carpet with each stomp.

He knew he couldn't take much more of this. Blood gushed from his mouth and nostrils. He felt weak, dizzy, light-headed and degraded beyond reason at the hands of a piece-of-shit-eating rat!

"You don't think I can kill? Well, you're about to see me kill! The only difference with me is this is simply business—never personal! I just need Toney out here more than I need your black ass!

"It's just a life for a life, that's all. Now for the last time, turn your pitiful ass over!" He watched as Drako complied this time, facing his death fearlessly.

He had turned almost halfway when Damien caught sight of the pistol in his hand.

"Your life, mothafucka!" Drako gurgled.

Blam! . . . Blam! He pulled the trigger.

Before Damien could flinch, he saw the fire leap from the large hole at the end of the barrel. The bullet exploded in the center of his chest and crushed his small body against the wall behind him where he slumped over face first to the floor.

Drako sat up and dumped seven more .40 caliber shells into the corpse, watching Damien's body jerk with every shot.

He lay back down and reached for his side again. He had spent all that time trying to wrestle the gun from his holster, but this time, he was really attempting to clutch his terrible wound.

Drako lay there and tried to gather some strength and composure. His mind raced between thoughts of Diamond and Wiz, and how he'd lost control of what should've been an easy task. He could have easily taken the first shot, but he felt he wouldn't have been satisfied. Damien had been right: greed for money had blinded him and greed for revenge had given the enemy a hair of a second to put him in the critical state he was in.

The wounded would-be assassin struggled to sit up. He had to call Diamond, clean his tracks and get to a hospital. Indescribable pain shot through his entire midsection with every move he made. He took one last look at Damien's lifeless body and the large pool of blood it laid in.

"Stunt . . . ya done!" Drako recited the gangster's slogan of victory to the corpse. He began to crawl toward the briefcase. He didn't even consider grabbing the duffel bags in his state; his body was weakening with every second.

Drako used a small table for leverage and pulled himself to his feet. He took note of his image in the mirror on the wall above the table. He saw his swollen, bloody face, and for the first time he realized how much blood he was losing. From the waist down, he was drenched in blood that dripped over his sneakers.

He turned from his image in the mirror. Holding firmly to the wall, smudging a trail of blood, he struggled to get to the front door. All he now wanted to do was get into the car, call Diamond, and meet her as close as he could to the nearest hospital. He was trying to will himself to go on, but his body was refusing to comply.

Drako hoped he had all the evidence as he fought with all he had left in an effort to reach Myria's car and sit down again. Drako realized that he was human, and although he was strong, he couldn't outmuscle a .357 bullet.

After what seemed like an eternity, he reached out and finally grabbed the front door handle. His legs trembled, and the feeling of faintness came upon him. He twisted the knob and barely opened the door.

For a moment, he felt a burst of relief. But his next moment was filled with complete darkness as he passed out, dropping the briefcase and hitting the hardwood floor.

Lewisburg Penitentiary
Chapter - 33

From the moment Deuce last hung up with Drako, pure rage consumed his thoughts. Drako's word was all the proof he needed to light his fuse.

Drako was a solid nigga who had stayed true; he showed unconditional love, even when he got out. As Deuce thought about the possibility of losing the only real friend he had left out on the streets, his relentless appetite for revenge grew with every second.

It was time to call a truce. The only way to reconcile this problem was to give Jet the 'real!' Jet had bad blood here as well, and it was time to bring the Bs and GDs together!

*****

Duece couldn't step to Jet without gaining the attention of every shot caller in Lewisburg, so he sent Dub-D to holla at Jet's top lieutenant, Chuck.

Chuck was a very sensible gangsta who possessed leadership qualities. He listened to Dub-D attentively as he studied his face. He weighed the seriousness of Deuce's request, and then chose to relay the message to Jet in full.

Jet, who never trusted Dub-D, Deuce, or anything resembling Red, listened with an attentive ear. He ultimately agreed to meet with Deuce, though it took some convincing from Chuck, who personally thought it was the best move.

After agreeing on several precautions, Chuck was on the way back to Dub-D. A meeting was set, but only on Jet's terms. There would be no "rockin' a fool to sleep," no unexpected ambushes. The only people who'd be present would be Deuce, Dub-D, Jet and Chuck.

The meeting took place where it had all started in Jet's mind. They were once again in the building that served as the chapel at Lewisburg Penitentiary. This time, they all stood face to face in a small bathroom.

In a million years, no one in the pen could have ever pictured this. For Deuce, or even worse, Dub-D, to co-exist with Jet in an area this small without anyone noticing would have been an all out war!

An eerie tension engulfed the room as these two sets of gangstas stared at one another only two-feet apart. Jet stood there with his signature broom straw dangling from the left side of his mouth while he stared Dub-D down. Dub-D returned the same glare.

Deuce stared at Chuck, a six-foot chiseled two-hundred-pounder. Chuck had brown skin, wavy textured hair, and wore thin wire-framed glasses that made him appear scholarly. He really was the graviest nigga a solid nigga would ever want to meet, but the moment one crossed that line of respect, irreconcilable death was Chuck's M.O. He was a legend to snitch haters, and was now sitting on seven consecutive life sentences.

Jet was the 'G,' and Chuck was the other component that put the 'D' in 'GD,' which brought them together as a force to be reckoned with.

Deuce's legacy was also a bloody one; he had the scars of war that said a million words as he raised his shirt to prove to Jet that he was clean.

"I come in peace," Deuce calmly stated to break the ice. "Dub-D, pull up yo' shirt!" he further ordered.

Dub-D complied. Both men were clean.

"Listen, gangsta, we got a problem! We got a rat in our cipher, and he's seen too much! The fool is having conversations wit' them folks, and he might use what he's seen

around here to help breath some clean air on the other side of the wall."

"Who you speakin' on?" Jet asked with a curious face.

"Toney Domacio."

Jet's face twisted up even more. "I knew somethin' wasn't right about dat proper-actin' mothafucka!" He pulled the broomstraw from his mouth and spat on the floor with disgust.

"I always felt uneasy about that fool, too! Dominicans ain't never ran wit" no black crews!" Deuce added.

"I told you he was a nigga hater!" Dub-D interjected.

"Look, gangstas, I know I came to you and stopped the beef when Drako did what he did," Deuce continued. "Ever since then, things ain't been cool wit' us. But you know what? I never saw that fool eatin' cheese! I „on protect rats in no kinda way, and running that fool up top ain't an option!"

"Lemme do dis' fool right!" Dub-D said, pacing the floor.

"Chill out, Dub." Deuce took control. "Gangstas, I made a bad call, and for that, I wanna right my wrong. That fool played me, and he tryin' to free his own ass and leave a solid nigga on stuck!" Deuce momentarily paused letting the GDs absorb his words. "Bloods can do him themselves, but all the bad blood we've had is 'cuz a him. I feel like he owe you a piece of his ass, too!"

"Dat" fool need ta' get stuck in his hot ass fo' he die!" Dub-D interjected with burning anticipation.

"Hold up, Dub-D! Don't move so fast. Dis" shit gotta go down right!" Deuce made clear.

"Listen, soldier, all I got is my word. Let's come together and do this right! I give you my word that from this day forward, y'all got the respect of all Bs."

Deuce studied their faces as Jet peered between him and Dub-D. Jet showed little emotion as he pondered the truce.

They all waited in silence until Chuck took a step forward. He extended his open hand in Deuce's direction. "Let's get these Bloods and Disciples together."

Deuce gave him a firm shake.

"All I see is Ds . . . Ds as in death! Toney Domacio's death— and anything standing in his path!" Jet pledged as he now extended his open hand to Deuce.

"Let's make them fools bleed!" Dub-D added.

"Hell yeah!" Chuck said. "Lewisburg may as well get ready for a mass lockdown, 'cause when they wake up tomorrow it's gon'' be a massacre like they ain't never seen before!"

"We ain't waitin' on this fool! We movin' first thing in the morning. When the doors pop, we pop!" Deuce shouted.

"He's eight cells down from me," Jet said. "I got a plan I already had just in case me and that rat ever crossed paths again!"

*****

At 5:30 a.m., at the loud, clanking sound of all the cell doors unlocking, Dub-D, who was fully dressed all the way down to his steel-toed boots, pulled the covers back and hopped to the cement floor. He left his cell and quickly started his job, except he was extra early this morning, just as the plan had called for.

Deuce and Chuck were already pounding the cement, swiftly moving toward Jet's cell, which sat only a few cells ahead of Toney's. The plan would be as easy as pie if executed right on time. Nobody in the pen knew what Toney had been up to, nor did they know what the Bloods and GDs had in store.

Ever since Drako had left, it was a known fact that at daybreak, when the cells were opened at 5:30 a.m., Toney's two main henchmen would head for his cell to make sure he didn't receive any unwelcomed visits. Their job was to hold post until he fully awakened, then escort him to the shower and hold post outside the door until his shower was complete. The shower

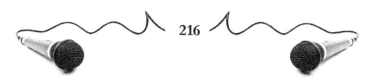

here, as in all pens, is a key spot for ambushes and penitentiary rapes.

This morning was sure to go different, because when the henchmen reached Jet's cell, they would be greeted with an ambush of shanks wielded by four real gangsters. Once that knife fight ended, the path to Toney's cell would be clear!

*****

At approximately 5:37 a.m., Dub-D was mopping the tier as normal. He dropped his focus to the floor at the sight of the first henchman approaching as he swung the mop from side to side and was only a few paces from Jet's cell. He looked as if he was making his best effort to happily complete his chore.

The henchman didn't give Dub-D a second thought as he neared. Dub-D had expected them both to come on time, but as fate had it, only one showed. As soon as the inmate passed by, Dub-D had made up his mind to take him on his own.

He reached into the mop bucket of soap water and pulled out a ten-inch rusty blade. Swiftly he trotted to catch up with his mark, and then he lunged forward with all his might, stabbing Toney's man just under the rib cage. He plunged the shank as deep as he could as he clamped his other arm around the man's body to brace him. Deep purple blood gushed down his back, proving that Dub-D punctured his liver.

The man only got one loud squeal out before Dub-D covered his mouth. He ripped the shank out and began to stab him viciously while shoving the man's body toward Jet's open cell door.

Chuck sprang from the cell and quickly assisted Dub-D. He snatched the bloody man inside, and then let his body drop to the floor. Dub-D fell right back on top of him, puncturing the man as though he were a pincushion.

"Work him, Dub-D!" Chuck chanted with cheer.

217

In a matter of seconds, Deuce was pulling the overly excited Dub-D off him. "We got him, fool! Get back out there and mop that blood up before the other one shows up!"

Dub-D quickly left the cell with his orders. He was mopping up the last traces of blood when the next henchman came into view at the end of the tier. As soon as he walked by, Dub-D reached for the shank, caught up with him and tore into him the same way.

The knife ripped through the flesh of his lower back, and shoved him forward. Dub-D tried to stifle the man, but this one was much larger and stronger than the first. As he shrieked out in pain, he spun around to contest his attacker. Dub-D stabbed the huge Dominican in his gut, but the big man overpowered him and held Dub-D's arms tight in his bear hug.

Chuck rushed to aid Dub-D again, burying another shank deep into the Dominican's back.

"Take that, since you wanna protect a rat!" Chuck yelled as he strangled the big man by his neck and dragged him into Jet's cell. As Chuck continued to squeeze the man into darkness, Dub-D stabbed away. When all forms of physical life seeped from his body, Chuck dropped him to the hard cement floor.

"Now the path is clear." Jet stepped over his body and peeked up the tier.

"Dub-D, go mop up the hall," Deuce ordered. "We got an hour before the guards come on the tier."

Dub-D quickly obeyed, and the storm of destruction was now headed on its short path just eight cells away

*****

"Ack!"

Toney gasped as he awoke and found himself being strangled. His eyes were brimming with fear as he looked into the faces of the four angels of death standing over him. He felt a surge of adrenaline and tried to sit up, but he found his

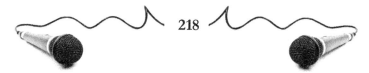

shoulders were being pinned down by Jet. He tried to kick his feet, but realized Chuck held them firmly. Attempting to wiggle his arms, he knew the death angel straddling him was indeed Dub-D.

"What the he—"

Deuce"s fist smashed into Toney's mouth and ended his words. "Soou-Woou, bitch!" Deuce announced with vengeance.

"No! . . . Please . . . wait—" Toney"s cries fell upon deaf ears as Deuce slammed punch after punch to his face again, while busting his mouth and swelling his eyes nearly shut.

He screamed in terror after each blow, swallowing pieces of teeth and blood.

"Ain't no plea bargains here! If you get a Rule 35, it'll be in hell, bitch!" Deuce said, pulling the shank from his side.

Just last night, Toney was lying in the same bed, clad in boxers and enjoying the promise of freedom. He never imagined that 'A Life 4 a Life' would bring the end of his own life.

Toney's brain raced at warp speed. He wondered how in the hell anyone could have known. Damien was the only person in the world helping him orchestrate his ingenious scheme. But he remembered that Drako was smart and had the ability to see things others couldn't. Yeah, it had to be Drako, he reasoned. He couldn't believe it; he had been done in by the man he had tried to set up. Toney braced with fear as Deuce raised the shank high above his head. He had once been a solid gangster, and knew all too well that there were no words to save him. There was no place for pity in this cell, and the only thing left to do was accept his death with dignity.

"Fuck you, you fucking nigger faggot!" Toney shouted with fear in his eyes.

Deuce grew even madder as he slammed the knife into Toney's chest. "This is for Drako, you hot mothafucka!" Deuce yelled over Toney's horrific screams as the next gushes of blood splurted from his body. Deuce ripped his shank out and stabbed him again. Jet stepped up to join him. "And this is from them Folks, you nigga hatin' rat!" Jet shouted as his blade slammed into Toney's side.

"Take dat'!" Deuce added with every jab.

"Put dat' work in, homie!" Dub-D encouraged as he watched the two shot callers administer the lethal wounds.

It wasn't long before Toney's mutilated body was lifeless.

When Deuce tore his shank from Toney's ribs for the last time, he spit right in his swollen, bloody face. "Look at you now!" His chest heaved up and down as he stared at the lifeless corpse.

Dub-D stepped closer, inspecting the holes and deep lacerations on Toney as he lie there in his own pool of blood.

"He da' best lookin' rat I ever saw!" Dub-D nodded victoriously.

"Go get dem' other bodies and drag „em down here, fool! We ain't got but forty-five minutes to clean up before the guards get on deck."

Dub-D, as always, said not a word as he eagerly took to his task.

"I'm going wit' you," Jet stated and disappeared from the cell right on Dub-D's heels.

Deuce went to the door and got ready to mop up the traces of blood tracks right behind them. Chuck stood over Toney's corpse and looked on in pure disgust.

"Here come Dub-D wit' da' first fool! We gon' be right on time," Deuce said as he knelt down on one knee, carefully peeking down the tier.

In a few seconds, he ran from the cell door and helped Dub-D drag the first corpse into the cell, where they dumped him on the cement floor.

Chuck, meanwhile, was busy yanking Toney's bloody boxers down. "What da fuck you doin' fool? What da fuck you into!" Deuce whispered sharply.

"We gotta send a real message to these rats! Look at the big man now!" Chuck replied at the sight of Toney's four-inch penis. Without another word of warning, Chuck reached for Toney's limp dick and stretched it out as far as he could. With his other hand, he slammed the knife into its base. Blood splattered the wall at the first incision. Chuck raised his knife and slammed it down again. By the third hack of the blade, he severed Toney's penis from his body and held it in his hand. He then stuffed the dick into Toney's mouth, making sure it was left there to dangle.

"Who dat" faggot now?" He snarled at the corpse. "Take dat, you hot mothafucka!"

Jet had just made it back through the cell door as Chuck was stuffing Toney's face with dick. He couldn't believe what he saw; Chuck had once again proved his pedigree.

"A'ight, das' enough! We gotta keep it movin'!" Jet announced as they looked at the three dead bodies for the last time.

By 6:30 a.m., all the traces of blood were mopped clean from the corridors. Jet's cell was cleaned of blood splatters and the four fiercest gangstas at Lewisburg were back in their cells as if they'd never even left.

The men had left a message to all rats to be discovered in none other than Toney Domacio's cell!

* * * *

Shortly after 7:30 a.m., work call was announced over the intercom. The scene of Lewisburg's worst massacre had been found. The prison was immediately put on high alert lockdown for an indefinite amount of time.

The prison officials began the standard investigation procedures. Although no inmates saw a thing, the never-sleeping ears of the prison walls had surely heard. To the real solid niggaz, this altercation would be labeled 'the untold story.' To the undercover rats, it was a warning to make them aware of the consequences if they were ever caught crossing lines. To the GDs and Bloods, it was a damn good day—the four fiercest gangsters" legacy lives on!

Diamond
Chapter - 34

Back at Reality Records, several hours had passed. Diamond had long grown tired of talking to Myria and hearing her high-pitched, annoying voice. The more time passed, the more she became worried about Drako. After two hours, there was still no word. Nevertheless, she did her best to remain optimistic.

But that was two hours ago.

Now that the sun was setting, Diamond began impatiently pacing the floor. Her composure was slowly but surely unraveling. She couldn't sit still, and Myria, who had been going on and on about Wiz, could tell that Diamond was no longer paying her any attention.

"Diamond, why don't you relax? You know Drako's gonna call. Him and Damien probably still talkin" and you know Damien's scary ass gonna listen to him."

"Yeah, I'm pretty sure of that." Diamond feigned a smile and tried to sound confident. She brushed past Myria and headed for the room that held Drako's wall safe. She went against his orders as her better judgment had her sneaking in that room for the fifth time to dial Drako's cell number.

"Dammit!" she huffed again at the sound of his automated voice mail service. "Turn on the goddamn phone!" She hung up and redialed again. Her nerves were shot. She knew Drako should've called her a long time ago. He was always punctual about business, and always put her feelings first! Something had to be wrong.

"Fuck this! This bitch is gonna take me to my man!" Diamond reasoned, lying the cell back down and stepping into the closet.

She slipped off her sandals before choosing a pair of jeans to jump in, and then slid her feet into a comfy pair of Air Max and grabbed her Gucci bag.

Before heading out, she reached into the wall safe. Seven handguns were left. She didn't know the names of any of them, she just chose the biggest one she saw.

Diamond knew how to use it. Drako had spent hours teaching her how to use the safety switches, pop clips, and all the basics. She quickly placed the chrome .44 Desert Eagle in her bag.

Diamond thought for a moment. She had no qualms about holding the pistol to Myria and making her drive if she didn't comply. *Hell no. Drako, wouldn't want her to see shit!* she thought. She decided it was best to leave Myria in the studio and go find Drako herself.

Myria's face was flushed with surprise when Diamond reentered the office. "Where are we going?" Myria got to her feet.

"Oh, *we* aren't going anywhere," Diamond said, stopping Myria in her tracks. "I just need you to stay here. Drako's been tryin' to call, and I had this damn cell phone turned off." She slipped her hand into her purse and clutched the gun. "Give me the directions to Damien's again."

"But I thought th—"

"Myria, give me the directions so I can go get my man!" Diamond's tone only perked an octave, but Myria's intuition knew the request was a demand.

Myria did what she thought best. She once again gave clear directions, which only prompted a flat "thanks" from Diamond.

"Come lock this door and stay put. You'll be fine if you just wait here." She prayed that Myria wouldn't try to leave.

Myria took the cell phone from Diamond"s outstretched hand, and then Diamond turned and headed for the door.

"Hurry back," Myria spoke with despair.

"You'll be fine," was Diamond's only response as she set the alarm system before locking the front door.

*****

As soon as the private jet's wheels landed on the tarmac in Atlanta, Wiz was dialing all of Drako's numbers all over again.

They deployed from the plane and settled into another Lincoln Town Car en route to Drako's house.

"South will take us to Stone Mountain, right?" Swirl asked from behind the driver's wheel as they approached the expressway.

"Yeah . . . south," Wiz said, adjusting his electric seat.

"Matter of fact, scratch all that. Take 285-North and get this shit downtown." He waved his hand in that direction. "Take me straight to Reality Records," Wiz ordered and lay back quietly in his own thoughts until he reached his destination.

*****

Diamond ignored everything about this cool, busy night as she whipped her fire red Lexus through downtown Atlanta. She nearly crashed twice, driving at top speed with hardly any regard to anything else on the road. Nothing was gonna keep her from Drako.

In about twenty minutes, Diamond found herself turning into Damien's neighborhood. Her small foot stayed heavy on the gas pedal until she reached his street. She turned down the seemingly quiet drive with caution.

Spotting Myria's car in the driveway, Diamond approached slowly. She cruised past the home twice before pulling in next to the Honda and killing her headlights.

Resting the heavy pistol in her lap, she thought of what to do next. She quickly took note that the house was dark. Common sense told her that if Damien had not yet returned, Drako would have surely been looking out and would have given her some type of signal when he saw the coupe.

She leaned forward and squinted to better focus in the dark of night. It was quiet outside; the eerie silence alone, felt creepy. She grew even more jittery when she noticed the front door ajar.

"Heaven help me," she whispered, clicking the safety from the pistol before cocking it. She got out of the car, holding the gun close to her side as she trotted to the door.

*****

When Wiz and Swirl pulled into Reality's parking lot, the only car they saw was Drako's black Bentley Coupe. Swirl whipped right up to the front door. He came around and helped Wiz out the car and up to the door a bit. Wiz's left arm was in a sling and he leveraged his weight with a cane at his right side.

They began to knock on the door loudly as their first few knocks seemed to go unanswered. Swirl flipped open his cell, handed it to Wiz to try Drako's number again, and then stepped up to the door and yelled Drako's name through the slit. For some reason he felt Drako was inside. After just one try, the last person he thought he'd ever lay eyes on in a studio, stepped timidly from the dark shadows of the hallway.

"Wait," Wiz said almost in a trance, closing Swirl's cell phone and staring at Myria's distant look as she approached the door nervously. Her eyes were on Wiz the whole time. It was as if she never blinked and her heart was beating extremely fast.

Wiz knew something was wrong. She stood on the other side of the glass looking almost petrified. Her heart hoped Wiz had come to save her, but her thoughts were so scattered that her mind wouldn't register.

"Open the door, Myria," Wiz spoke easily. "Tell me what's goin" on."

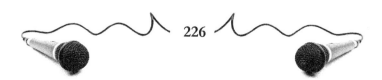

She fumbled with the locks nervously as the tears spilled down her unmade face.

As soon as she unlocked the door, she rushed out and hugged Wiz tightly, as she bawled into tears.

"Shh . . . Shh . . . don't worry, baby. I'm here." He steered her back into the entrance and nodded for Swirl to relock the door.

"Where's Drako?" he asked, rubbing her shoulders and looking in her puffy, tear soaked eyes. Myria was out of it.

"Come on, Myria, I need you to be a big girl and pull through," he said, trying to persuade her to calm down a bit.

A few patient moments later, she was doing her best to relay to Wiz all she'd relayed to both Diamond and Drako.

"It's okay. It's gonna be fine. Just get us over there," Wiz said. In the next moment, Wiz was settled in the backseat, while Myria rode up front giving Swirl the fastest route to Damien's house.

*****

Diamond leaned against the cracked door again, only to realize it was barricaded. As she took a small step back, her foot slid on the ground. It was then that she realized she had stepped into a pool of liquid. She bent over to get a closer look. The substance was dark, and she couldn't see it, but the iron laden smell was unmistakeable. It was certainly blood seeping from beneath the door.

She shoved the door harder, and this time she heard a moaning sound. Her body didn't stiffen, as she could never mistake the distinctive sound of Drako's voice! She leaned into the door until she wedged enough space to slip through, and when she did, her worst nightmare became her reality!

She could see that Drako had been shot. The dim light coming from the bedroom was enough for her to recognize his swollen face.

Dropping to her knees, she cradled his head in her bossom. His eyes were open, but he was barely responsive as he struggled to pronounce her name.

"Shh, shh," she whispered as heavy tears began to run down her face. "Is anybody here?"

Drako slowly shook his head no.

"Oh God, Drako! What happened?" she cried with deep sorrow, like a mother holding her dying child. She began rocking him. "Hold on. Be strong. I'll get you to a hospital, okay? Please don't leave me." Diamond hugged him even tighter as she felt his hand clench her waist. She knew at that moment that nothing in the world could ever mean more to him than her, and she felt exactly the same way.

"Get up, baby. I gotta get you outta here!" she ordered as she tried to help Drako sit up.

"Ahh!" Drako's murmered cry rang out.

Diamond could hardly budge him. And as hard as he fought to, he could barely muster the strength to breathe. The air traveling in and out of his lungs caused him unbearable pain.

"Wait!" Drako's weak, trembling voice managed to say. "I ca-can-can't make—" His words were cut short by a fit of coughs that caused him to spew gobs of blood to the floor.

"No, Drako! Don't give up, baby!" Diamond shouted, frantically struggling to lift him up by his armpits.

"N . . . Nooooo!" Drako stammered out with what sounded like the last traces of strength and oxygen in his body.

"Okay, baby, okay!" She let him go. "I'm calling an ambulance!"

"No!" Drako cried as his hand clenched Diamond's arm tighter.

"Drako, I don't know what to do! Baby, I'm scared!" Her mind began to race. "Honey, just let me get you outta here! I'll

get you somewhere else and tell 'em you got robbed! Anything is better than lying here!"

Drako fought to smile; he barely made a smirk. "I-I-I lo-love you."

"And you know I'll always love you. Now help me, Drako!" she demanded with tears.

Drako's grip slightly tightened. "You got 'erything. Save yourself and save Wiz . . . C-c-clean these tracks up and k-keep."

"No, Drako, no!"

Drako coughed up more blood as tears soaked his face. Diamond had pulled the cell phone from her pocket when she felt Drako squeeze her arm as hard as he ever had. She looked down at him. He stared back up at her; it was as if he were looking into her soul. Diamond leaned closer as he struggled to speak.

This time, his voice was even weaker. "P-please, ma," he whispered in pain as he held his side. "Clean up and k-keep playin' da game raw."

"No, Drako!"

"Let my D-Diamond shine . . ." He could barely studder through the pain. Drako was so weak; he could no longer hold the half smirk. He choked up even more thick gobs of blood from his mouth and his nose.

"I love you, baby! I love you!" Diamond pleaded as she held Drako tighter. She could feel him reciprocate, and then suddenly, his body went limp.

No more muscles moved.

"No, no, no!" Diamond wailed uncontrollably. This time she used all of her might to lift him up by his armpits. Drako felt like dead weight for real. Diamond began to cry even more but she never let up. Again, she found herself asking, *What would Drako do?* And like always his voice rang clear to her. She rolled him over on his back and tried to check his pulse. She was so nervous she couldn't tell if there was one or not. All she knew is that if he were to be pronounced dead it would be at a hospital. She pulled Drako closer to the door by an arm. Drako felt like he weighed 300 pounds, but she got him there and leaned him up against the wall, and then made sure the pistol was secured on her side.

She saw the bloody suitcase Drako was trying to flee with lying on the floor. She was sure there were lots more in the house as well. She hoped she could make her way back to clean up before the authorities discovered the crime scene, or either she'd just have to face the consequences later. Right now, she was about to drag Drako out of that house.

She took another deep breath and creaked open the front door. She leaned over and hoisted Drako out onto the porch with hope now on her side. In the very next instant her heart dropped. Her world came crashing down again. She let Drako go and reached for the heavy pistol again when the Lincoln's headlights flashed her directly in her face.

*****

Swirl, whose street instinct was all too familiar with gunplay, quickly read her body language, just like he'd read the rest of the scene as soon as his lights settled on the doorstep.

"Diamond . . . wait!" he yelled, killing his lights as fast as he could.

"It's family, lil momma!" he said, taking his chances and hopping out the car. He'd surely saw the deranged look on her face when she glanced back.

"Swirl?" she said, her voice cracking in a whisper.

"It's me," he said, bringing relief to both their hearts.

Diamond was glad it wasn't any of Damien's connected friends, and Swirl was just happy that no sparks flew in his direction.

"Oh shit!" he said as he trotted over and looked down at Drako.

"I gotta get "im to the car!" Swirl said, already lifting Drako by his armpits. He wasted no time getting him into the back of the Lincoln.

Wiz had stepped out and Myria stood there with her hands covering her mouth in pure disbelief.

"What? Oh God . . . What did I do?" Myria began to cry, regretting what she told Drako and wishing she'd have kept driving right past Reality Records.

"Myria, be quiet and get back in the car," Wiz ordered evenly. He turned to Diamond. "Is anyone else in the house?"

Diamond didn't respond, the hollow eyed look she gave told it all.

"Okay, this is what's up." He looked at Diamond with all the trust and confidence he could muster. "You and Myria get him over to the hospital. I'll stay here and clean this up. You gotta stick with your story." Wiz stepped closer to Diamond. "Someone tried to rob him for his jewelry and he resisted." He nodded.

She didn't say a word, but that knowing look was in her eyes. "I got everything off of him." Swirl stepped over, nearly out of breath. He had a few clips in his hand, Myria's car keys, and a wad of money.

"Y"all got to get movin"!" Swirl hissed. "Myria, can you drive?" He looked her way.

"Yeah, I can." She nodded weakly then proceeded to the driver's side with haste.

"Don't worry. I got this," Wiz said, closing the door and slipping the pistol from Diamond's lap. "We'll find ya' when were done."

Wiz and Swirl watched the Lincoln pull off and head for the hospital. Wiz said a small prayer and headed into the house. He knew in his heart that things didn't look good at all for Drako.

*****

Swirl led the way down the hallway. Diamond's Desert Eagle extended in front of him. They followed the heavy splotches of blood on the floor and the nasty trail Drako"s hand streaked along the wall. The trail led back to a small home office just as Myria had described.

"Uh . . . Shit!" Wiz cursed at the repulsive sight of Damien's contorted, perforated corpse. There was a huge blood splatter on the wall, just above where he'd obviously fell. His eyes were still wide open and his face was now a pale blue.

"Don't look at dat' wench, man," Swirl told Wiz, turning away. "Let's clean this shit up and get lost." He reached for the blood stained suitcase Wiz passed him. He quickly stepped over to the desk and popped it open. He picked up the knife in the Ziploc bag and set it aside first. Then Wiz stepped up and began whisking through a few pages with numbers and things that didn't ring much of a bell, other than Bless' private number in which was circled. He sifted through all the pictures of Drako and knew exactly who Diamond was, even behind the blonde wig. He quickly nodded his head, staring at the pictures of him standing with Damien's friend. The pictures were taken in Wiz's own mansion from obscured views that Damien must've watched from. Wiz didn't want to see anymore.

"Close that shit up," he ordered, "No need to see anymore." He glanced around the room and saw the two large duffel bags sitting oddly in the middle of the floor. "Open these for me," he told Swirl. He nodded his head, not surprised at all at Damien's deceit. Reality had long ago become ultimate for him. He'd seen Damien's intention on tape and now it all rang clearly. Damien not coming to the hospital to visit him. He realized it was

Damien who kept him and Drako's wires crossed up from the start. He remembered just how hard Damien coerced him not to give Drako a lot of money, and even recently it was Damien's corecion that brought the brilliant idea of signing Big Turk to Red Rum Records.

Wiz felt disgusted inside. But it, in time, would be okay. He was not reporting any of this as he'd instructed Swirl to find cleaning supplies. They were doing their best to rid the house of all fingerprints and traces of blood. They'd torn every nook and cranny for any and all evidence that would tie Red Rum, Drako or Diamond to the Feds. Wiz felt they'd had it all and just like the incriminating evidence Damien had planted in his house, this too would settle at the bottom of the ocean just a few miles out in front of Wiz's mansion, resting with the fish and severing all ties once and for all. They decided that the X-pills would be left behind to stink along with Damien's corpse. Perhaps when the neighbors finally complained of his horrible stench it would be an open and closed drug related file.

They double-checked their tracks one last time, and then made their way out. Swirl jumped into Diamond's coupe and Wiz trailed him in Myria's little Honda, leaving the worst chapter in their lives far, far behind . . .

Drip
Chapter - 35

"Everything"s gone be all right." Drip had just swallowed a lump in his throat, and then spoke in a hope filled tone from the passenger"s seat as he realized Ebony was still muffling back tears from the seat behind him.

It had been just hours ago when Drip had received the terrible news that somehow last night Drako had become the victim of a robbery that went horribly wrong. Now with it being more than twenty-four hours later and hardly any progress to his condition being reported by Swirl, things were looking worse than anyone could"ve ever imagined for everybody at Reality"s camp. Drip had finally told them Drako was surely the man behind Reality Records. Of course, Drip could run it. But without Drako, the true vision that birthed Reality Records would never be the same.

"Man, this shit is crazy," Save huffed, clenching the steering wheel tighter as he nosed the black Escalade into heavy traiffic and sped off toward Grady hospital. He too was still trying to put it all together. Things seemed to move at warp speed as he thought about how fast Drip nixed all plans of the concert they were set to perform in Scottsdale, Arizona, and only hours later another charter jet had landed them safely on the tarmac in ATL once again.

"Yo, fa"real, son." Save nodded his head. "This the shit I be talkin" about. . . . I mean, I know what I did was bad, but it"s like yo, you give it or you get it!" He glanced at Ebony through the rearview mirror as he made the next turn. "I just wish he"da squeezed first." He sounded disappointed. It was to go without saying. Save had mad respect and admiration for Drako.

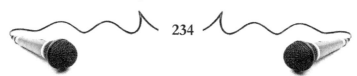

A LIFE FOR A LIFE II

"Hmph . . ." Drip huffed, sounding both defeated and confused. "I don"t get it. This one has me beat. I don"t have to tell a real nigga nothin". We both know that man is a cold gangsta!" Drip reared back calmly, and then slid his long fingers together before resting them on his stomach. "But you ain"t got ta" worry „bout this here." He sucked at his teeth sounding sure. "We will get to the bottom of it and when I do, it"s gonna be handled like only a gangsta can." He promised with ice in his tone, and then glanced at the navigation"s screen. "Just a few more blocks . . ." He perked with hope and began another silent prayer as Save cut into the left lane, ignoring the sounds of honking horns in his rear as he threaded dangersously through traffic to his destination.

*****

"Fuck 'em! Park this shit right here." Drip motioned his hand as Save brought the Escalade to a screeching halt right in back of an ambulance parked near the emergency exit.

"Let's go," he said, having already hopped out the front seat and was now giving Ebony a hand to help her step down safely in the spiked heels and tight leather pants she never got a chance to change out of. "It's gonna be heavy security, and he's registered under an assumed name, but they know we're here," he added, closing the door behind her, and then moving on course to the hospital's emergency entrance.

No sooner than Drip's foot pressed the rubber mat that made the electric doors slide open, he was relieved to be met by Swirl, Thump, and several security personnel.

"What's up, bruh!" Swirl spoke first and extended a hand as soon as Drip stepped into his space.

"Man." Drip sighed, giving Swirl dap and realizing Swirl's attention was on Save and Ebony, just behind him. "It's, it's still unreal," Drip admitted, unable to focus on anything else.

"I-I know what you mean." Swirl shot back, still gazing over Drip's shoulder. He had never been so close to Save in person and it was simply second nature for the gangster in him to size Save up. His eyes had quickly shifted to Ebony and even with all the shit that was circulating, he still couldn't stop the feelings of astonishment her curves and swagger sparked in him.

"Well." Swirl cleared his throat and did his best to swallow any thoughts of beef he may have harbored for Drip and the people who he now knew meant so much to Drako and Diamond. "This shit is unreal to everybody," Swirl confessed, taking a step closer, now giving his full attention to Drip.

"All that shit ain't 'bout nothing," he said.

"Shit don't look good. Diamond tryin" to be strong. We all prayin' but . . . but he still ain't breathin' on his own." He paused, vaguely hearing Ebony gasp at his words and quickly trying to wipe the small tear that trickled from beneath the dark wide framed shades she wore over her chocolate skin. "Diamond knows Drako wants you here. She speaks proudly of you. And me and Wiz got some things we want to run by you." His squint was subtle, but Drip knew it held something very important behind it.

"Cool . . . no problem." Drip nodded his confirmation. "But right now I need to see him. I need to see Diamond, and I need to know what the doctors are trying to do. We're gonna get him the best surgeons money can buy." He pledged.

Swirl cut his eyes at Thump, and then back to Wiz. "Say, man, that's all around the board. Wiz got his hand over everything here. All you can do is fall back and join us in prayer." Swirl's words defeated Drip's enthusiasm, but he knew it was true. No matter how large or sincere his intentions were, they'd never size up to Wiz's. Wiz was the closest thing to Drako, other than Diamond. And he was filthy rich!

"It was a single gut shot." He laid a comforting hand on Drip's shoulder. "But it shattered his spine on the way out. He definitely lost a lung and they have only small hopes of repairing his intestines, and man, if he even walks again it'll be . . ." Swirl's voice trailed away and he could hardly look at Drip with all the pain each word brought to Drip's face. "Look man. Let me just get you inside."

Swirl turned, said a few words to security and sent one off with orders to get clearance, allowing Drip and crew into the private waiting room.

Drip immediately stepped closer to Swirl. "Sheeit!" he slurred his trademark curse in a whisper. "Somebody finna' give the cowards up who did this shit!" He knew with one glance into Swirl's eyes that this soldier in red was more than ready to handle up.

Swirl slightly turned his head, looking straight at Drip with a nod. "Wiz gone holla at ya." He sucked diamonds with a smirk and strolled away, leaving Drip stunned by his response.

What the hell? Drip thought, feeling more confused than ever. He knew by Swirl's response, that Wiz had already known exactly who had to be behind this.

"Let's go. He said follow him," Thump spoke, breaking Drip's thoughts as he stepped up and gestured an arm for Ebony to walk ahead of him.

"Yeah . . . yeah," Drip mumbled, trying to clamp hold of the many racing thoughts now in his head. "Just get me upstairs." The entourage rushed down the busy corridor and piled into the elevator, en route to the twelfth floor.

*****

After gaining a quick clearance from Wiz's added security, they all were led into the family's private waiting room. Immediately, Drip spotted Diamond sitting next to Wiz and headed straight over to her, ignoring everybody else as he looked down at her still puffy red eyes.

"I-I-I'm sorry. I-I don't know what else to say." He choked on his words and hugged Diamond tight.

"I-I-know how you feel." Diamond sniffled, still clearly distraught. "I just wanted you here. I knew Drako would want you here, and . . . and I think Wiz can explain better than me. Right now, we just all need one another." Diamond loosed a heartbroken sob and hugged Drip even tighter.

He could feel every bit of the pain, sorrow, and fear that wracked through Diamond's body as she failed to stifle her trembling.

"I-I understand, Diamond." He patted her back gently. "I'm here till the end. We're all gonna be here! There is no Reality Records without you and Drako around. Don't worry, it's gonna work out." He let Diamond go and watched her sit back down, and then his eyes finally settled on Wiz.

They spoke no words as Drip sat down and made himself comfortable for what would become a stay for as long as it would take. He'd never planned on fraternizing with Wiz at anytime soon, but the stake of losing someone like Drako far exceeded the altercation they were once facing. Blondelle had no ties to Drako whatsoever, and regardless of the tragedy at hand, she just refused to allow Drip to drag her anywhere close to where Wiz would be. As soon as they deployed from the charter, Blondelle was chauffeured in the opposite direction back to Drip's estate.

"We here now," Wiz said in a calm and sincere tone to Drip. "Those are the exact words Drako spoke to me after I came to my senses. We left the past in the past and we pushed forward. No games, no lies, no deceit." Wiz sat up a bit and looked Drip deeper in his eyes. "Now, I'm sayin' the same to you because we all have the same interest here, ya dig!"

Drip nodded, not quick to be sold with words, but he knew to comply was only right. "I gave Drako my word from day one. I trusted in his word just like he trusts in mine. I'm surely gonna see this and everything else all the way through."

"Good." Wiz nodded and reared back in his seat. "Good." He nodded once more, now feeling he could trust in Drip to do what he needed, just as Drako once had. And now as Diamond believed, this would be all the added precaution to ensure the safety of everything at risk.

"I think we better get comfortable." Diamond's voice cracked, seeing the sullen look plastered on the doctor's face as he came strolling into the waiting room with a clipboard in hand.

He stopped right in front of Diamond, placing his pen into the upper pocket on his white smock and peered over the top of his wire-framed glasses. "I'm confident that we've done all we can for now." He sighed and tightened his saggy jaws with a smug smirk. "He's stabilized. Not yet responsive, but he is surely a fighter. He's breathing again; however, the damage to his spine seems to be far beyond the work of my scalpel." He huffed with disappointment.

"What we need here now is patience and tons of faith. All we can pray for is that he recuperates well, even if he's immobile. I'm very optimistic that there won't be any form of brain damage, temporary or permanent. The head trauma he suffered was not nearly as severe." He concluded, watching the tears soak Diamond's face as she took in the ultimate reality of Drako's condition.

Seeing as though she was unable to respond, Wiz cut right in. "Thanks Doc. Keep doin' all you can. I want a list of the world's best surgeons and I want them all to take a look at his chart." Wiz's instructions were firm.

"Will get it done, simultaneously," the doctor added, and then turned away with Wiz's orders. He knew exactly who he was dealing with.

"He's gonna make it." Wiz wrapped an arm around Diamond and sat beside her. "I did and so is he! It's just gonna take some time." He sounded sure, but felt just like the looks that everyone had on their faces after hearing what the doctor revealed. They all knew that even if God brought Drako through, he'd never be the same.

"Well . . ." Wiz stood to his feet. "It's my turn again. The media knows we're here, so I"m tryna' keep this security blanket tight. Everybody present now will have authorization to rotate around the clock." He was ready to lead, just as Drako did when he was hospitalized. "And as soon as we can, we'll be wheeling him out of here." He looked around the room and made sure his plans were clear to everyone.

A short while later, he dismissed Swirl, Thump, and his security, as did Drip excuse Ebony and Save. Wiz then explained to Drip that Diamond revealed to him her knowledge of Drip's genius as an accountant, launderer, and a mastermind of Contractual Law. He further revealed part of the plot Damien had set out for Drako and Red Rum. To Drip's astonishment, Damien"s plan could've destroyed Reality Records as well.

"Get the fuck outta here!" was all Drip could say, totally blown away behind a set of wide eyes.

"Yeah . . . and the guy on the inside's name was Toney Domacio," Wiz said.

Drip felt like his brain was gonna burst. He couldn't believe it. Wiz didn't give it all to him just yet, but he told him enough to assure him that Damien had been taken care of the right way. Wiz also informed Drip that he obtained lots of paperwork from Damien that he didn't understand clearly, but he wanted to make sure nothing was left floating to ever tie the Feds back to Red Rum, nor Reality Records in any way.

"Shit ain't a problem. You can't hide behind paperwork with me. Numbers or letters, I find flaws," Drip said with his gaze still glued to the cold tile floor. He was reflecting back to the days when he served time in prison and recalled how Drako had looked up to Toney Domacio like the father he'd never had. Drip's skin felt like it was burning with vengeance. He couldn't wait to gather the full story. He knew there was much more.

"Just secure everything. Once we get a break from here, I'll make sure everything on our end is airtight." He slid his fingers together again and gave Wiz his first proud wink, hoping that Drako and Wiz's move had ultimately saved his life and all he'd worked for as well.

"I'm sure." Wiz winked back, pulling out his iPhone to send Swirl the message that all was well. "Everything's safe." He pecked Diamond on the forehead and walked off, leaving her and Drip a quiet, private moment to talk and gather themselves for the saddest days that were sure to come. Then Wiz made plans to see Myria and give her the apology she'd long ago deserved. He hoped they could somehow make amends.

Diamond
Chapter - 36

Monday night marked seventy-two hours since Drako's near fatal incident. Regardless of what the doctors predicted, the one thing Diamond was now certain of was that God's hands were the only merciful hands still keeping Drako alive.

Diamond stood gazing through the observation glass outside of the Intensive Care Unit, praying for Drako to catch his breath and to find some strength once again. Tears seeped from the wells of her eyes as she stared between Drako and the graph on the screen of his heart monitor. She was praying that this time the dot would continue to bounce across the screen to the same steady rhythm and not slip back onto the same flat line she'd witnessed just last night that caused her to belt out the shrill scream that rang through the whole floor.

Banging at the glass and yelling in hysteria, Diamond had alerted every ICU personnel.

"Oh, God . . . please. Save him. Get in there." She'd tried to rush in behind the doctors as they hurried to Drako's side. "No . . . No!" She kicked and screamed as strong arms quickly restrained her and pulled her out of the staff's way.

"Clear!" she heard a voice yell. Then she heard the electric shock of the defibrillator trying to jolt life into Drako once again.

"Please God, please!" Diamond prayed aloud as strong arms held her tighter in front of the window again.

"Go!" the surgeon instructed as the next volt surged through Drako with such force that his chest bounced off the gurney and the heart graph came to life with a sharp beep and springing white dot.

"Thank you God!" Diamond sighed with relief, praying as hard as she'd ever prayed. That time, and from the moment she'd heard the doctor yell "clear," all she could envision was the first night they'd wheeled Drako in on that blood drenched stretcher. His head was swollen and covered in blood. He was unresponsive, and his vitals were so shallow that the EMT had surely thought he was dead.

She remembered the EMT yell, "One more. Let's give it a final try." Diamond knew if that volt hadn't sprung life into Drako that time, her life too would've ended in that next instant.

Last night, she felt she was back in that same place. She prayed the same prayer, and again God spared Drako another moment of life. Diamond was now staring at the oxygen mask covering his mouth and the tubes that were now shoved up his nostrils. She'd seen the looks on everybody's faces when Drako's vital signs unexpectedly plunged into darkness. They'd all lost hope. But Diamond still believed that under his bandaged head and through all the IVs, Drako was still fighting for life again. Her hope was that his eyes would soon flutter open. She'd spot that glint in his eyes, followed by his warm smile if he just held on.

Just then, she raised a hand to her forehead. The heavy scent of the hospital's antiseptic floors that made her feel faint.

"You okay?" Wiz stepped right up and gently wrapped an arm around her shoulder when he noticed her slightly sway, then placed a hand on the wall for leverage.

"I'm-I"m fine," Diamond stuttered out a lie.

"Come on, sis. You gotta sit down. You haven"t hardly slept since you been here." He began coaxing her to a row of padded seats. "I understand how you feel. I do. But this here, we can't fix what God is already workin" on." He finally sat her down and looked into her puffy red eyes.

243

In all honesty Diamond was a wreck! She looked like shit and had surely put herself through sleep deprivation.

"I-I-know." She sniffled, looking at Wiz and refusing to accept the same reality he had. Diamond needed Drako. She had to talk to him. Hold him once more, and more than anything she wished she would have gotten the opportunity to tell him she was pregnant.

All the signs had been adding up, and she'd had that gut feeling for weeks, but now she was certain. The smell continued to make her want to vomit, but she suppressed it along with the urge to tell Wiz her condition. She'd prayed hard, and this surprise would be saved for Drako to hear first.

"I'm gonna be strong." She sat up a little straighter and tried to compose herself like she knew she had to. "I really appreciate y"all being here." She glanced over at Swirl sitting next to Thump, who was thumbing away on his Droid. "They really are like family too," she admitted. Diamond reflected on how they, just like Drip, Myria, Ebony and Reality's top security personnel had frequented the hospital with support from the moment they arrived.

"It"s time to go and wrap things up," Diamond said softly, spotting Drip the second he stepped off the elevator that was a short distance down the hallway. Ebony pranced behind him in another pair of tight jeans and a fitted top that was a bright, irritating shade of pink one couldn"t ignore. "I believe in my prayers. I know if he falls, he"s gonna fall forward."

"Huh?" Wiz huffed with a confused stare.

"Just somethin" he always told me." She tried to smile, reflecting on Drako's jewels of wisdom. She knew Wiz didn't understand. "See about it, then destroy it. You're right. This is already taken care of." She patted his hand just as Drip stepped within earshot. Diamond wanted closure as well.

"How"'s everything?" Drip smiled warmly, quickly shaking Wiz"'s hand and nodding in Swirl and Thump"'s direction. Then he turned to hug Diamond.

"Hi," Ebony chimed in right after him as she sat down and crossed one leg over the other politely.

Diamond casually took notice, from her nice matching boots all the way to the thick coat of lip-gloss and eye shadow that accented her smooth complexion. *What the fuck did she plan to dress for?* Diamond thought, which caused her not to even return the greeting. It was something else about Ebony that turned Diamond's gut and made her warm.

"Stable," Wiz said happily to Drip. He noticed the sudden change in Diamond's mood. "Peter Gilcrest is listed as the best in the business. He practices at Duke Medical Center, and he's now here to oversee Drako the rest of the way." He smiled with hope, knowing he"'d summoned the best to carry out any further surgeries.

"Great." Drip nodded, exhaling his own breath of hope. "Well," he said, trying not to stare at the dark bags under Diamond"'s eyes or the unprimped strands of hair that nearly covered one side of her face, "I think maybe you should get some rest."

His tone was calm. "You don't have to leave. They can make arrangements for you to rest here, I'm sure." He looked over at Wiz for confirmation.

"Of course." Wiz flashed that dazzling diamond smile in Drip and Ebony's direction. "Lil sis gone be fine. She"'s still the toughest lil momma I know!" He winked and stood to his feet.

"I need ta" speak to you," Diamond said sternly to Wiz. Her tone let everybody know she meant privately before he and Drip were to depart.

"Cool." The smile vanished from Wiz's face as he gave Swirl a chin-up, which clearly meant clear the area. "I'll see you in a minute." Wiz gestured his head in the direction of the waiting room to Drip, who in turn stood to his feet and followed Swirl and everyone else in that same direction.

Diamond crossed her arms over her chest. Her tiny nostrils flared with a disgusted look as she watched Ebony strut away as if she was dazzling the camera on a set.

As soon as they stepped through the door, she turned back to Wiz. "I know I'm handling a lot right now, and I also realize my thoughts and hopes may not be in the same place as everyone else's at this point." Her voice cracked and she nodded her head. "But for that man lying there, I know what's good for him *and* to him." She had a cold glint in her eyes.

"Don't worry, sis, this doctor is—"

"I ain't talkin' ,,bout no doctor!" He noticed her hand clench into a fist.

"I'm talkin' 'bout this silly bitch that keeps struttin" her hot ass up in here for all the wrong reasons!"

Her thought took Wiz by complete surprise. She didn't give him an opportunity to even respond. "Her intentions ain"t right! I ain't want to make a scene and I can't tell her in a decent way."

Wiz nodded agreeingly. He knew Diamond meant business, and her female intuition was telling her something.

"It don't need to be but one woman hoping for Drako's recovery. I see the larceny in her eyes when she looks at my man. I've sensed it several times as we've spoken about him, and I know she wants more than just the Chief Executive to recover. What that woman ,,thinks" she wants is enough to get her killed." A new strand of tears slipped from Diamond's eye.

Wiz reached for her hand, but Diamond pulled away, determined with her intuition. "This is a place for family. Tell Drip to get that bitch outta here! Make sure she doesn"t return, and if I had any inclination that she'd been with Drako it would take another act of God to bring her out of this place alive."

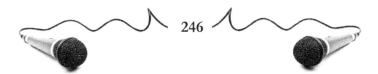

Diamond wiped away the angry tears as her declaration held promise to Wiz's ears.

"Don't trip, lil sis. You got enough on you as it is," Wiz said sincerely."She just young and new to this shit, but you know just as I know, Drako ain't got eyes for nothing beyond you . . . nothing."

"Uh huh," Diamond said, gazing blankly down the hall with her own deep thoughts reeling through her mind. "Just handle it!" she muttered dismissively and watched Wiz step away.

Moments later, they were all exiting the waiting room and strolling off in the opposite direction. Drip had an arm draped around Ebony, who didn't seem so perky anymore, nor did she attempt to glance Diamond's way as she was led back into the elevator.

Oh God, Diamond thought, feeling a sharp pain course through her lower stomach. She realized she had to find some restraint; if she added any more weight to her already heavy burden, it could easily lead to a miscarriage. It was just hard to shake the visions of her strangling Ebony until she foamed at the mouth with a set of bulging eyes, if she were to ever find out there had been anything between her and Drako. She trusted Drako for certain, but for that level of deception to have taken place right under her nose, she knew she'd carry out her promise whether Drako lived to see it or not!

Exhaling another breath of hope, Diamond stood. This time she was going to the nurse"s station. She wasn"t ever going to leave his side, but it was time to get some rest and some attention toward her own condition as well.

"I need a few hours of sleep and I need some fluids," Diamond said, leaning over the desk.

"You sure do, baby," the friendly, heavyset nurse replied quickly, coming to Diamond's aid. She led Diamond to a private room, and in no time Diamond had eaten, climbed onto the small bed, and claimed some sleep. She knew it was finally time to let go and let God.

Wiz
Chapter - 37

"So, what the hell does that mean exactly?" Wiz's baffled expression made his forehead wrinkle as Drip anxiously crunched another sequence of numbers into the laptop, trying to decipher info from the pages he'd sorted and chosen from Damien's files.

"Just be patient," Drip said, growing irritated with Wiz hovering over his shoulder and staring at the screen in wonderment. In rare form, Drip sat staring wide-eyed at the screen and hardly even blinked as his long fingers tapped quick relentless strokes at the keyboard. Wiz knew Drip was certainly on the trail of something he'd surely missed.

Tap, tap, tap. "Yeahh!" Drip sang after the stroke of one last key. "Right there!" He pointed to the screen with a sure nod. "He's been robbing you blind!" Drip was ready to reveal his findings after deciphering Damien's spreadsheet. "He's been bouncing money from the label's account to create a paper trail of these frivolous accounts for the IRS to probe and track you." He nodded with a knowing smirk. "Simple shit to do if you don't have a meticulous accountant on top of your shit," he explained, pulling up his next target.

"These accounts here, you sure you don't recall them?" he asked.

Wiz promptly replied, "No!"

"He's opened several more and all of them lead back to Red Rum's holdings." Drip was now starting to sweat, as he tried vigorously to hack through security codes and see what each account held.

The task had proven to be tedious, but with a bloodhound as thorough and as keen eyed as Drip, there would be no backing down until everything was on the table and wiped squeaky clean!

Watching Drip work, Wiz now felt a bit more confident. He knew that had he not turned to Drip, his past would have eventually caught up to him again. Drip had to find out where else Damien's tracks would lead, which turned out to be Wiz's biggest fear. It was certain that if those paths weren't cut off, the IRS would soon find them.

Wiz and Drip were the only two present in the plush executive suite of the Westin Hotel overlooking downtown Atlanta. Two chairs sat close to the huge table now littered with audio tapes, pictures and piles of documents that Drip's heavy pistol lay atop of. Settled at their workstation, Wiz continued to reveal to Drip all he'd discovered and thought of Damien's scheme. Other than knowing the scheme was named 'A Life for a Life,' Drip understood Damien's intentions clearly! He'd read up on case law and saw firsthand the workings of Rats during his term of imprisonment.

He also knew Diamond's assumption was right. Damien had to be working under Toney Domacio''s thumb! A lot of things about Toney never added up to Drip. But back in Lewisburg he had no reason or need to press those assumptions. It had often struck him in a peculiar way as to how Toney only gravitated to one particular black man, but had always and so easily shunned the others.

Wiz's revelation had sounded so twisted from the start. The bloody knife he described, the heavy surveillance Damien had put down, and even how he hid the secrets of him cutting into Myria. Then came Raoul and the connection of the ecstasy ring, which all made sense to Drip.

"Wait a fuckin' minute . . ." Drip stumbled on to something else with the most astounded look he'd had yet. "This . . . this . . . neither of these accounts is attached to Red Rum." Already, he

was trying hard to crack the pass codes just as he'd eventually done to every account he'd laid eyes on so far.

"Haa!" he gasped, looking wide eyed as he hunched forward to get a closer look to assure he was reading the numbers correctly. "Seven million, six hundred sixty-four thousand dollars and zero cents!" He moved the cursor along as he read out the mindboggling balance to Damien's secret offshore holdings. "Damn!" he huffed, trying to gather his thoughts, but quickly took aim at what had to be Damien's other account. Breaking the next code seemed to take even longer because of the anticipation. But in reality, Drip had cracked it open even faster. This time, another just over four million dollars grand total was winking back at him.

"Man! That little bastard was caked tha' fuck up!" Drip sat up with a smirk, now certain he'd deciphered all they needed to know.

"So . . ." Wiz cracked his knuckles and asked, "What can you do? Can you close out these accounts or what?"

Drip reared back in his seat for a moment in silence, but his mind had already jumped several moves ahead. "Sheeit . . ." he slurred, locking beady eyes with Wiz. "I"ma clean it up, then I"ma clean his bitch ass out!" He bellowed with a scowl. "Dead men can't testify, nor do they have the need to keep this kind of money." He sat back up, picked up his handkerchief and wiped the sweat from his forehead. "Yeah, I'll snip those accounts, retrace his steps and wipe free all tracks. Then I'll return those funds to where he stole them from." The first part of his strategy came easy. "Then comes the big part, I'm gonna bounce what's nearly twelve million out of those accounts and into the hands where it belongs—our hands!" Wiz only responded with an understanding nod.

"These holdings are in Latin America. I'm very familiar. Their well placed, but I have a few connections that I can pass this by. It's gonna take some hard work, but it'll be taken care of."

Wiz didn't even think twice. He was certain Drip played his game well, and taking anything that bastard Damien left behind was surely the right thing to do.

"Fuck that piece of shit!" Wiz barked. "Clean 'im out! I know this could never take the place of Drako, but we can use it to help look after Diamond." Wiz's voice was laced with defeat at his last remark, but both he and Drip had to face reality. It was only logical to presume that if Drako didn't bounce back in the next few days, his time in this life would be over.

"Yeah. I know. That's my only intention," Drip said, meaning every word."If it comes down to that we'll just handle our business. No need to tell her where it came from."

"And there's no need to hide it from her either." Wiz made clear. "Ain't no more secrets between us. Trust me; she can handle more than you'd ever believe."

"Cool." Drip nodded. "Cool. This one"s for Drako."

Wiz smiled inwardly, hearing Drip's unspoken pledge. He knew if anybody deserved that money, it was most definitely Drako.

Moments later, Wiz began to place all the evidence back into the suitcase where he'd kept it stashed.

Turning back to the laptop, Drip resumed stroking the final touches on his keyboard that would eventually snip all ties to these ugly memories of their lives for good. As he did so, they both milled in deep thoughts, silently praying for Drako's miracle. Their hearts spilled over with sympathy, love and respect for Diamond as they shared some warm memories about the two. But even with Wiz now being a lot more open, Drip still wasn't completely sold on him. He didn't look forward to any lone business ventures in their future, and the reason he'd decided to handle the business to the utmost surely wasn't

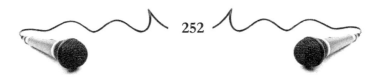

because he liked or respected Wiz. It was first on the strength of Drako, and even further, because he now possessed leverage heavy enough to anchor Wiz and any of his future antics down for good!

Standing to his feet, Drip gave a look to Wiz that told deep inside they'd both counted Drako out. Neither of the two could even fathom uttering such an assumption, but the grim reality was still there. They knew only a miracle from high in the sky could save him.

Still in a semi-haze, Wiz watched Drip swallow the lump in his throat and fold his laptop, just before reaching behind him and tucking his semi-automatic back underneath his shirt where it had come from.

Taking his stance as well, Wiz knew it was time to return to Drako's side, and this time only time would tell the tale of Drako's life.

Epilogue

It was now finally April 14th, which marked five months later. Wiz's waterfront mansion was decorated more festively and lively as it had ever been. Massive flower arrangements were everywhere. Long white, cloth covered tables were topped with silver catering trays on one side of the pool area. The other side was lined with comfortable white padded chairs for all the guests. There was an elegant grade of red carpet that rolled out from the mansion's door, all the way to the podium that was placed just in front of the estate's beautiful waterfall.

Drako was parked at the end of that carpet. Wiz stood to his right and Reverend Armstrong stood next to him. Drako looked over at all the many faces in attendance as Jesse Powell belted out the first note to "You." The entire guest list stood to their feet in awe as his soulful voice serenaded Diamond down the red carpet. Two small flower bearers in lavender satin dresses led her down the aisle. Their wedding had to be postponed in light of Drako's injury. She never thought she'd have a spring wedding, but thanks to Diamond's strong prayers, she finally got to wear her gown. Until she made it about two yards in front of him, Drako had forgotten she was even pregnant. She was so beautiful when he looked up at her today, that a single tear left Drako's eye. Choked for words, he was filled with more appreciation than ever now. He'd surpassed the ten million dollar goal and Reality Records was making legimate money hand over fist. It seemed as though for the moment the Hip-Hop Task Force lightened up on Wiz. Oh, they were still around, focusing on a new target everyday, but it just felt good to know Wiz was no longer their sole focus. Drako looked out as his entire camp was in attendance and most of Red Rum. Not to mention the host of other celebrities and artists who came to show their support. Life had been great and Drako had taken lots of chances. He had a chance to make much better choices. He realized this, now that he was given a moment to sit down and think about where he'd gone wrong. Well, he'd pretty much already figured it out, but how long he'd be sitting down only God could determine. Every since the accident, Drako had been paralyzed from his injury. Those final steps he'd taken into Damien's foyer may have been his last. Wiz had basically convalesced himself back to health, but for Drako's injury it seemed hopeless.

He experienced sudden muscle spasms resulting in hard tremors and he had to urinate with the help of a catheter, but at least he was still breathing. He still had Diamond, who took care of his every need, and as life turned out, he realized he didn't need as much as he thought. Wiz never found out about his white-collar schemes, so that was money only he and Diamond knew of.

Diamond released her album under Reality Records, but Wiz produced most of the songs. She was doing well for her first album, which sold over 500,000 units. Reality and Red Rum were now doing things together and the game of hip-hop was back on track for everyone.

Well, that was the reality for everything going on around him. And Drako's ultimate reality was that his greed for money and greed for pain had both bitten him in the ass at the same time. All he had to do was take the shot and go. He"d made his choice and today he'd have to live with the consequences.

Diamond glared down on him with teary eyes as Reverend Armstrong read the list of vows Drako had written.

"I, yes . . . I do." She choked a bit.

Drako heard the list she'd prepared for him and spoke his heartfelt, "I do . . . Always have, always will."

The reverend said, "You may now kiss your bride." He smiled warmly as she leaned over and kissed Drako passionately for a long while.

Everybody clapped, but then to her surprise Lloyd stepped from out of seemingly thin air with a mic in his hand. He performed a song Neyo had penned just for Diamond. The song was titled "Forever." The guests once again found themselves gasping in awe.

Soon, Wiz had pushed Drako and his wheelchair over to the table so that he and Diamond could share the first slice of cake. Drako slid the knife into the almost four-foot tall tiers of a cream, yellow, light pink and light blue frosted work of art. That was their final step into their official union on paper.

A few moments later, they moved to a nearby table. Drako pulled his wheelchair up close and locked its wheels. Diamond sat down on the end of the bench beside him, and from there they enjoyed the sight and soaked in the day they'd waited to come for so long.

Soon, Drako stretched an arm out. He gently placed his hand on top of Diamond"s that rested on her inflated belly.

"You know I"ma get out this wheelchair one day." He smiled with hope and rubbed her belly lovingly.

"I know you will, baby. And I"ma be right there when you do. You just lead the way and I"ma keep following." She squeezed his hand and winked just like old times.

Just then, Drako felt Wiz rest a firm hand on his shoulder. "Look at you two," Wiz said and smiled sincerely. "Man, if I knew you'd look like a church boy in that tux, I'da bought you one the day you came home." Wiz chuckled, but was no doubt giving Drako props for how clean he really did look in his all white tuxedo.

"Yeah . . . whateva." He waved the remark off. "And you still ain't no gangsta." Drako smiled warmly at him this time.

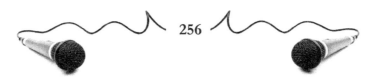

"Bullshit, and you know it." Wiz held his glare. "I"ma get missing for awhile. I just wanted to let y"all know."

Drako nodded dismissively as Wiz turned to leave.

"Hey, bruh," Drako called out, causing Wiz to stop and look back. "I just wanted to say thanks. I appreciate all you done here today . . . And I love ya, bruh."

"Man, don't sweat it. It is what it is. Shit gone always be real between us."

He gave a cocky suck to his diamond grill, shot Drako a wink, and then limped off in Myria's direction with a smile.

*****

Well, till this day, Wiz is still crankin' out the hardest beats money can buy. Red Rum is squeaky clean, running straight and legit. Diamond never thought she and Myria would ever become best friends, but they have.

With Drip still at his side, Drako silently runs Reality Records right from his wheelchair. And the Feds, along with the Hip-Hop Task Force, are all still spending millions of hard earned taxpayer's dollars to follow, launch investigations, and harrass blacks with too much money and/or influence over hip-hop culture. Y"all better wake up! Open your eyes to reality. Shit is real out here.

Well as for me, I'm just glad their attention is no longer focused on Red Rum or Reality Records. I hope they both keep putting down gangsta lyrics over them hot ass tracks, and I hope Diamond keeps nailing that melodious voice forever!

Stay up, keep making your next move your best move, and don't forget to 'play da game raw!'

ONE....

The Ultimate Reality.

By: Mike Jefferies

Afterthought

First of all I"d like to thank you for your support. I really hope you enjoyed the conclusion of this sequel. It was killing me not to reveal the true meaning of "A Life For A Life" until now. Well, just like in this tale all of my future novels will have their own authentic plotline leading up to a shocking conclusion. It is my intention to entertain you and be the author you can always look forward to. Keep believing in your dreams. It"s not always what you know, it"s oftentimes what you can imagine . . . Think, pray and hope good things into existence. What you just read is the evidence.

Now to address the concern of my current situation. Yes, I am incarcerated. And, no, I didn"t try to avoid the question; I just didn"t mention it (smile). Summer 2013 it is finally over! Sixteen years straight, in the feds. I"m a battle tested, stand-up soldier beyond any shadow of a doubt. That is for certain! However, I didn"t want my personal or past history to create any contrast with my art. I wanted my art to grow legs of their own. Well, by now you see there are many layers to my genius, and believe me, this is only the beginning! My sincerest hope is that if you truly enjoyed this story you"ll keep it player and share the good news with at least one friend. I"m trying to take a crack at doing the right thing and come up clean. Help spread the positivity. Send your review to Amazon.com. Tweet someone the title to this true and certified Hip-Hop Fiction and visit me on Facebook. I look forward to meeting you at one of my many booksignings. The time has finally arrived. You"ve just read the first installment of something amazing. My calling . . . I"m not just talented, I"m God-gifted. Recognize the difference!

258

Much Respect Always,

Mike Jefferies
To write the author,
Sent mail to:
C/O Mike Jefferies Fan Club
60 Evergreen Place
Suite 904
East Orange, NJ 07018
Also visit my fan page on Facebook, Michael Jefferies.

Group Discussion Questions

1)   Did you ever imagine 'A Life for A Life" being Toney's ultimate plan, and what did you think of it being the climax to this two part series?

2)   How did you feel about Toney's betrayal toward Drako?

3)   Did you ever suspect Damien for being as deep in deceit as he was, and overall what did you think of his character?

4)   Did you enjoy Swirl's character and the way he handled business?

5)   What did you think of Myria, after falling on all the bad luck in her past, being the one to first discover Damien's deceit?

6)   Do you think Myria should give Wiz another try after all he put her through?

7)   Did you feel bad for Wiz when he got shot? And how do you feel about Drako's incident leaving him confined to a wheelchair?

8)   Did you like the feel of what Drako and Drip built at Reality Records, and which label did you look forward to the most?

9)   What did you think of the new characters, Save and Big Turk? Did you like the way their beef unfolded?

10)   How did you feel about Drako and Ebony"s encounter? Was he to blame and should that be considered infidelity?

11)   Would you like to see this series continue?

12)   After all was said and done, do you believe either Wiz, Drako or both, may have changed their ways for good?

13)   Out of the whole series, which character grew to become your favorite?

14) If the series continues, which characters do you look forward to seeing?

15) On a scale of 1-10 what would you rate this series? And what do you think of this author's writing style?

WAHIDA CLARK
PRESENTS
BEST SELLING TITLES

Trust No Man
Trust No Man II
Thirsty
Cheetah
Karma With A Vengeance
The Ultimate Sacrifice
The Game of Deception
Karma 2: For The Love of Money
Thirsty *2*
Lickin' License
Feenin'
Bonded by Blood
Uncle Yah Yah: 21st Century Man of Wisdom
The Ultimate Sacrifice II
Under Pressure (YA)
The Boy Is Mines! (YA)
A Life For A Life
The Pussy Trap
99 Problems (YA)
Country Boys

CPSIA information can be obtained at www.ICGtesting.com
Printed in the USA
BVOW06s1422171115

427217BV00007B/73/P

9 780982 841464